Trixie Travers is Captured in Time

Abbie L. Martin

Book 1 - A Trixie Travers Time Travel Mystery

TRIXIE TRAVERS IS CAPTURED IN TIME

ISBN: 978-1-7644050-0-3
Abbie L. Martin Paperback edition / December 2025
Abbie L. Martin books are published by Abbie Allen Publishing

Preface

She stood on the hill overlooking Wattlebury, her white dress flapping in the breeze.

It was the moment of calm she needed before her big day - she just hadn't expected it five minutes before she was due to walk down the aisle.

Feeling the panic rising, she began to focus on her breathing. In, out. In, out. Then the familiar feeling of nausea and tingling washed over her.

"Oh, thank goodness, you're back!"

Her mother was there, standing on the verandah of Silver Gum Cottage, bouquet in hand, as if nothing had happened.

"Let's hope that doesn't happen again today," she said.

Taking the bouquet, she looped her arm through her mother's and together they walked down the steps.

Chapter 1

"We can't be late for the first day of school!" Trixie Travers grabbed a brush she found lying next to the toaster and swiped it through her chin-length pewter hair, before dropping it into the fruit bowl and taking a sip of her coffee. "Uggh." It was already cold. "Meg! Joe! Have you brushed your teeth?"

Today, Trixie had chosen a pale green tea dress and cream canvas shoes. It was an important day, so she had chosen her favourite dress, in the vintage style she was known for in Wattlebury.

She popped an apple into two lunch boxes sitting on the sink and snapped them closed. Once they were in cooler bags, these and the matching water bottles were pushed into the school bags hanging on coat hooks at the door. With all the back-to-school preparations she had done, Trixie was surprised at how disorganised she felt that morning. Then again, it was something she'd struggled with her whole life.

"Mum," said a young girl with brown hair, which in its current state could only be described as a bird's nest. "Do you think chickens remember their mums when they get taken to a new home?"

The questions this seven-year-old came out with never ceased to amaze her, even when they were entirely off topic and unrelated to getting out of the door in ten minutes.

"Meg," said Trixie. "I have no idea, but maybe you can ask your teacher when we get to school. Now, where was that brush?"

Trixie spun around, knowing she'd just brushed her own hair but with no recollection of where she'd put it. "Meg, can you go and find a brush and come right back!"

Her daughter was at the kitchen table, working on a colouring she'd started when she woke up.

"Meg! Brush. Now!"

Meg glanced up at her mum, a confused look on her face, before she understood what she was being asked and raced off.

"Right, where was I?" Trixie was prone to talking aloud to herself. It was how she attempted to make sense of the buzzing in her head, especially when she had a list as long as her arm to complete. First on the list, get the kids to school, with the rather large stipulation of not being late for Joe's very first day. Second, open her brand new vintage store and repair shop, Paraphernalia.

"Joe! Have you brushed your teeth?"

Joe, the five-year-old with a head of straight blonde hair, ran into the kitchen.

"Yep! See!" He smiled a broad smile. Trixie grinned at him before noticing the huge glob of toothpaste down the front of his brand-new school polo shirt.

"Oh, Joe! Tomorrow you have to brush your teeth *before* you get dressed. Hang on, I'll grab you another top."

Trixie stepped into her tiny laundry just off the kitchen and pulled a shirt from the clean clothes basket. "Here, arms up, arms up," she said, tugging Joe's jumper over his head, before replacing it with an identical one, albeit toothpaste-free.

"Meg! Did you find a brush?" she called over the top of Joe.

Joe went to dash out of the kitchen, but Trixie grabbed him by the arm. "Nope, you're not going anywhere. We have to do your hair, get your shoes on, and then we *must* have a photo."

She would not forget the first day of school photo. Even if it meant they were a few minutes late.

Meg thankfully strolled back into the kitchen with a brush and handed it to her mum. "Mum, do you know there's a brush in the fruit bowl?"

Trixie sighed. "Of course there is."

The pair were pulled into line with the strokes of the brush, and Trixie eventually pushed them outside, school bags on their backs, placing the siblings in front of a lavender bush.

"Smile!" she called, holding up her phone to capture this momentous day; both children were finally at school.

The three Travers piled into the front of Trixie's 1950s Morris J Type van, Meg in the middle of the bench seat, and Joe in his booster seat. Trixie loved her van. It was navy blue and had Speckled Hen Farm painted in white on both sides.

Speckled Hen Farm, along with the barn that housed Paraphernalia, was only five minutes out of town. They lived on the outskirts of Wattlebury, a lovely Adelaide Hills village, which most weekends and holidays was filled with tourists. Today it was slightly quieter, with many people also headed towards Wattlebury Primary School for the first day of the school year. It was the very end of January and not quite as hot as it could have been, but they were still in for a stunning summer's day. As was usually the case in the Hills, the air was cooler that morning, but it would be hot by the time the kids were let out at recess to play.

"Your hats are in your bags," said Trixie "They've got your names on them, but please don't lose them. Joe, yours is brand new! Put it straight in your bag. Ok?"

"Ok," said Joe, staring out the window.

"Mum," said Meg. "Do you think my teacher will give us

homework, now that I'm in year two?"

"I have no idea," said Trixie. "I'm sure you'll find out soon enough."

"I hope so," said Meg. "Last year, I had to make up my own homework."

Trixie smiled. Her daughter sure was one of a kind. And Meg wasn't stretching the truth. Trixie had to purchase her daughter multiple homework books throughout the year, because the reading and spelling words her teacher gave her each week simply weren't enough for Meg.

"Mum, is Dad going to be home tonight?" Joe asked.

"I believe that's the plan," said Trixie. "But you know that things can change at the last minute. We'll just have to wait and see."

Her husband Kirby was a helicopter pilot. He was often away on unusual projects, and for the past two weeks, he had been helping transport materials from the mainland to a small island just off the Eyre Peninsula, where they were completing the renovations of a lighthouse. He was due home that day, but a lot depended on the weather. The kids were used to it, but of course, it would be nice for Kirby to be there to greet the kids after their first day of school.

They walked Meg to her classroom first, who had her new teacher bailed up within seconds. Trixie smiled and waved goodbye. Joe was next, and although he feigned shyness, it wasn't long before he found some kindy friends and was sitting at a table playing with the magnetic blocks. Trixie stood and watched him for a moment, tears pricking her eyes. She knew she had a busy day ahead, but for once she made herself stand still and soak in this moment, even managing to sneak a photo without Joe noticing.

She wished Kirby could be there. She knew he wished the same thing. But they had accepted long ago that his job was unpredictable. It afforded them the ability to have Trixie home with the kids and live in the rambling farmhouse they owned without too many worries, at least financially. It also meant she was able to dive into some of her own crazy schemes, with today's soft opening, as she was calling it, of Paraphernalia being one of them.

Smiling and waving at parents she knew, Trixie made her way back to the van. It was tempting to stop in the main street and grab a coffee, but with a scheduled opening time of ten, she ignored the urge and continued driving.

Trixie pulled up in front of the barn that housed her new business. She was not surprised to see three women standing out front, one carrying a large basket, one holding a huge bunch of flowers, and all three beaming and waving. They were quite the spectacle.

They were The Silver Ladies, and they were her family.

Chapter 2

"Come on, Trixie! You only have half an hour before people are arriving," called out a woman wearing a long white linen dress and bright red glasses. Her curly grey hair was cut short, and a large raffia bag was slung over her shoulder.

"I do realise that, Mum," said Trixie, bending to pull up the floor lock before hefting across the large corrugated iron sliding door to reveal Paraphernalia.

The walls were iron, the floor rustic timber. The space was filled with vintage treasures of every kind. Tea cups. Pigeon holes. Typewriters. Vases. Tea spoons. Jars of nails. Fruit crates. And oh so much more.

Fern strolled in ahead of her daughter and began making her way around the room, leaving the other women to follow.

"Oh, Trix! This looks amazing!" A slim, tanned woman, with a ponytail of platinum blonde hair and wearing burnt orange active wear, took Trixie's arm as they walked into the space.

"Thanks, Maggie," said Trixie, accepting the flowers thrust into her arms. "I can't believe people are finally going to see it." Maggie was her mother's best friend and as much family as the other two women.

"Wait for me!" called the third woman. She had steel grey short hair and wore a set of ring-tailed possum earrings.

Trixie turned around. "Sorry, Nan," she said. "Here, let me grab that." She reached out for the basket, but Rhada pulled it away from her.

"I'm perfectly capable of carrying a basket," Rhada said. She was well into her eighties, but you wouldn't know it. She wore jeans, silver sneakers and a loose navy blouse.

"And you're sure about the name?" Fern asked, walking over to the women.

Paraphernalia: Originally: items belonging to a particular person, esp. articles of dress or adornment; trappings, bits and pieces, accoutrements. Subsequently, the miscellaneous items needed for or associated with a particular activity. - Oxford English Dictionary

Trixie rolled her eyes as she placed the flowers into a large milk jug. "We've had this conversation a million times, Mum. If they can't say it or spell it, then I don't want them here anyway."

"But Paraphernalia. Is it the right choice?"

Trixie ignored her mum and walked to a room in the back. She pretended to be searching for something, but really she just needed to get away before she said something she didn't mean. When it came to naming her business, all Trixie knew was that when the word Paraphernalia came to her, it was the one. Something about the implied chaos, but also a treasure trove of discoveries. It was exactly what she wanted her store to be. Surprising, fun, mysterious and without limitations, so it could evolve into whatever Trixie needed it to be. She knew she got bored easily and wanted to feel confident that Paraphernalia would move with her.

Fortunately, her trip to the back room wasn't wasted. She found the 'Open' sign she wanted to hang out the front. Returning to the main shop area, she found Rhada laying out champagne glasses on the counter, a large rustic carpenter's bench, and two bottles already on ice.

"I hope people will want to drink bubbles at ten o'clock," said Trixie with a smile.

"Of course they will," said Maggie, who was pouring water into the jug of flowers. "At least I will!"

One wall was lined with clocks, but only a few held the correct time. Trixie knew the original railway clock from the old Wattlebury Station was correct and was surprised to see it was already quarter to ten. What if people arrived early? She began to feel a familiar flutter of panic in her throat. Where should she stand? At the door? Behind the counter? Near the wine?

"TRIXIE! THIS IS SO EXCITING!"

She didn't have time to decide. A group of mums from the school had already arrived. The gaggle hugged her and exclaimed, and exclaimed and hugged, and then made a beeline for the champagne, which Maggie happily handed out.

Rhada came to stand by her granddaughter. "You should be very proud of yourself," she said. "I know how hard you've worked, not only to get this set up, but with your kids, and managing the farm when Kirby's away. Soak this all in. Enjoy it." Rhada took Trixie's hand and squeezed it before going to regale the group with the banter she was known for.

"Don't forget to look at the tea cups!" Rhada called. "I've already got four sets at home!" Trixie's Nan grabbed the elbow of one of the women and dragged her over to the table of tea cups.

Trixie smiled. Trust her nan to start selling. She felt tears prick her eyes for the second time that day. Rhada was right. She should be proud of herself and all that she had done to get here. But she didn't want to get ahead of herself. This could all be a complete flop. The hard work might end up being a waste. Maybe no one cared about vintage things as she did.

But perhaps they did.

"Trixie! A sale! Come and ring them up!" Rhada was waving at her. Trixie broke into a grin. She felt sorry for the women who had arrived first. They had no chance against her nan.

On the long timber counter was an old-fashioned cash register. But it held a secret. Behind it, Trixie had set up a stand so that her iPad sat securely on the front, and if people waved their card or phone at the top, their payments would be taken. She had even rigged it so that she could open the cash drawer and take payments that way as well. Trixie was quite proud of it and hoped people would ask questions. She'd tell them that she wasn't only selling vintage items, she was also repairing and restoring them.

"I hope Rhada didn't force you to buy this," said Trixie to Janine, who passed her a teacup and saucer.

Janine laughed. "Not at all! I mean, she is very good at her job. But this is the perfect gift for my friend. She's having surgery this week and is going to be bed-bound for a while. She loves reading with a cup of tea, so this will be a treat for her."

Trixie smiled. A lovely, meaningful gift, which perfectly summed up her goal for Paraphernalia. "Would you like it gift wrapped?"

"No, thank you," said Janine. "I'm going to the second-hand bookshop next, so I'll add a few things to the gift first."

Trixie carefully wrapped the set in tissue paper and then butcher's paper, before placing it in a brown paper bag with the shop name stamped across it. She and Meg had spent hours over the weekend preparing those bags.

"Thanks for being my first customer!" Trixie grinned as she handed the bag to Janine.

"First sale, ladies!" Janine called out, waving her bag. Trixie gripped the benchtop, fearful the teacup and saucer would come unstuck. But all was well, and the women cheered, even breaking out into a round of applause which the Silver Ladies happily joined in.

Feeling her face go red, Trixie didn't quite know where to look. Being applauded was unfamiliar. Should she take a bow? Make a speech? Fortunately, one of the women brought an item up to the counter, and Trixie got busy putting another sale through the cash register.

Trixie hadn't been expecting a busy day. It wasn't meant to be a grand opening. She had only invited a few friends and acquaintances to pop in, to help her find her bearings, not anticipating that almost all of them would come through the barn door at some point during the day.

Yet, just an hour before she would have to shut shop for school pick up, a woman she didn't recognise walked in. Trixie glanced at her mother, who gave a slight smile and nodded. It seemed Fern knew the person standing in the middle of the room, looking around apprehensively, holding a large box. Trixie smiled at her, and the woman walked up to the counter.

"Do you mind?" the woman asked, indicating she'd like to put the box down.

"Of course," Trixie nodded, reaching out to assist.

"They were my mother's," the woman explained, pulling apart the box lid, each flap tucked under the next. Tucking her straight brown hair behind her ear, the woman pushed the box closer to Trixie.

Trixie peered over the top and saw it was full of cameras of all shapes and sizes.

"Do you think…" The woman paused and looked into Trixie's

eyes. "Do you think anyone would want them? To buy them, I mean?"

"Oh," said Trixie. She hadn't anticipated anyone bringing in products for her to sell. She supposed she shouldn't be surprised. If she'd allowed herself to think more than a few days ahead, of course. "I imagine *someone* would be interested."

"Maybe I can leave them with you to have a look through? Then you can let me know?"

"Ok," said Trixie. "Sure. I can do that. Ah, what was your name?" Trixie took a pencil and a notebook that she had set up behind her cash register.

"I'm Anna Treloar," she said before giving Trixie her phone number.

"Give me a few days," Trixie said. "I'll let you know what I think."

Anna smiled and turned to leave without even taking a moment to explore the shop.

Trixie's mum made her way to the counter.

"Do you know her?" Trixie asked as she watched the woman walk through the barn door.

"I knew her mother," said Fern. "She died a few months ago. What did she bring in?"

"A box of cameras," Trixie replied. "I know a little bit about cameras, but I'm going to have to do some research." Trixie began pulling them out of the box. Some were zipped up in leather cases. Others appeared quite old and delicate. Then she excitedly pulled out a camera she recognised.

"Look, a Polaroid camera!" She held the camera up to her mum before everything suddenly went black.

Chapter 3

Trixie staggered, feeling the camera almost drop from her grasp before she took hold of the strap. The blackness began to fade and, shaking her head, her vision returned. There was just one problem.

Paraphernalia was nowhere to be seen.

Her heart began to race, and she spun in a circle trying to recognise her location. Where was she? Instead of talking to her mother in the barn, she was standing on a street that seemed somewhat familiar. People were walking down the footpath, going in and out of shops. There was a chill in the air, and she noticed most people were wearing jumpers and jackets. On a hot day in January? Trixie was confused.

It wasn't until she began to take notice of the cars that she finally realised what had happened. Watching each one that drove past, Trixie realised that not one of them was new. Not one of them was older than-

"The eighties," she sighed. "You've got to be kidding me."

Trixie let out a loud groan, startling a bleached-blonde, spiked-fringed woman, walking with a brown side-by-side stroller. Trixie attempted a smile before quickly heading in the other direction. She found a bench flanked by two bright yellow lions and sat down.

She cradled the Polaroid camera in her lap. "I bet you're the culprit," Trixie said. "I suppose I'd better try and get back."

Lifting her head, she looked at the world around her. Behind her was a cafe proudly proclaiming its specialty was German bee sting cakes, and the lunch of the day was quiche and salad. Next door was Nancy's Haberdashery, which was looking rather run-down and quiet. Across the road, in front of a Shell Service Station, was an orange telephone box. Down to the right was a newsagency that doubled as a video rental store.

"I can't believe this has happened, today of all days," she thought. "It's been forever. I thought I was over this. I'm nearly forty for goodness sake."

The only thing she could think of to do was wait. Resting her head in her hands, she began to take deep breaths, hoping that calming herself would reverse what had happened. She breathed, waiting for the nausea to subside, keeping her eyes closed. Just as she felt like she was getting back to normal, her stomach suddenly dropped. "Oh, thank goodness!" It was her mum's voice.

Once again, Trixie found herself staggering, but this time she was quickly held up on either side by supportive arms.

"Trix, are you ok?" Fern asked.

Trixie blinked her eyes and took another deep breath. She saw she was once again in the barn, in Paraphernalia.

"Yes, I'm fine," she said. "I think. But what happened?"

"Sit down, dear," Rhada said. "Get your strength back. Maggie, can you go and make her a strong cup of tea with lots of sugar?"

Rhada and Fern led her over to the tan Chesterfield sofa that had a sign propped up on the back. 'Not For Sale'. Slumping into the seat, Trixie rubbed her eyes and ran her hands through her hair before suddenly standing.

"What's the time? The kids!"

"It's ok, it's ok. You don't need to leave for fifteen minutes," said Maggie. "And I can go and grab them if we need."

Trixie glanced at the railway clock, confirming Maggie was correct, before sitting back down. "So, I was only gone for ten minutes?"

"Yes, if that," said Rhada. "Was that what it was like for you?"

"I think so," said Trixie. "I think it was the same."

"Ok, well, at least that's good news."

"Good news! Good news!" Trixie stood up again and started pacing the barn. "How on earth is this good news?"

"Now come on, Trixie," said Rhada. "It's nothing to worry about."

Trixie turned, face ablaze, hands on her hips.

"Are you trying to tell me that spontaneous time travel is nothing to worry about!"

Rhada and Fern, sitting on the sofa, looked at each other and shrugged.

"You're back in one piece," said Rhada. "And no one really noticed."

"No one *really* noticed?" said Trixie. "So people did notice something?"

Maggie swooped in and wrapped her arm around Trixie. "Trix, there's nothing to worry about. Your Mum distracted the people here and explained you had to pop out for a bit. We even made a few sales!"

Fern stood up. "Yes, in fact, I sold a painting and some of those tools you have." She looked so pleased with herself. Trixie wanted to shake her.

"And then we just took down the open sign and shut the door," Maggie grinned.

Trixie rolled her eyes, groaned, and went to grab her handbag. "We'll talk about this later. I have to pick up the kids."

"Trixie, do you think-" Fern was cut off by Rhada putting her hand on her arm.

"Meet you at the Cottage?" said Rhada.

Trixie nodded. "Can you pull the barn shut on your way out?"

"We'll sort it, Trix," called Maggie. "Go find out how the first day went."

Trixie got into her van, clicking her seatbelt into place. Before she started it, she rested her head on the steering wheel and took a few deep breaths. The day had become something she wasn't ready for. And yet she knew this would happen again, eventually.

Chapter 4

The time travel was unexpected. Inconvenient. Annoying. But it wasn't shocking. Not to Trixie, not to Fern, and certainly not to Rhada. To anyone else, it would be unexplainable, requiring a trip to the doctors for a full medical.

But for the Travers women, it was their condition, their legacy. They were time travellers. Or time slippers, as they preferred to call themselves. The thing was, Trixie had managed to avoid a trip for so long she had convinced herself the affliction had disappeared. To discover, today of all days, it was very much still running in her veins, was a bitter disappointment.

She was worried, concerned, and most of all, angry. Why was it back? Could she keep her children safe if she kept suddenly disappearing? Could she find a way to control it? And what about Meg, her daughter, who would no doubt have the same condition?

Trixie shook her head, an attempt to expel the thoughts from her mind. Now was the time to focus on her children. It was Joe's first day of school, his first day of Reception.

Trixie also had plans for herself this year. She was getting her time back now that both the kids were at school. She wanted to keep on top of the house as well as work on her passion project, Paraphernalia. Her love of vintage items, as well as her keen eye for a bargain, and her hands adept at repairing or adjusting the items, was all being channelled through the barn. Time travel was not on the agenda. The only thing she could hope for was that today was some sort of weird glitch.

Parking further from the school than she would have liked, Trixie walked briskly toward Joe's classroom, hoping the bell wouldn't go before she got there. Yet, despite her best efforts, as she strode, puffing, up to the classroom, the tiny reception kids were already running to greet their parents. Joe was holding the teacher's hand, eyes wide, searching for his mum.

"Joe!" she cried, bending down, arms out. He ran as fast as he could, his large backpack swinging from side to side, his face beaming. "How did you go? Did you have fun?"

As they walked to find his sister, Joe regaled Trixie with stories of sitting on the mat on their own name, what he did at recess and lunch time, and confirmation that he didn't have any homework, much to his relief.

"Mum, Miss Banks gave us homework!" Meg exclaimed as Trixie and Joe walked up to her classroom. "And lots of it! I can't wait to get home." Trixie had Joe's backpack swung over her shoulder, and they all walked hand in hand back to the car.

"Mum, can we go straight home, so I can start my homework?" asked Meg.

"No." Trixie shook her head. "We're going to the Cottage first."

"Do we have to?" Meg usually loved going to Silver Gum Cottage, but today, homework had priority.

"Granny's making an early tea for us all. But I'm sure she won't mind if you set up at the dining table and start your homework," said Trixie, buckling Joe in as Meg climbed across the driver's seat and into the middle.

"Yes! Great idea!" said Meg, her bag on her lap, pulling out her homework book.

"Mum," asked Joe. "Is Dad going to be home today?"

Trixie smiled. Good news to share. "Yes, he is, but he isn't quite sure what time. He promised you'll see him before bedtime, though."

"Yay!" Joe cheered, his little fists in the air. Meg was smiling as she read her homework sheets.

Trixie drove through the streets of Wattlebury to Silver Gum Cottage. The white picket fence was lined with salvia, its purple flower spikes arching over and through the timber slats, with white alyssum lining the bottom. The front garden was filled with grevillea, lavender, daisies and the Cottage's namesake, a proud Silver Gum tree, as well as many other plants that attracted a bevy of bees. The van squeezed through the front gate, and they trundled their way down the gravel drive, stopping behind Maggie's Jeep.

By the time the three had tumbled out of the van, both Rhada and Fern were on the front verandah waiting for them.

"Granny! Nan! I've got so much homework!" Meg ran excitedly towards them. Fern swept up Meg whilst Rhada pulled Joe into a big hug.

"That's wonderful news, Meg," said Fern. "And how about you, Joe, do you have any homework?"

"Uh uh," Joe said, shaking his head, equally pleased to have nothing. "My teacher said all I have to do is play and have an early night."

"An early night, hey," said Trixie. "That sounds like a great idea."

"What does everyone say to a milkshake?" Maggie asked, poking her head out from behind the screen door.

"Yay!" Joe and Meg cheered before squeezing past her and thundering down the timber hallway to the kitchen at the rear of the cottage. Maggie jogged after them whilst Rhada, Fern, and Trixie took their regular places on the front verandah.

"How are you feeling now?" Rhada asked Trixie.

"Honestly, I'm feeling rather annoyed and a touch worried," Trixie replied. "I thought I was past all this time slipping nonsense."

"What, you thought you'd grown out of it?" Fern said with what Trixie could only call a smirk.

"Actually, yes!" said Trixie. "I mean, I haven't travelled in years. Not since before the kids were born. So why on earth would it happen today?"

"We have actually been talking about this," said Rhada. "And your mother and I think it may have something to do with the fact that today is quite a significant day. Your youngest child's first day of school. The first day of your new business. Time has shifted in your world, and it's reignited your time-travelling abilities."

Trixie's eyebrows raised, but she also nodded. It made sense. It *was* a particularly significant day. And as she recalled, one of the last times she travelled had been an equally significant day. Her wedding day.

"But if that's the case, why didn't I slip when my kids were born? They were just as significant as getting married, and much more so than today," she quizzed her mum and nan.

"I doubt your body would have been in the right condition to travel," said Fern. "There's a physical element to time slipping, and your body wouldn't have been aligned."

"Well, I wish I knew how to make my body permanently unaligned," Trixie sighed.

"But wasn't it fun?" asked Rhada, leaning forward. "I haven't travelled in years. I so wish I could!"

"Yes, Trix," said Fern. "What was it like? Where did you go? What *time* did you go?"

"I'm pretty sure it was Wattlebury," she said.

"Is that all?" Rhada sounded disappointed.

"Yes, but it was the eighties. That was pretty cool." Trixie had to admit seeing all the eighties cars, the fashion, not to mention the hair, had been fun.

Fern and Rhada laughed. "The eighties! That was only yesterday!"

"Ah, it was forty years ago," Trixie said. "That's certainly not yesterday."

"But I wonder why?' asked Rhada. "What were you holding again?"

"A Polaroid camera."

"Well, that explains it," said Rhada. "Everyone had Polaroid cameras in the eighties. They were a bit of an eighties icon."

"But I hold things from the past all the time," said Trixie. "I mean, think about all the items I've held just in the last few weeks, getting Paraphernalia set up. What's so significant about the Polaroid camera?"

"Maybe the camera holds a particular story," said Maggie, who was walking through the front door, holding a tray of cocktails.

"Cocktails? Really, Maggie?" Fern asked.

"They're mocktails!" Maggie laughed. "A raspberry and basil sparkler!"

"That does sound delicious," said Rhada, taking a glass from Maggie.

Trixie reached for hers and, after peering at the purple-tinged basil leaves mixed with the crushed raspberry, she took a sip. "This is delightful! A hidden talent, Maggie?"

"I do work in a pub, remember," said Maggie. "But I really should use my skills at home more often."

Each woman had their own chair, a set lineup on the verandah maintained for years. Many a deep conversation had been had on the front verandah of Silver Gum Cottage, as well as lots of laughter, not to mention a few tears.

Today, Trixie was worried that life as she knew it had changed forever.

"So Mum," said Trixie. "Whose camera was it? What was her name? Anna. She said the box belonged to her mum. Did you know her?"

"Well, yes, as much as you know most people who live in the same town," replied Fern. "Sharon Stewart."

"And does she have a particular story? Were cameras of particular importance to her?" Trixie sipped her mocktail, eyes on her mum.

"Well, no, not that I know of," she said. "She had a lot of jobs. She worked at the bakery for years and years. She took in boarders. Maybe she was a photographer too."

"But there was something that happened, wasn't there?" said Rhada, pulling a piece of raspberry from her drink and popping it in her mouth. "To one of her kids?"

"Well, yes," said Fern, a frown on her face. "She went missing."

Trixie gasped. "What?"

"It was her eldest," said Fern. "I can't think of her name. Maggie, do you remember?"

"Let me think," said Maggie. "It will come to me. I'm just going through the alphabet." Maggie closed her eyes, mouthing A, B, C as she tried to remember the girl's name.

"She was fifteen, I think, or sixteen, and disappeared," said Fern.

"The police are pretty sure she's dead. But Sharon never gave up. I think maybe that's why she worked at the bakery for so long. Dreamt of her daughter walking back through the door."

"Tanya!" Maggie cried out. "It was Tanya." She looked at the group, proud that her memory method had worked.

"Yes," said Fern. "That was it. Tanya Stewart. Her name was everywhere. All the towns in the Hills had her poster plastered on windows and stobie poles."

"Sharon was a single mum to Tanya," Fern explained. "I don't think I ever knew who the father was."

"And what about Anna?" said Trixie. "She was Tanya's sister. Who was *her* father?"

"Their father," said Fern. "There are two more kids. Anna and her brother Jason. They were born a lot later. But their dad was Ron Kovac. Sharon and Ron never married, but they lived together until Ron died, maybe ten years ago."

"So Tanya just went missing one day? No clue why?"

"It was a long time ago, Trixie," said Fern. "You were a newborn. I don't remember much about it."

"But that must be why I slipped, right?" said Trixie. "Because the camera's connected to a tragedy."

Rhada nodded. "It does tend to happen that way."

"Are slips always connected to tragedies?"

"Not necessarily tragedies. But significant events. It's like the strong energy of that moment makes slipping to that place and time easier."

"Well, then the solution is clear," said Trixie, standing up and leaning on a verandah post. "I just have to tell Anna I can't take the cameras. I'll give them back to her and put this all behind me."

"Perhaps," said Fern, glancing sideways at Rhada.

"What?" Trixie frowned. She'd seen that look between mother and daughter before.

"It may not be something you're ready to hear," said Maggie, shrugging her shoulders as she finished her mocktail.

"Well, I wasn't ready to time slip today, but I had no choice in that," said Trixie.

"How about we just sleep on it," said Fern.

"What if I travel in my sleep?" asked Trixie.

Rhada and Fern laughed.

"Wouldn't that be fun!" said Rhada.

Trixie groaned. "You two are impossible," she said, before glancing at Maggie, who was smiling too. "You three. You're like a secret club that thinks they know what's best for me."

"No," said Fern. "We don't claim to know what's best for you. That is up to you. But we do have life experience and generations of time slippers before us. And I can tell you, it is highly unlikely you will travel in your sleep. In fact, I don't think I've ever heard of that happening. Have you Mum?"

Rhada shook her head. "No, but it is a fascinating thought."

"Mum! We're hungry!" Joe and Meg appeared at the door, both sporting substantial milkshake moustaches.

"Well," said Fern. "We'd better do something about that."

"Don't let them eat too much before tea, Mum," said Trixie.

Fern scoffed. "Of course not," she replied, taking the children's hands. "Now, does anyone remember where the biscuit barrel is?"

"I do!" "Me!" the children cried, and once again their thundering footsteps could be heard, Fern calling out to them to slow down as she followed.

Chapter 5

They sat down to dinner in the backyard under the wisteria-covered pergola. It was a simple tea of cold meats and salad, as well as cut-up mango and strawberries. The sun was still quite high in the sky, and the air was warm. But sitting in the shade with the wisps of a breeze, there couldn't have been a more perfect summer evening. Only one thing could have made it better.

"Are there any school kids around?" a man's voice called from inside the darkened house.

"Dad!" Meg and Joe leapt from their chairs just as Kirby Whifield-Travers walked through the door. He pulled them into a hug and managed to swing both of them off the ground at the same time.

"Perfect timing as always, Kirby," said Fern. "Pull up a pew and tuck in."

Kirby, a tall man wearing jeans and a light blue T-shirt, bent down to kiss Trixie on the cheek, his stubble brushing her skin. "I don't mind if I do."

Joe and Meg fought to sit on Kirby's lap, and somehow he managed to seat the two of them, one on either knee, and load his plate with food.

"Now, what job were you just on, Kirby?" Rhada asked her helicopter pilot grandson-in-law.

Kirby replied with a mouthful of silverside, pushing aside the dark brown hair that had flopped in his face. "The lighthouse reno."

"Oh yes. I bet that was tricky. I imagine there was a lot of wind to contend with."

Kirby nodded. "Yep, and the weather took a turn for the worse over the weekend, so we were grounded until it cleared up. Last night

I thought I might be stuck there for a few more days. But when we woke up this morning, the sun was shining, and we got the last lot across just after lunch."

"Well, your family is very glad to have you home," Maggie said, smiling at the two children on his lap.

"But, enough about me," said Kirby. "How did the big opening go, Trix?"

"It was a huge success!" Fern said, clapping her hands together.

Trixie couldn't help but roll her eyes.

"It was somewhat of a success," said Trixie. "With one major hiccup."

"Oh?" Kirby turned to Trixie, a frown on his face. "What happened?"

Trixie shook her head. "I'll tell you later," her side eyes indicating the children.

Kirby nodded, furrowed his brow, and returned to eating, instead asking the kids about their day.

Kirby knew about her time travel. She had slipped away a few times when they first met each other, and less frequently once they were married, before they had kids. Rhada used to say that the more settled you become in your life, the less time slipping you did. She said that's how she knew Kirby was the one for Trixie and liked to remind them that she knew this before the couple did. Trixie let Rhada believe she was first, but she knew Kirby was the one the day they met.

It was a set-up between two friends. There had been a group of them, a mix of friends coming together, organised intentionally for Trixie and Kirby to meet. They'd spent the afternoon at a local winery, the sun shining, wood-fired pizzas eaten.

Over the years, Trixie had managed to keep her time travel a complete secret from most of her friends. She'd convinced them that she often got overwhelmed in social situations and would take herself off to a quiet spot. Fortunately, back then, she could usually feel a time slip coming on and would abruptly get up and walk to a secluded location.

That day, she had been sitting next to Kirby, having quite a deep conversation, desperately trying to ignore her friends who were smiling at her and nudging each other in approval. She had felt a slip coming on, the nauseous feeling rising in her throat, and quickly excused herself. She'd only been gone for five minutes. She was out of practice now, but back then Trixie could pull herself back to the present fairly easily if she wanted to. And that day, she had really wanted to get back to Kirby. Yet, she also knew how rude she would have appeared, so she sat back down apprehensively. Kirby just smiled at her, squeezed her knee, and continued their conversation as though she'd never left. She didn't know if it was the smile, the squeeze, or the fact that he didn't question her departure or return, but at that moment, Trixie felt a clench in her chest and knew he was the one. It certainly hadn't been completely smooth sailing between Trixie and Kirby, but here they were, with a beautiful home and family, doing what they loved.

Yet, Trixie wasn't quite sure how Kirby was going to take the news that she had time travelled again. It had been years. They'd discussed it, and both had concluded that she'd grown out of it, as a child grows out of sucking their thumb. It had been a relief to both of them, although Trixie hated to admit she had grieved it for a time. Losing her ability made her realise that, although she resented it, there was a part of her who treasured her uniqueness, her wild ability, even though she kept it hidden from almost everyone she knew. Time travel had caused her much pain and distress.

"Mum, can I go and finish my homework?" asked Meg. Trixie almost laughed at how eager she was. "Are you full?" she asked, ensuring her daughter's dinner was finished before should could have this 'treat'.

"Yes," said Meg, her hand rising to her throat. "I'm full right to the top!"

"Off you go then," Trixie smiled.

"Can I watch TV?" Joe asked. Trixie repeated the same routine before the two children disappeared inside.

"Right, well, Trixie, you'd better tell Kirby what's going on," said Fern.

Trixie sighed, picked up her serviette and wiped her mouth. She turned to Kirby, who took a sip of his beer, preparing for whatever his wife was about to say.

"So, slight hiccup today," she said. "Right in the middle of serving all the customers who had kindly come into Paraphernalia, I picked up a camera and time slipped to the eighties."

"What?" said Kirby, coughing and thumping his chest. "But you haven't time slipped in years?"

"Uh-huh," said Trixie. "And I am not thrilled about it."

"But why? Why now?"

"We have a theory," said Rhada.

"You and Mum have a theory," said Trixie. "I'm hoping it's a glitch that will never happen again."

Rhada shook her head. "It's not a glitch, my dear. And you know your mother and I have talked this over. We think it has something to do with today being such a significant day."

"Significant day?" Kirby asked.

"You know, two kids at school, opening of my shop," Trixie explained. Kirby nodded.

"But," said Fern. "We think it's more than that. We think it has to do with the camera itself."

"Camera?" asked Kirby.

"I time slipped after I picked up a Polaroid camera someone had brought in."

Kirby turned to Fern. "And you think the camera caused the time travel? Is that normal?"

"Quite normal actually," she said. "And as we were explaining to Trix earlier, items with significant events, tragedies, strong energy connected to them, cause time slips quite frequently."

"And this camera has a significant event attached to it?"

Fern told Kirby the story of Sharon and Tanya, and how Tanya was still missing.

"And I believe that's the reason you, in particular, time travelled," said Fern, turning to her daughter.

"What do you mean?" Trixie asked, picking up a cherry tomato and popping it in her mouth.

"Not only does the Polaroid camera have a tragedy attached to it, but it is an unsolved tragedy. It's a mystery."

"Yes, and will probably remain a mystery," said Trixie.

"Unless," Rhada chimed in. "You solve it."

Chapter 6

Trixie laughed at Rhada's declaration.

"Unless *I* solve it? Me? What are you talking about?"

Maggie was nodding. "It all makes sense, Trixie," she said. "Even I can understand what they're saying, and I still can't quite make heads or tails of this time travel business."

"So the Silver Ladies are sitting here telling me they think the reason I time slipped today is because I have to solve a mystery?"

"Exactly!" Fern said, taking a sip of her mocktail and smiling.

"It's official," said Trixie, looking at Kirby and rolling her eyes. "They've all gone mad. Bonkers."

Kirby squeezed her knee. "It does sound bonkers. But I think you should hear them out. I mean, it's pretty strange you time travelled again, after all this time. Seems there might be something to this mystery theory."

Trixie groaned. "Not you too! Look, there's a completely obvious solution to this. I return the box to Anna, and we can forget all about this."

"I don't think that's how it works," said Rhada.

"How what works? Have you or Mum ever had to time-travel to solve a mystery?" Trixie leant back, folding her arms, feeling rather self-assured.

"Actually," said Fern, catching her mother's eye.

"What? You two have solved a mystery?" asked Trixie.

"Yes, we have," said Rhada. "More than one, actually. We can tell you another time. But what I will say is, what happened to you today is very similar to what has happened to us before."

"And when you try to avoid fate, it has a habit of tapping you on the shoulder again and again until you listen," said Fern.

"Or whacking you in the face," said Rhada, raising her eyebrows.

Trixie knew there must be a story for Rhada to tell, but she most certainly did not want to hear it right now.

"Look, let's leave it for today," said Fern. "Sleep on it. Don't go making any rash decisions. I have a feeling the answer will come to you one way or another."

Trixie shook her head, despairing, and glanced at the vintage gold watch on her wrist. "We'd better get these kids to bed."

"Righto," said Kirby. "I'll clear the table if you want to round them up?"

The couple stood, Trixie happy to make her way inside the cool, dark cottage, away from the Silver Ladies and their bewildering theories.

She wondered why this was the first time she'd heard of her mum and nan solving mysteries when they time travelled. She didn't think they'd lie to her, but were they embellishing the truth just so she didn't return the box of cameras and go back to her normal, non-time-slipping life?

As Trixie helped Meg repack her school bag, found Joe's on the verandah, and coaxed him from the television, almost asleep, she went over the words of the Silver Ladies again and again. And she concluded that the whole idea was preposterous. There was no way a Polaroid camera and a touch of time travel in any way meant she was to become an amateur sleuth, solving crimes. The women really were bonkers.

Kirby helped strap Joe into his car seat, and then he and Meg hopped in his ute. Joe was asleep by the time they got home, and together Trixie and Kirby got him out of his seat and into his room, where they put on his pyjamas and tucked him into bed. They stood at the doorway for a moment, arms around each other, watching their big school kid sound asleep, just like they had when he was a baby.

Trixie let a few tears roll down her face. It had been a big day. For everyone. And it seemed more things were changing in her future than she could have possibly anticipated.

Finally, Kirby and Trixie were able to curl up on the lounge next to each other after Kirby had brewed her a pot of chamomile tea. She sipped the hot drink as the fan above them ticked, sending a refreshing breeze onto their bare arms and legs. Kirby watched a replay of the cricket. Trixie pretended to, but found she couldn't stop thinking about Tanya Stewart.

Ignoring the fact that there was no way she was getting involved, the idea that this fifteen-year-old girl had been missing for forty years was staggering. It seemed obvious she must no longer be alive, and yet, if what Rhada and Fern said was true, was there a reason her first time slip in years had occurred when she held that particular Polaroid camera? It was surely a coincidence. A rather inconvenient coincidence. Or was it?

Trixie used to time-travel a lot when she was younger. And whether it was obvious at the time or not, there always seemed to be some correlation to the time and location she jumped to, and the current situation she was in.

She recalled a time when she had been at her friend's grandfather's funeral and had to abruptly leave the church. As soon as she had made her way behind the Sunday School building, she had travelled back to the very same church, sixty years earlier. It turned out a wedding had just ended, the final car leaving just as she had appeared. Before returning to the present day, she had poked her head into the church only to find a program for the wedding of the very man whose funeral she had just been at. She'd held onto that program, bringing it back with her, even though her mum had severely reprimanded her when she found out.

"You must never, ever take anything with you!"

"Oh Mum, what's the harm?"

"Only the state of the world as we know it."

Trixie had rolled her eyes. That was Fern, dramatic as always.

"I'm not playing, young lady," Fern had said, even though Trixie was around nineteen at the time. "You've heard of the butterfly effect, haven't you?"

"Yes, of course, you never cease to remind me of it."

"Well, you just can't know how one action could change everything. Someone might have put it down and come back for it only to find it missing. That could set in motion them questioning their own mind, and change everything for them, and anyone in their world. You cannot play with these things. As time slippers, we have a huge responsibility."

"I never asked to be a time slipper," said Trixie. "Maybe I'm *meant* to change the world. One wedding program at a time."

"You're impossible," said Fern as she moved to the kitchen sink, picked up a box of matches, and set the program on fire.

"You're destroying it!" Trixie cried. "Who's to say *that* won't change the world as we know it?"

"It seems a lot safer than someone one day finding this in your belongings and wondering how on earth it got there."

Thankfully, she had so far never known anything to be directly impacted by her decision to take the program that day. However, it was a constant reminder that the time slips she had experienced were usually, if not always, related directly to something in her life. She just wasn't always privy to exactly what that was.

Yet, how did this relate to the dramas of the day? Was it simply that she was holding a Polaroid camera that was used by Sharon in this town in the eighties? Or was it more significant? Was it trying to tell her something about what happened to Tanya?

As she began to feel drowsy, she told Kirby she was heading to bed. Lying down, she reminded herself that Rhada and Fern had told her it was virtually impossible, if not completely, to time-travel in her sleep, and with that thought, she was able to fall soundly asleep.

Chapter 7

Trixie would have liked to have been able to say the next day's school drop off was much smoother with Kirby home. But that would be a lie. As she packed their lunchboxes, she discovered all the forms both children had been given on the first day back. So, whilst Kirby got them dressed, she sat down to complete them. If she had learnt one thing since her children had started school, it was to return the forms immediately. Otherwise, they would disappear forever into the vortex that seemed to engulf Speckled Hen Farm.

Kirby was more than happy to do the school drop off today, and although Trixie would miss seeing Joe arrive at his classroom for the second day, she knew there were many more opportunities for her, but fewer for Kirby, who was often away. Trixie took the chance to get to Paraphernalia early. She had decided to open between ten and two on weekdays for a while, to test the waters. She was giving herself full permission to change this at any stage, but for now, she was happy to spend time in the barn, even if she was mostly by herself, and give this business a go.

This morning, she did have specific plans in mind. An experiment. And with Kirby leaving the house just before eight thirty, she hoped she would have enough buffer time in case anything went wrong.

Anna's box was on the counter, just where Trixie had left it the previous afternoon. She was pleased to note that the Silver Ladies had locked up correctly, and everything was neat inside. Feeling the need to steel herself before embarking on her test, she made herself a cup of tea.

For ten minutes, she simply sat, sipping her tea and staring at the Polaroid camera. It was almost as though she wanted it to communicate something to her. Perhaps she could learn to 'read' objects, allowing her to avoid any that would cause her to time slip simply by picking them up. But it gave her nothing. Trixie noticed scuff marks on the top and side, as well as a peeling sticker on the front. She couldn't tell just from looking if there was any film loaded or, for that matter, if it even worked. To evaluate that, she would have to touch it, and she wasn't quite ready for that.

"Knock, knock!"

Trixie jumped, narrowly avoiding spilling the half cup of remaining tea down her blouse.

"Professor Crowe! What are you doing here?"

In walked an elderly man, nimble despite his age. Even though it was going to be another hot summer's day, he was wearing a full three-piece suit, tweed, a preference he and Trixie had in common. His white hair sprang wildly from his head, and he was carrying a large brown leather caddy.

"How many times do I have to tell you to call me Sutton?"

Professor Crowe asked her to call him by his first name every time they met, but Trixie knew he loved being called Professor, so she would never change. However, in her own mind, she actually called him The Engineer.

Sutton Crowe was an eccentric and, for reasons unknown to Trixie, rather well-off Wattlebury resident. He had been an engineering professor at prestigious universities throughout the world, but now that he had retired, he was fascinated with inventing things, both theoretical and physical, without the constraints of academia. The pair had a love for visiting clearing sales and estate sales, and after running into each other on numerous occasions, had gradually built a weird and wonderful friendship. Trixie could only imagine what he had brought in to show her today.

"So, what's in the box?" she asked.

"I'll get to that momentarily," he said. "But first, my dear, how did it go? The big opening?"

Trixie smiled. Despite being rather eccentric and dishevelled most days, Trixie had come to know him as a very caring man who remembered everything she told him about her life and her family.

"Oh, not so big, just as I wanted it," she said. "I made a few sales, which was lovely. The real test is going to be the next few weeks."

Professor Crowe clapped his hands together, smiling broadly. "Wonderful news! I have no doubt you'll be a huge success."

"Ok, you can't delay any more. What's in the box?"

Trixie felt a bit miffed that her experiment with the camera had been interrupted, but she quickly realised the engineer's arrival was a rather weird coincidence.

The Professor lifted his box onto the counter and walked around to stand next to Trixie.

"This is something I've been working on for a while, and it certainly isn't finished. It may never be finished. But I just had to share it with someone. I only hope you don't think I'm crazy."

"Why would I think you're crazy?" Trixie asked. Although if pressed by someone other than the Professor, she would have admitted he did have a touch of the bizarre about him.

Without replying, he opened the leather straps at the front before turning a coded lock. Lifting the lid, the four sides fell away, and a curious contraption appeared before them.

There were a lot of shiny silver cogs, a row of buttons at the back, wires everywhere, and in the middle a large digital clock displaying the date alongside twenty-four-hour time. If Trixie didn't know better…..

"It's not a…" she trailed off, indicating an explosion with her hands and mouth, not wanting to say the word.

"A bomb!" Professor Sutton laughed loudly. "An absolutely valid assumption. But no."

Trixie allowed herself a grin before asking, "Then what is it?"

Lifting his head, the Professor caught Trixie's eye and held it before finally speaking. "It's a time machine."

It was Trixie's turn to laugh. And not for the reason the Professor believed.

"I know it probably seems fantastical to you," he said. "But I assure you, this is backed by the best science."

Trixie smiled and shook her head. "No, no, that's not why I am laughing. I do not doubt with your expertise that you could very well create a time machine. Sorry, I didn't mean to laugh. It's just a coincidence, that's all."

"A coincidence?"

Despite telling him a lot about her life, Trixie had never once ever so much as hinted at her family's propensity to time slip. And after yesterday, she was certainly not about to reveal it here and now.

"It's just my family happened to be talking about time travel last night," she said. "Somehow it came up in conversation. It was all very silly. I just couldn't believe the coincidence."

"Well, my dear, I certainly don't believe in coincidences, so it is bound to mean something."

"Possibly," Trixie agreed, albeit reluctantly. She had experienced too many coincidences in the past twenty-four hours to feel comfortable with that assumption. "So, you say it doesn't work yet?"

"Not yet," he said. "But I have finally managed to get the epoch regulator to communicate with the anachromometer."

Trixie frowned. "The what communicating with the what?"

"Forgive me," said the Professor. "I've had to invent the names for the various parts. There are not that many time machines around to work with." He chuckled. "In layman's terms, the dials where I input the target date and time are now talking to the clock."

"Ah, I see," said Trixie. "But what about the location. Do you put in a target location?"

"Location?" The Professor frowned. "Well, that is another story. I was anticipating the first trip would simply be a jump to the same location where the time machine was. Just a different date and time."

Trixie nodded. "And how do you get back?"

"Well, you are asking the tough questions! I knew I liked you for a reason."

Trixie smiled. Little did he know. However, she was relieved to acknowledge that his answers, or lack thereof, didn't indicate he wasn't going to be meeting her in 1980s Wattlebury any time soon.

"It sounds like you've made great progress," said Trixie. "Just imagine if you cracked it!'

He smiled, nodded, and packed the box back up. "I've also brought something for you to work on. A paid job, please. For Paraphernalia."

"Of course! What is it?"

The Professor reached into his breast pocket and pulled out a small transistor radio. "Do you think you can fix this?" He handed it to

Trixie.

"Well, I'm not sure," she said. "But you're more than capable of fixing this, aren't you?"

"My mind, yes," he said, tapping his temple. "My fingers," he held them up to show Trixie the slightly swollen knuckles. "Unfortunately, they aren't what they used to be, and for the delicate work this job requires, completely inadequate."

"Well, it would be my pleasure."

"Thank you," he said. "It was my Mother's. I am hoping I can take it to the cricket. My niece is taking me to the one-day match at Adelaide Oval next week."

"And are you working on any other inventions, aside from the time machine?" Trixie asked, as she went to her iPad to start booking in the transistor radio repair.

"Well, now that you ask," he said. "I am trying to create a machine that will manoeuvre across the shelves of my library and dust."

"Now that sounds like a genius idea! Will it only dust bookshelves?"

"It's not even really doing that, at least not well enough to my wife's liking," he smiled. She had only met his wife, Jean, a few times, but knew she was a lovely yet fastidious person. Trixie wondered how she put up with the Professor.

"Well, when you're even close to Jean being happy, I would like to order one in every colour!"

"You're on!" The Professor patted Trixie on the shoulder before grabbing his caddy and moving out from behind the counter. "Wishing you a very successful week." He waved as he left the barn.

Trixie shook her head, marvelling at this encounter. It took her a moment to remember the Polaroid camera. What was the time? Ten past nine. Was that cutting it too close?

"Oh, what the heck! I doubt anyone's going to be knocking on the door on the dot of ten."

Without hesitating, she moved to stand in front of the camera.

"Right, let's do this," she said aloud. "One…two…three!"

Trixie closed her eyes, snatched up the camera and waited. She couldn't bring herself to open her eyes for a few moments.

"Seriously!"

When she did, she found she was still in the barn, and nothing had changed. Trixie quickly checked a clock on the wall to ensure the time and date were the same. They were. She was utterly confused and, if she was honest, a little disappointed. She plonked the camera in the box, shoved it under the counter out of the way, and looked around for things to do.

When she finally put the Open sign on the door, no one came.

Chapter 8

Trixie tried not to feel despondent. It was only day two, and it wasn't as though she had made a big hoo-ha about the opening of Paraphernalia. She didn't doubt word had gotten around, and she had shared a few things on social media, but it was only the second day of school. People were getting back into the swing of things. A visit to Paraphernalia wouldn't be top of their list.

Trixie sat at a wooden table she had set up in the window, displaying old tools, and watched a blue wren and his three brown females flutter around the rosemary bushes outside. It struck Trixie that she was rather like the wren, with three females who were always on the periphery of her life. In general, Trixie had gotten used to them popping into the farm, making suggestions about her life, or doing things they believed were helpful. Of course, she mustn't forget how much support the Silver Ladies gave her, especially when Kirby was away for work. She had learnt to dismiss most of what they said and did, whilst also trying not to come across as rude or ungrateful. It didn't always work.

Today, she was wondering if she should ignore their comments as usual, forget about solving a mystery, and arrange to return the box of cameras to Anna as soon as possible. Normally, she would have laughed off this ridiculous idea, not mentioned it for a few days or weeks, and hoped they would have forgotten, which they usually did. Yet, Trixie couldn't seem to get Sharon and Tanya out of her mind. How could it be that a fifteen-year-old girl could go missing without a trace? Even if she were deceased, the idea that her body hadn't been found was devastating. And to think Sharon herself had passed away, never knowing what happened to her own daughter.

Trixie stood and went over to the camera box. She brought it back to the table and began to pull out items. If she time slipped, so be it. There was no one to see her disappear anyway.

The Polaroid camera was first, which she pushed to one side. When all of this kerfuffle was over, she was looking forward to testing it out. Next, she pulled out a small leather case that contained an Olympus Trip 35 with the flash that attached to the top. Looking at the back, it didn't appear to contain any film. Laying it to one side, she found a slightly more modern Canon Snappy 50. Underneath, Trixie couldn't help smiling at a long, thin, bright pink Hanimex camera. She imagined a teenager in the eighties would have adored it. There was a selection of different film canisters, along with a packet of Polaroid film. She wondered if it still worked.

The remainder of the box was filled with multiple packs of negatives in all different shapes and sizes. Trixie thought it must contain every single film photo Sharon Stewart ever took! She wondered if Anna had known these were in the box. She picked up one set that had been slid into a plastic sheet, with rows of the processed film laid out one below the other. Taking it to the window, she pressed plastic to the glass, examining the images.

It had been many years since she had looked at photo negatives. At first glance, they were just a lot of sepia and cream blobs until your eyes focused. The sky was black. Grass was white. And faces glowed. A moment in time, captured but colours reversed. Yet despite the altered perspective, you were still able to make out most things in the tiny, postage-stamp-sized images.

The negatives Trixie was looking at appeared to contain crowds of people. An event or a celebration. Individuals couldn't be made out, but groups clustered, most facing in the general direction of the camera, as if the photographer was a part of the main action everyone was watching. She went back to the box and took out another packet. The film was different, as though from another camera. Yet when she held these negatives up to the light, again she saw crowds of people. Was it the same event, or a different one?

Next, she picked up a spool of film, one not cut up or slid into a plastic protector but curled up. She felt like a photographer in their darkroom, images revealing themselves as the sepia plastic unfurled. It was harder to get a good look, but this one appeared to only have a few photos of a crowd, with the others showing a variety of scenes. A dog and a cat asleep on a mat, a young boy blowing out a birthday cake, and what appeared to be a family photo at Christmas time. These were all quite different to the ones in the sheet protectors. Trixie wondered what that meant.

"Lunch time!"

The voice of her husband startled her. Trixie smiled, looking over to the man who was strolling into the barn.

Kirby was carrying a bundle of paper bags. "I've been to the bakery! Couldn't stop thinking about their custard berliners."

Trixie laughed, placing the film back in the box. "I hope you got me one!"

"Of course! I also got you a cornish pasty with sauce," he said, handing her one of the warm bags.

"Perfect!"

They decided to take them outside and sit at the small wrought iron garden setting she had at the front. It meant they could brush the crumbs to the ground, and perhaps the blue wrens would snack on them.

"Have you been busy today?" Kirby asked, leaning over as he took a bite from his steak and mushroom pie so it didn't land in his lap.

Trixie sighed. "Not a single visitor."

Kirby glanced up at his wife. "Oh, that's no good."

She shrugged. "I obviously have to do some work to get the word out there." As she'd spent the morning looking at the negatives, the time had passed quickly, and she wasn't too concerned that the day had been quiet. Long-term, she hoped to keep herself busy with repairs and renovations.

"Actually, I forgot!" she said. "The engineer popped in. He's given me my first repair job."

"Well, that's better! See! You've not only had a visitor, but you've had a customer." Kirby smiled at her, clearly proud.

"It was only Sutton," she said. "But you're right, it is better than nothing. I have to repair his mother's old transistor radio."

They fell silent as Trixie finished her pastie, and Kirby devoured his custard berlina. "That's the stuff!" he said, using the back of his hand to wipe sugar from his face.

"So, what are you up to for the rest of the day?" Trixie asked.

"I've got to plan the job up at Wilcannia," he said. "Doing some mapping work for a station manager up there. As soon as the weather cools down, he'll want me over, so I thought I'd better be ready."

"Any more flying before then?"

"Yep," he said. "I'm going to have to head off the day after tomorrow. Mount Gambier airport for some training."

Trixie nodded. She was used to her husband's schedule. She didn't love it, but she understood and appreciated how hard he worked for their family.

"Thinking I'll get the laundry painted tomorrow," he said.

"Oh no, have a rest! You're barely home. You can take a day off, can't you?"

"Maybe," he said. "Thought I'd paint and have the cricket on in the background. That won't mess you around too much?"

"As long as I can use it when you head off, it would be amazing to finally cover up the mould stains."

Kirby nodded before standing. "Well, I'll head back to the house. And you'll pick up the kids? Or would you like me to?"

"I've promised them a visit to The Chocolate Bar, and Mum and Nan are planning to join us.

"Well, I'll leave that to you!" He grinned. Trixie knew coffee with the Silver Ladies wouldn't be his preferred way to spend the afternoon.

Pecking her on the cheek, he made his way down the track that led to the farmhouse. Trixie sat outside for a bit longer, wondering how the kids were doing at school, trying to remember what her Mum said she was up to today, and racking her brain for marketing ideas so people knew Paraphernalia existed.

"I have absolutely no idea!" she said loudly to herself. Walking back inside, she wanted to take another look at the box of negatives, but knew that wasn't achieving anything.

"I'll bring them up to the house tonight and take a look," she told herself. Instead, she picked up Sutton's radio and placed it at her repair bench, all set up with a magnifying lamp and tools for small jobs like this one.

Putting her head over the lamp, Trixie turned the transistor over in her hands, analysing the best place to start. To her right was a small tray divided into sections. With a screwdriver, she began to dismantle the transistor, placing the screws into one section of the tray before carefully lifting the back off. Small pieces of lint and debris were inside. Spinning around on her stool, she blew as much as she could away from the radio, dust particles slowly floating to the floor.

For the next few hours, she pulled apart the transistor, taking photos, making notes and drawing sketches as she went, to ensure everything was returned to its original place.

Her alarm on her phone rang, the school pick up alert, scaring her as she attempted to lift the tiny speaker from the front plate.

"Wow! Hours of peace, quiet, and concentration," she said to herself. "I can't remember the last time that has happened."

Clicking off the lamp, Trixie stood, carefully placing all the pieces into a plastic container before pressing the lid down securely.

It was time to pick up the kids and head to The Chocolate Bar.

Chapter 9

The Chocolate Bar was a local establishment in Wattlebury. It was run by a quirky couple called Odette and Rupert Zima, who, despite possibly being in their late sixties, always seemed young, hip and up with the latest trends. They would often travel, seeking out different ideas for their business. Every item on their menu either contained chocolate or had some chocolate connection. There were the tried and true items like their chocolate torte or truffles. But then they did things such as turning a black forest cake into lava cupcakes, where the cherry filling exploded from the centre as you bit into it. Or serving chocolate fettuccine with sun-dried tomato pesto alongside a chocolate red wine.

As Trixie ushered Joe and Meg inside, they spotted Rhada and Fern at their usual table towards the back. Odette and Rupert tended to leave these seats free for the locals, letting the tourists fight it out for the spots at the front or on the street. The locals preferred chatting with Odette and Rupert over people watching.

"So what flavour have you got today, Nan?" asked Trixie, pointing to the slice of chocolate cake in front of Rhada, cockatoo earrings dangling from her ears. "Raspberry? Banana? Mint Caramel?"

"Odette has gone back to classic chocolate fudge cake today! Delicious as always. She's got cupcakes, too. I'm taking a box home."

"Of course you are!'

Trixie got the kids seated, and before she herself could sit down, Rupert was bringing the kids' milkshakes over.

"Oh Rupert! Amazing service as always."

"Don't worry, Fern gave me the heads up," he said. "Luckily, I know their usual."

Meg loved the caramel-choc milkshake, whilst Joe always opted for a straight chocolate, both with a chocolate flake bar crumbled on the top.

"And Trixie, what can I get for you?"

After her bakery lunch, she knew she shouldn't indulge too much. "What savoury items do you have on the menu today?"

"We have a crostini with prosciutto, goat's cheese and a chocolate balsamic glaze."

"That sounds perfect!"

Rupert smiled and took Trixie's order to the kitchen.

"How did you go today, Trixie?" asked Fern, who was wearing thick green glasses and a burgundy dress.

"Only one customer, first thing," said Trixie, before telling them all about Professor Crowe's transistor radio.

"So, what did you do with yourself all day?" asked Rhada.

"Fixed Sutton's radio, of course," said Trixie. "Well, at least I got most of it pulled apart."

Fern and Rhada laughed.

"That was the whole day?" asked Fern.

"Kirby brought me lunch from the bakery."

Fern nodded.

"And ah," Trixie hesitated. "I did have a bit of a look in Anna's box."

"Stop!" Maggie had arrived, dressed head to toe in mint green active wear, even finishing off the look with a matching cap through which she had pulled her blonde ponytail. "Don't say another word until I can listen." Maggie twisted around and called out to Odette. "Could I please have a lavender hot chocolate?"

"A hot chocolate in the middle of summer?" said Fern, raising her eyebrows. "Really, Maggie?"

Maggie ignored her friend. She did the occasional shift in The Chocolate Bar, especially when they were getting slammed during the height of the tourist season. So if anyone knew the menu, it was Maggie. Today, one of their bespoke hot chocolates was top of her list.

"Back to the box," said Maggie. "Did you…you know?" She tilted her head and raised her eyebrows, which Trixie knew meant she was being asked if she time slipped.

She shook her head. "Nope, not even an inkling."

"Was there anything interesting inside the box?" Rhada asked.

"Some nice vintage cameras," said Trixie. "A cool, bright pink one from the eighties. Probably a teenager's."

"Probably Tanya's," said Fern, picking up a chocolate truffle and placing it in her mouth.

"Oh! Gosh, I didn't even think of that," said Trixie. She put her head in her hands. She'd been having such a lovely time going through the cameras, checking all the negatives. Not once registering the possible connection to the decades-long missing girl.

"What else did you find?" Maggie asked.

Trixie took a few moments to respond before taking a deep breath. "There were two other cameras and lots of negatives. Quite a few in those plastic protectors where you can look at them in rows. Others just still rolled up and tossed in."

"Anything of interest on the film? Any clues?" Fern asked.

"Clues!" said Trixie. "Don't start with the mystery thing again."

"Ok, ok," said Fern. "But what were the negatives of?"

Trixie described the many photos of some sort of event or

celebration and the differences between the sheets of negatives and the rolls.

"An event," said Rhada, putting her fingers to her lips. "I wonder…."

"Your crostini," Odette placed a plate in front of Trixie. "And a lavender hot chocolate." She handed this to Maggie before sliding a plate of chocolate strawberries in front of the two children. They grinned at her, straws still in their mouths.

"Odette," said Maggie. "Do you remember Tanya Stewart, the girl who went missing?"

"Yes, of course I do. She'd just started working here a few weeks beforehand."

"And the day she went missing, wasn't there some sort of event on?"

"Well, yes, it was the town's 150th anniversary celebration," said Odette. "Tanya didn't show up for her shift. That was one of the reasons Sharon realised something was wrong."

"There," said Maggie, turning to face Trixie. "That's what those photos would be."

Odette didn't ask what Maggie meant. She just smiled and went back to serving customers.

"What makes you so sure, Maggie?" Trixie asked.

"They'd be photos of the last day Sharon knew Tanya was alive," she replied.

Rhada and Fern both let out noises of understanding.

"What?" asked Trixie. "What are you talking about?"

"That's Sharon's box, right?" asked Maggie, sipping her hot chocolate.

Trixie nodded.

"It was her search. Sharon was using the photos to try to work out what happened to Tanya."

"Really? She took all those photos?"

"No," said Fern. "That's not what Maggie means."

Trixie frowned, confused, her mind going back to the negatives. She remembered the negatives hadn't all been the same. Maybe they were different types of film. For different types of cameras.

"You mean, they were from other people's cameras?" she said.

"Exactly," Maggie said. "I think what you've got is Sharon's collection of photographs from that day. Sourced from as many people as were willing to help her."

"And I imagine that was quite a few," said Fern. "The whole town was in shock. I mean, it wasn't like today. There wouldn't have been a huge number of people with cameras. But being such a big event for the town, I'm sure there were more than usual.

Trixie picked up her crostini and took a crunchy bite. She was shocked Anna had simply handed Trixie a box that would have been so significant to her mother.

Yet, it obviously didn't hold the clues Sharon was looking for.

That night, as she had planned, after the kids were in bed, Trixie went to the barn and brought the box back with her to the house. Her initial curiosity was now tinged with a feeling she couldn't quite put her finger on. Guilt? Concern? Invasion of privacy?

Should she even be looking at these negatives? She had to remember that most, if not all, of them had been given to Sharon. At least, that was what she and the Silver Ladies had deduced. So, if Sharon had permission, it surely meant it was ok for Trixie to look at them? Although they did now belong to Anna. Perhaps she hadn't realised the negatives were in the box. Perhaps she didn't care.

Kirby had already gone to bed after snoring on the couch for half an hour. Trixie set herself up at his desk with the lamp on. One by one, she pulled out the negatives, this time looking at them differently.

Maggie was right. It very well could be the day of the centenary celebrations, the day Tanya went missing. As she held up negative after negative, what convinced Trixie that the Silver Ladies were right was spotting various people in old-fashioned dress; much older than the eighties era these negatives seemed to depict. No, this looked like people dressed up in outfits they would have worn a hundred years prior, at the time the town was formed.

Trixie worked her way through the box of negatives, confirming to herself that all of the negatives in the protective pages were photographs of that day. Of the centenary. Of Tanya's last known day in Wattlebury. Looking at the loose negatives, Trixie realised none of these contained images of the 150-year event.

"What does all of this mean?" thought Trixie. "And what on earth does it have to do with me?"

Trixie had laid everything out on the desk, now at the bottom of the box. She went to move the box out of the way, but it was heavier than she expected. It was at that moment she realised. The box wasn't as empty as she'd thought. There was something concealed at the bottom, fitting perfectly.

Tipping the box upside down, the mysterious item landed on the desk with a thud.

"Oh my goodness!" It was a photo album.

Chapter 10

Trixie opened the album and quickly flicked through the pages. She wasn't surprised to see that many of the photos were prints from the negatives inside the box. All were of the same day. That day. The town's anniversary. There was no doubt. Each photo was different but similar. And many had a handwritten note next to it. There were even notes slipped inside some of the pages.

Maggie was right. Sharon was using these photos to find any trace of Tanya, any clue that would lead to her missing daughter.

Deciding she needed to relocate for this, Trixie picked up the album and went into the kitchen to make a cup of tea before settling herself in the lounge room. She turned the ceiling fan to low so it wouldn't disturb anything inside the album, and got comfortable.

The first thing she noted was that some of the photos had a time written next to them, most with 'approx.', but some times were underlined. These, Trixie could see, were photos of the formal proceedings of the day. People making speeches, a plaque being unveiled, and what appeared to be a group of school children singing. These were obviously moments in the day when Sharon could be more certain of the timing. Flipping through, Trixie saw that it was roughly in order of the day, although some times appeared to have been crossed out and updated later, which did disrupt the timeline somewhat.

The next things she noted were names written by the photos. Trixie guessed Sharon had worked on identifying anyone she knew or Tanya knew. Perhaps they were people Tanya could have been with that day? Trixie wondered who Tanya's friends had been and if they were still alive.

"Still alive? What are you thinking, Trixie?" she said to herself. "Stop acting like you're actually going to investigate this."

Trixie sighed, realising The Silver Ladies had gotten into her head. Yet, she returned to the photos. Arrows were pointing to people, and some individuals were even circled in pen, on the actual photos, which, for some reason, shocked Trixie. Most had question marks next to them or even 'who is this?'.

Some photos featured Tanya herself, or at least, this is what Sharon had noted. It wasn't very clear to Trixie, but she did begin to recognise the repeated denim skirt and fluro-pink oversized t-shirt, tucked in at the front, that Tanya had worn. Trixie went back to the beginning of the album and started to look at each image meticulously, particularly those with Tanya identified. In some, she appeared to be with friends. Others, she was in the line at a sausage sizzle, or listening to the singers. It was often next to these photos where Sharon had more detailed notes on paper slid into the album. Trixie found some of the writing hard to follow, almost as if Sharon was writing a train of thought, not coherent ideas. They didn't appear to be of much use.

"I might go back to the notes later," she said, realising she was beginning to feel tired and needed to go to bed.

It was then she saw it. Something that shocked Trixie so much she let out what could only be described as a yelp. Tossing the album to one side, she quickly stood up. Her heart was racing, and she could feel her palms getting sweaty. Any other time, Trixie might have believed she was having a heart attack, and perhaps she was. But after what she had just seen, it was much more likely this was the beginning of a panic attack.

"Now, Trix, you've got to calm down," she said out loud. "You were probably seeing things. You're tired. Not thinking straight. Take a few deep breaths, sit down, and look again."

Trixie ran her hands through her hair, then shook them out in front of herself in an effort to dissipate the energy that was coursing through her body.

"Ok, ok, you can do this," she said out loud again. As she often did, she used vocalisation to help herself process this bizarre revelation.

Taking ten intentional deep breaths, she let out a loud "whoosh!" on the final breath. Trixie felt ready to sit down and pick up the album again.

Of course, the page she had been on was no longer open, so she had to take her time, looking for the photo again. Where was it?

"See, you were dreaming, Trix! All in your imagination," she spoke aloud.

But she knew it wasn't in her imagination. Page after page, she couldn't see it, so she went back to the start again. Finally, five pages in, she saw it.

"Bloody hell!"

There it was, not in black and white, but in full colour. In fact, it was in full Polaroid colour. On one of the pages, within the time frame of the formal proceedings, was a Polaroid instant photograph. As was typical, it was tinged orange and ever so slightly blurry. But there was absolutely no mistaking what it was. In that photo from 1989, as clear as crystal in the upper right-hand corner, was what had shocked her to her core.

It was a photograph of herself.

Chapter 11

"What do you mean, you're in the photo album?" asked Fern.

Trixie had rallied the troops the next morning, asking them to meet at Paraphernalia before it opened. She needed the insights of the Silver Ladies. She needed their support. At this stage, she didn't believe it really was her in the picture. At least, she didn't want to believe it.

Not that there was any doubt.

Trixie pointed to herself.

"Oh!" said Maggie. "It flippin' well is you!"

It was clearly Trixie. She wasn't obscured in any way, and she was big enough that there was no major distortion. Looking at the photo and then at the Trixie of today, there was absolutely no difference. Same pewter hair, a legacy from greying in her twenties. It was even the same length, probably to the millimetre. Aside from the surroundings and the quality of the photo, it could have been taken today.

Or tomorrow.

Rhada was walking around Paraphernalia, peering into boxes and drawers.

"Nan, what are you doing?" called out Trixie.

"Surely you've got a magnifying glass somewhere in this place!" she said, slamming a box closed and bending down to peer under one of the benches.

"Why do you need a magnifying glass?"

"We've got to analyse all these photos," she said. "What if your mother or I are in them too?"

"I don't think you're in there, Nan," said Trixie. "I've gone through these photos so many times."

"At least we know now what you're meant to do," said Fern, leaning back in her chair, hands now resting on her lap.

"We do?" asked Trixie, who hadn't been able to stand still since the Silver Ladies arrived and was currently rearranging a table filled with baking equipment.

"Of course we do, Trix," said Maggie.

"Don't say it," said Trixie. "Don't even think it."

Rhada had found herself a pair of giant retro glasses and was trying to use them as a magnifying glass.

"Even if we don't use the words," said Fern. "It doesn't change the facts."

"But don't you all see how crazy this is?" said Trixie, shaking her head. "It's weird enough that we can time travel. Now you want a mum of two, who's trying to start a vintage shop, to turn detective?"

Fern shrugged, Maggie smiled, and Rhada flipped to the next page of the photo album.

"This is ridiculous!" said Trixie.

"I could be persuaded to believe you-" Fern was cut off.

"Thank you!" Trixie responded.

Fern shook her head and then tapped her finger on the album. "*If it wasn't for the fact that you're right there. In this photo album from the eighties! You were a newborn baby. Yet here you are, as clear as crystal.*"

"Maybe it's just someone who looks like me. A doppelgänger."

"Trixie," asked Maggie, tilting her head. "Why are you fighting so hard against this?"

"I don't know!" She raised her hands before placing them on the top of her head. "It's too much. I've got enough on my plate. Why is this even happening?"

Maggie walked over and put her arm around Trixie's waist. "It's a sign, Trix. A big, fat, time travelling sign."

"Uuuggh!" She walked away from Maggie and flopped down onto the Chesterfield couch, lying across it, forearm on her brow.

"Maybe we should just leave her to have a little think," said Rhada

"Thinking isn't going to change anything," said Fern, pushing her chair back and standing up, hands on her hips. "Trixie, you've got to buck up and get on with things." She walked over to the couch and sat down on Trixie's feet, forcing her daughter to sit up.

"She's right, you know," said Maggie. "The answer is in the photo. You've already time travelled. It's a fact. So stop making it harder than you need to. You never know, it could be fun!"

Trixie was about to have another outburst, but Fern put a hand on her arm, stopping her in her tracks. "Maggie's right, Trixie. Stop trying to change things. It is inevitable. It's now time to prepare."

Rhada picked up a bentwood chair and placed it in front of the mother and daughter. "Your mum's right. Gosh, there's so much we've got to do. It will almost be like starting from scratch."

"Starting what from scratch?" Trixie asked.

"Your training! You've got to do this properly and safely. Otherwise, devastating things could happen."

"Devastating," she moaned. "See, this is a bad idea. We should just completely forget it. I'll take the box back to Anna and leave it all alone."

"Snap out of it, Trix!" Fern was stern yet again. "You've got to focus. And right now you've got to focus on the fact that it is past ten o'clock and you have customers waiting."

Trixie jumped up. "I do?" She was genuinely shocked, but as she pushed the sliding barn door open, she saw Fern was right. There were two customers parked next to her mum's Volvo.

"Ok, you lot need to leave. You'll only distract me."

Trixie ushered them out, with Rhada confirming they would work on a training plan. "Shall we get started tonight?"

"No!" Trixie said rather quickly. "I haven't told Kirby about the photo. I don't want to bother him. He leaves tomorrow. We can think about it then."

The Silver Ladies left in Fern's car, and Trixie welcomed inside a woman searching for milk glass lampshades - Trixie showed her a small collection - and a couple who wanted to use old keys as part of their wedding decorations. A large glass jar full of keys kept them entertained.

They all made purchases, and Trixie was beaming by eleven o'clock when she sat down to work on Sutton's transistor radio. Unfortunately, thinking of the Professor reminded her of time travel, which in turn brought back memories of her own jaunt and this morning's conversation.

She knew she would have to accept it, but she'd never truly come to terms with her time travel abilities. The *whole family's* time travel abilities. Fern had always revered time travel. Trixie had just felt weird and uncomfortable about the whole thing. Fern had continued to travel throughout Trixie's school years. Longer even. It wasn't until she'd had a bout of pneumonia in her fifties that Fern lost her abilities. She'd been devastated when they'd never returned.

Rhada's abilities were similar to Trixie's, losing them once she was married and settled down. Hers had never returned. Rhada and her granddaughter were similar. Neither were obsessed with time travel. Trixie had often wondered if that was why their abilities had left earlier than Fern's.

Trixie had assumed that, like her Nan's, hers would not return. Now she was questioning everything she knew. It seemed time slipping had only been lying dormant inside her; it hadn't died. It had reactivated for a reason. Unfortunately for Trixie, it was becoming impossible for her to deny that the reason was Tanya. And Sharon. And Anna and Jason.

Her family had always talked about time travel as something to be proud of, that they'd been blessed ("Inflicted!" Trixie would retort) with it for a reason, and it was up to them to use it the best way they could. Trixie had never been able to manipulate it to her whims like Fern had become adept at. Her mum always said Trixie would be able to if she actually tried, if she actually cared about learning. It was Rhada who always backed her up, supporting her decision not to embrace time travel. Eventually, although she never understood it, Fern accepted it. Trixie suspected it was only because she had hoped that would change one day.

Had that day come?

Chapter 12

Trixie was thrilled that a few customers trickled in during the day. Not everyone bought something, but they were so enthusiastic about the shop, oohing and ahhing, as well as commenting on the sign she had added to the counter announcing her repair and renovation services.

"Amazing! I have a tiled coffee table that was my Great Aunt's, but some of the tiles are lifting or cracked," a young woman told her. "Would that be something you could fix?"

"Absolutely," said Trixie. "And depending on the tiles, it is possible I could source new ones to replace the cracked ones."

"That would be brilliant!" she said. "Shall I send you a photo?"

Trixie gave the woman her phone number and smiled as she waved at the door.

Just as she was about to sit back down to the Professor's radio, Kirby strolled in. He was covered head to toe in paint.

"Whoa! So, the laundry's going well?" She couldn't help but laugh.

"So good!" he said, grinning. "I'm on a roll, so I won't have time for a lunch run today."

Trixie smiled before shouting, "No!" He was about to sit his paint-covered butt down on an upholstered stool.

"Oh, sorry," he said, spinning in an attempt to check if he had paint on the back of his pants. He did indeed. "I have absolutely no idea how that got there."

"No problems about lunch," Trixie said. "I don't need another bakery lunch. I'll grab something from the fridge."

"I think I'm going to warm up some soup," he replied. "Just one more coat to go. I've already built the new counter, so I'll slide that in, but I might not get to the shelves today."

Trixie came over and gave him a big hug, despite his paint-covered clothes. She hoped he knew how much this meant to her. How he cared for her and the kids without her having to ask. It was all the little things he did to make her life easier that made him so special.

"Thank you for getting all this done today," she said. "I can't wait to have a functioning laundry!"

"And how has business been today? I've heard a few cars."

She told him about each customer, what they'd said and what they'd bought. Sharing it with someone made Trixie feel quite excited about Paraphernalia. Yes, it had been a crazy few days, but despite the time slip element, this new business was showing it may actually have legs.

After putting a "back in 15 minutes" sign on the door, she walked to the house with Kirby. He made soup while Trixie pulled together an egg mayonnaise sandwich. She took it back to the Barn, and with her plate next to her on the counter, she pulled out Sharon's photo album and grabbed her notebook. If she was going to have to investigate, she might want to find out exactly what Sharon had discovered first.

Having looked at the album numerous times, she knew Sharon had marked certain names with a red star. Going back over these, Trixie realised that it wasn't a whole lot of different people. It was just two. Two men whom she'd identified in multiple photos. Unless she was mistaken, these two men were Sharon's suspects. But who were they?

"Might need to use Rhada's trick," Trixie thought, smiling as she got up to find the glasses her Nan had been using earlier.

Trixie peered at the photos, but she still had no idea who they were. Not that they were bad photographs. Quite a few had a clear shot of each of them. But the photos were forty years old, which meant the suspects, as she had begun to call them, were forty years younger than they would be today. Fortunately, she knew three women who might recognise them.

Continuing, Trixie made sure to write in her notebook anything significant she could take from Sharon's notes. It wasn't much, and some of it she didn't understand. What surprised Trixie was that there was nothing in the album or the box aside from the photos, cameras and negatives, and the few scrappy pages from Sharon. There were no newspaper cuttings. No reports about Tanya going missing. Not even a notice about the 150th anniversary celebrations.

"I think I'm going to have to visit the library," she said. Even if she had tried to search online, Trixie knew she wouldn't find much. There might be a snippet in one of the smaller papers, but she wanted to look at the local paper, The Lilly Pilly Creek Chronicle, which covered the towns in their district. The paper had closed down about ten years ago, and she doubted that much, if anything, would have been digitised.

Trixie got up to grab a drink and stood in front of the fan she had set up. The day was warm, and they were reaching the hottest part. As she rested the cool glass against her cheek, she couldn't help but remember her Nan's comment about training.

What exactly did she mean? Trixie had time slipped plenty of times. Ok, none were deliberate, but that wasn't really possible, was it? It was just something that happened spontaneously. Or maybe you *could* encourage a time slip? She didn't really know. But surely it wasn't anything that needed official training. Surely it was just practice. And she'd had no trouble getting back the other day. Although she'd almost forgotten what to do, muscle memory had kicked in. All she'd had to do was relax, take some deep breaths, and visualise. She'd been taught how to do that when she was a little girl, when Fern and Rhada were preparing her for her first slip. They'd told her your first time slip could happen around the age of nine. They'd then gone on to tell her about their own slips and what they did to get back. From about five, they sat her down to practice her breathing and picturing home, just in case she got herself in a really sticky situation. She knew this. She knew how to return.

So what else was there to learn exactly? Training made it sound like she was going to get roped into a fitness regime of some sort, and that was not something she was signing up for. Perhaps it was theoretical? Did she need to know the science behind time travel? The thought made her head feel heavy. This was not her strength.

As Trixie tidied up and closed the shop, she wondered, would she have to accept that the role of time travelling detective may be her destiny? Or could she just ignore it and move on with her life? Despite everything, she had to admit there was a curiosity to discover what really happened to Tanya. If she were unfortunate enough to have the time slip affliction, it would be heartening to use it for good, to make a difference in someone's life. And surely someone should ensure the work Sharon did in her lifetime wasn't for nothing. Was that person her?

Chapter 13

"The library? Yes! I can do my homework there." Meg was thrilled when Trixie let them know where they were headed after school. Joe was less enthusiastic.

"Can't I just play on the playground?" Joe looked up at Trixie, pleading. "I'll be good. I promise."

"Sorry, Joe, I can't see you from the library," Trixie replied. "There are games in the library, aren't there, Meg?"

"Yep! And there's Lego. You like Lego, right, Joe?"

Although Joe wasn't pleased, Meg's suggestion of Lego did seem to appease him. Trixie grabbed their bags and led the way to the Community Library, which was connected to the school. Fortunately for Trixie, once they got inside, one of Joe's friends was already there, and they raced to the Lego box together.

Meg set herself up at a table near the microfilm viewer and drawers. Trixie found the drawer with the Lilly Pilly Creek Chronicle rolls and searched for March 1989. She quickly found it and went over to the machine. It hadn't been since university that she'd used one of these, so she forced herself to slow down and read the instructions very carefully.

"Oh Mum! Are you using that!" Meg had managed to pull herself away from her homework and raced over when Trixie started feeding the narrow brown film into the reel. "Can I help?"

"Careful, Meg, hang on," said Trixie as she pushed the reel into place with a click. "Just let me get it set up. I haven't used one of these for years." Trixie sat down on the stool, and Meg pulled a chair across, kneeling so she could see the screen.

At first, it was black. Trixie twisted the advance dial slowly, on, off, on, off, moving past slide after slide of black before suddenly they were almost blinded by a white page with just a few words identifying the contents of the slides.

"We have to find the year 1989," Trixie explained to Meg. Meg peered at the screen, determined to be the first to spot it. Trixie held the dial in the on position for longer as they skipped through the decades. They then reached the eighties.

"1985……..1986……...1987……1988…...1989!" cried Meg. She was right, they were in the right year. But they were much too late in the year. They needed to go back to March.

"Why are you looking at this?" Meg asked as Trixie stopped and started the microfilm, trying to narrow in on March 1989.

"I want to find information about the 150-year celebrations that were held for Wattlebury," said Trixie. "And any information I can find about who girl who went missing that same day."

"A girl went missing?" Meg asked, eyes wide.

"Yes," said Trixie. "No one knows what happened."

"That's very sad," said Meg, shaking her head and turning back to the screen. "Why are you looking it up?"

"Well, that's a little hard to explain," said Trixie. "Let's just say, I'd like to help their family and see if I can work out what happened."

"That would be a very nice thing to do," said Meg.

"Yes, I think so too."

Trixie wanted to share more with Meg. More about the reason why she felt compelled to research this mystery. The fact that she had time travelled holding the Polaroid camera. That it seemed she was destined to find out more about Tanya Stewart and apparently had no choice in the matter. But Trixie hadn't spoken to Meg about time travel.

Meg hadn't shown any signs of time travelling, the nausea, the dreams, the de-ja-vu. Plus, she was only 7. Trixie had been well over 10 before she first slipped, albeit only briefly, so she thought she had plenty of time.

Meg would no doubt think the whole thing was pretty cool. She'd probably be more like Fern when it came to time travel. Perhaps that wasn't a bad thing. But Trixie still worried about her daughter. Yes, time slipping could potentially be fun, but it could also be dangerous, especially when it happened spontaneously, and you didn't know where or when you would end up.

Trixie paused for a moment, panic rising in her. A thought had occurred to her that she couldn't believe she hadn't already considered. What if she time slipped when she was alone with the kids? What if they were left all alone in an instant, confused and scared? Maybe she was going to have to talk to them about time travel, sooner rather than later.

"There!" Meg cried, pointing at the monitor. Trixie was immediately pulled back to the present and let go of the dial. Yes, they had reached the month of March. "What date, Mum?"

"Well, the celebration was on the 11th of March, a Saturday. So just after that," said Trixie. "But they only published this newspaper once or twice a week, I think. It may have been different back then, though."

Trixie once again twisted on, off, on, off until they reached the 15th of March, the first edition of the Lilly Pilly Creek Chronicle after Tanya went missing. She wasn't surprised to see that a large black and white photo of adults and children dressed in old-fashioned clothes covered the front page.

WATTLEBURY CELEBRATES 100 YEARS

"Why do they look so strange?" Meg asked. Trixie explained the event to her as she pressed the advance button to flick through each page. There were lots of photos of the celebration. There was even a centre spread with multiple gallery pages. Trixie selected all the pages relating to the 150-year celebration and sent them to the printer. She then went back to the start to search for anything on Tanya Stewart.

"Surely there has to be some mention of her?" said Trixie.

"What is the name you're looking for, Mum?"

"Tanya," said Trixie. "Tanya Stewart. I think we'll have to go to the next edition."

Trixie quickly flicked through the back pages before arriving at the next front page. If she had been expecting a full page about the missing girl, she was sorely disappointed. Instead, the page was about an old gum tree that was cut down by developers. Quite the outrage.

"Not much has changed," thought Trixie. She slowly went page by page until she got to page six. She was startled to see Tanya Stewart staring back at them.

TEENAGER MISSING FOR OVER A WEEK

"Is that her, Mum?" asked Meg, pointing at the photo of the smiling girl with dark curly hair and a face full of freckles. "She looks nice."

Trixie smiled. Even in the low-quality image, a school portrait, Tanya looked like a happy and kind girl. The article was short, no more than a few paragraphs, with a request for anyone who knew about the missing girl to contact the Mount Barker police station.

Trixie pressed print and continued through the paper to see if anything else had been written about Tanya. There was nothing.

"Next one?" asked Meg. Trixie nodded and spun the dial. The pair of them went through the papers for the next few months. There wasn't something in every edition, but the paper appeared to keep on the case for at least six months before there was nothing else newsworthy to report. They did find an update on the first anniversary, and then on the anniversary for the next four years. After that, it was on the tenth anniversary and the twentieth anniversary. As they moved forward in time, there were some age progression photos included. The gist of each story was always the same. The case was still open, but there had been no new leads.

"Mum, can we go home?" It was Joe. They hadn't heard a peep out of him for at least forty-five minutes, but it appeared, as Trixie looked around, that it was now only them and the librarian remaining.

"Yep, as soon as I've picked up my printing," she said. They headed to the counter, where Meg enthusiastically greeted Mrs Masters.

"Hello Meg! Back again," she said. "And who have you brought with you?"

Meg beamed. "You know my little brother Joe. He's just started in Reception."

"Welcome, Joe! I barely recognised you in your school uniform," she winked at Trixie. "Now, how can I help you?"

"Mum needs to pick up her printing from the microfilm," Meg said.

Mrs Masters nodded and went to the back of the office. She returned holding a decent stack of pages.

"Working on a project?" Mrs Masters asked Trixie.

"Something like that," said Trixie, trying not to stammer. The thought hadn't crossed her mind that she might need to explain why she was researching Tanya Stewart. Fortunately, Mrs Masters didn't ask any more questions, but simply showed Trixie how to pay.

"See you next time!" the librarian called as the Travers family left the building.

"What are we doing now, Mum?" asked Meg.

"I think it's time to head to Silver Gum Cottage."

Chapter 14

"You're saying it wasn't reported in the newspaper immediately after she went missing?" Maggie asked.

Trixie shook her head. "This page is the first reporting we could find," said Trixie, pushing a piece of paper towards Maggie as she glanced at her co-researcher Meg, who smiled back.

"You mentioned suspects," said Fern, flicking through the pages. "In the paper?"

"No, from Sharon's album," said Trixie. She bent to pull the album out of the seagrass bag she had brought with her. Carefully laying it out on the dining table, she turned to the photographs Sharon had marked with an asterisk. "Do you recognise these men?"

Fern, Rhada (after putting on her reading glasses) and Maggie all stood around the album, peering at the suspects Trixie was pointing at. They were all quiet for a few minutes, which was quite disconcerting, before stepping back and returning to their seats.

Trixie frowned, looking at each of them. "So, do you know them?"

The three women glanced at each other, communicating silently. Fern nodded and began speaking.

"Yes, we know both of them," she admitted.

"And?" Trixie couldn't understand why they were dragging this out.

"So, the older guy is Kev Carrington. He runs the used car lot," said Fern.

Trixie shrugged. Was this shocking in any way? Why were they hesitating so much?

"Ok."

"The second one, the younger guy," said Fern. "Well, he's a bit more interesting."

"He is?"

"It's Mitch Lawson," said Fern.

Now Trixie was shocked. "Mitch, President-of-the-footy-club, Mitch?"

Maggie nodded. "Yep. Mitch, who also owns the family law practice. And the same guy who I may or may not have had a fling with once upon a time."

Trixie laughed. "Really?"

Fern rolled her eyes. "Is it all that surprising? I mean, this is Maggie we're talking about."

"Well, not surprising," said Trixie. "But potentially interesting considering he is currently a murder suspect."

"Murder? We don't know Tanya was murdered," said Maggie, almost defensive.

Trixie smiled. "Ok then, a kidnapping suspect."

"Enough of that, you two," said Fern. "This is serious. These two men were at the top of Sharon's list of suspects. At least, it appears they were at some point in time. So, I wonder if they were also on the Police's list?"

"Well, who would know that?" asked Trixie. "And what exactly are we going to do with this information?"

"I have absolutely no idea," said Fern.

"But you three are the ones who want me to investigate! How could you not have any idea of what to do?"

"We're time travellers, Trixie," said Fern. "Not private investigators."

Trixie groaned. Sometimes her mother was absolutely impossible.

"You said you two had solved mysteries!"

Rhada laughed. "Not deliberately, dear."

"What do you mean, you solved them by accident?"

"Exactly! We were sent there, we saw something or heard something, and it solved whatever mystery or question we had back in the present. We didn't actually investigate."

"I cannot believe you two! And you've roped Maggie into this, too. Expecting me to find out what happened to a missing girl from forty years ago, all because I held a camera."

"How about I get you a glass of wine, Trix," said Maggie. "Everything's easier with a glass of prosecco."

"I'll take the drink," said Trixie. "But I will not gloss over this. I've just had a very awkward encounter with Mrs Masters in the library. I can't imagine how many people she's gone home to tell that Trixie Travers was printing out newspaper articles about the missing girl. Can you imagine? What if it gets back to Anna?"

"You're panicking, Trixie," said Fern. "You know you do that. But just calm down."

"Arrgh! And you know how much I HATE to be told to calm down!" Trixie said, flinging her arms in the air. She decided now was the time to storm outside before she said something she might regret.

It was warm and quiet outside, only the sound of a lawnmower in the distance, cars, and a few birds. She strode through the garden to the back corner, where a garden bench sat underneath a Japanese Maple. At times like this, Trixie needed peace and calm. She took a few deep breaths before looking around her. A bee was buzzing at a lavender bush, so she focused on it, attempting to tune out all the voices in her head.

It seemed to her that the Silver Ladies' visions of her investigating the missing person could, in fact, be meddling. Sticking their noses where they were not needed or wanted. Why were they so adamant that Trixie should get involved? If the police hadn't found Tanya, why did they think time travel would make a difference?

Then there was the matter of 'how'. How would she know when and where to look? Time slipping was not an exact science. In her own experience, it had always been accidental. And yes, perhaps there was a way to intentionally time travel, to make a slip more likely. But could it be precise? Precise enough to be useful?

Trixie began to wonder how much there was that she didn't know about time slipping. She'd always had a bad relationship with it, and had made this known very loudly to her mum and nan over the years. Did she therefore have a large gap in her knowledge? Had she pushed it away from herself in her anger? And if that was the case, was she now ready and willing to receive it? Would she be able to handle it?

"Have you had long enough?"

Trixie heard Rhada's voice but didn't look up.

"I'm not sure."

Rhada sat down and put her hand on top of Trixie's, remaining quiet.

Still watching the bee, Trixie allowed time to pass before turning her hand and gripping her Nan's fingers.

"It's scary, Nan," Trixie said.

"I know it is," said Rhada. "But anything worth doing is scary, wouldn't you agree?"

"Maybe," said Trixie. "But I don't know if this *is* worth doing?"

Rhada nodded. "Mmmm."

"Is it?"

"I think it's up to you to make that decision, Trix."

"I don't even know why we can time travel in the first place. What's the point? It's scary, it makes me feel queasy, and you all seem to think I can just choose to time travel to when and where I want. But I can't! I have no idea what I'm doing!"

"The time travel. That can be taught," said Rhada.

"Can it?"

Rhada nodded. "But for it to truly work, you do have to actually *want* to travel. There has to be emotion around it. Haven't you found that? Haven't you found that the times you've accidentally travelled are when you've been feeling a lot of emotion?"

Trixie looked up at the leaves rustling gently in the breeze and thought. The day of the Polaroid camera, she had been feeling a lot of emotions. Two kids off to their first day of school and the launch of Paraphernalia. The day of the funeral had been emotional too, even though it was only her friend's grandfather. You couldn't help but get emotional as you pondered your own mortality. Then there was her wedding morning. One of the most emotional of all. Her mind flicked back to all the times in her youth she could remember slipping, and yes, she could identify many emotional events.

Turning to her Nan, Trixie nodded. "Yes, you're right. I don't know why I never thought of that before."

"Because you were always so angry when it happened," said Rhada.

Trixie snorted. "I was, wasn't I?"

Rhada laughed. "Oh my gosh, the way you would storm in here when you'd just travelled. Your Grandpa got quite a kick out of it.

Which only made you angrier, of course."

Trixie couldn't help but laugh, too. She remembered as a teenager being furious because she'd finally been talking to a boy she had a crush on when the feeling of an oncoming slip came over her, and she had to leave.

That day, she'd ended up in the middle of a scrub, surrounded by scratchy tea trees and the sound of birds. In any other circumstances, it might have been peaceful, but she had no idea what period in history it was or where she was. She at least presumed she was in Australia based on the landscape.

Trixie had walked slowly through the trees and come out to see a grassy plain stretching before her. The sky was blue and filled with marshmallow clouds. She knew to stop and take her deep breaths, but it had taken her a long time for her heart to stop racing. One moment she had been with her friends, nervously close to a boy, the next minute she was in another time and place, completely alone. It was extremely disorientating, which made the whole thing very scary.

That time, it felt as though she had been away a long time, and this was proven to be correct. After what felt like an eternity, she had managed to calm herself down enough to slip back to the present day. Yet, she had discovered it was twilight, and all her friends had disappeared. Time travel had caused her to miss the chance to talk to the boy, and Trixie had made sure to make her fury known when she'd stormed into Silver Gum Cottage.

"Well, I guess I can understand there's a way to deliberately travel," said Trixie with a sigh. "But is there a way to stop a slip when the feeling comes over you. That's what I wish I knew how to do."

"Don't you remember?" asked Rhada.

"Remember what?"

"What we taught you as a kid."

Trixie frowned, scrunching her eyes. She had no idea what Rhada was talking about.

"You taught me how to get back, that much I know," said Trixie. "But I don't think you ever taught me how to stop it."

"But it's exactly the same!" Rhada exclaimed. "Trixie, *you* know. You just have to calm yourself down, take deep breaths, and centre yourself."

"You never told me this!" Trixie stood up. "You never told me how to stop it!"

"Well, now might be a good time to practice," said Rhada, raising her eyebrows.

"Seriously! Are you honestly telling me to calm down? When you and mum have kept this information to yourself for all these years!" Trixie was facing her Nan, frowning, hands on her hips.

"Trixie, I know you don't want to hear this. But we did tell you what to do. You were a teenager when most of this was happening. You weren't known for your great listening skills, especially when we were talking about time travel. You just wanted to say your piece and end the conversation. Your mother and I decided it might be best for you to learn things for yourself."

"Learn things for myself! Well, I never learnt it. You can be sure of that." Trixie pouted.

"I know you have a lot of anger around your time slipping abilities, Trixie. I know you think it's not fair and hate that it's a part of your makeup. But it is. And you need to accept it. You were lucky to go for so many years without slipping. Now, though, it seems you are destined to time slip, at least some of the time. So it's up to you how you handle it. And getting angry about it is only going to make it worse. We can't fix this for you. There's no cure. So it's time that you behaved like the adult you are, and worked out what you're going to do about it."

Rhada stood up and patted Trixie on the shoulder. Trixie, channelling her teenage self, spun herself out of her nan's reach and stood with her back to her. Even as she did it, she knew she was being ridiculous, but for now, there was nothing more she could do. She heard Rhada walking away up the brick path.

Chapter 15

Trixie took the kids home to have tea with Kirby. She was quiet, but Kirby chatted with the children, asking lots of questions about school and then playing the alphabet game. Tonight, they had to go around the table naming as many foods as they could, starting with K. Trixie declined to play, preferring to eat her tea in silence, but she did manage to laugh a few times, especially when Joe said "Quinoa."

When the kids were in bed, she took a glass of wine and sat at their outdoor table with Kirby, enjoying the cool breeze and the buzzing of insects. They were both quiet, content in each other's company. Trixie felt very frustrated with herself. She was often prone to letting her anger get the best of her, much more frequently than she liked. Her family understood her well enough, but that didn't make it ok. It was something that constantly made her feel guilty and inadequate. Sipping her wine, Trixie tried to focus on what was important. Aside from her kids and her husband, and getting through each day, it seemed at the moment, the most important thing was the fact that Tanya Stewart was still missing, and she may be the only one who could solve the mystery.

She couldn't bear to imagine what it had been like for Sharon for all those years. Her precious daughter missing, and absolutely nothing she could do about it, no matter how hard she tried. Based on the photo album, it appeared Sharon had done everything in her power to find Tanya.

Maybe the Silver Ladies were right. Maybe she was destined to solve this. There was a reason the Polaroid camera had caused her to time travel instantaneously. Yes, the emotions of the day would be connected, but perhaps it wasn't her own emotions that had caused the slip. Could it be Sharon's emotions infused in that Polaroid camera, the entire box, that had sent her to the past?

Did she just have to accept that the universe needed her to solve this? And the fact that she had this crazy ability to time travel, which had previously served no positive purpose in her life, was the driving factor.

Trixie stood. "Just going for a wander," she told Kirby.

He smiled, knowing this meant Trixie was going to take a stroll through the garden. It was one of her favourite places on the farm. When she and Kirby had bought it just before they were married, the backyard was bare except for various fruit trees connected by a dripper system. They had loved the fruit trees, but since then, Trixie had turned it into a rambling cottage garden filled with a mix of natives and classic English plants that thrived in the Adelaide Hills. She also had pockets of vegetables. She loved having spinach growing in the same bed as a daisy, tomatoes next to the native sarsaparilla, and some corn popping up with the kangaroo paw. It was always fun to wander through her garden and see what flowers or veggies were growing. And the joy of picking apples or peaches from your own trees would never get old.

Turning, she looked back at the house. If the garden was rambling, the house was a mishmash, but in the best possible way. The original four-bedroom stone cottage had had many additions over the years. Nothing quite fit together, and as you walked through the house, you would find yourself stepping up into one room, and back down in the next. There were tiny passages connecting some rooms, or you would have to walk through multiple rooms to get to others. The weird and wonderful floor plan was why they got such a good deal on the house.

It certainly wasn't to most people's taste.

Trixie and Kirby had loved it, and as each child arrived, the whimsy of the house grew. Currently, Joe and Meg had their own rooms, but they were connected by a playroom, and Meg had to go through both rooms to get to her own. But she loved it because her room was more of a sleepout, with timber panels on the walls, and a big window where she could lie in bed and see the stars.

Her daughter was currently sleeping soundly, oblivious to the worries of the world, just content that her teacher was giving her enough homework. She could hardly imagine being a mother like Sharon, who had looked out at the stars, wondering if her daughter was looking at them too, or whether her eyes had long since shut forever. Having no idea where she was or what had happened to her. Trixie felt tears in her eyes. The pain Sharon must have felt for the remainder of her life, even if it was tempered by the arrival of Anna and Jason. The not knowing must have been heart-wrenching, weighing on her constantly.

What made it all worse was that Sharon had left this world, never knowing. But would it serve any purpose to find out now? How would it impact Anna and Jason's lives? Or was it best to leave sleeping dogs lie?

"No," Trixie said aloud. "Surely the truth can only be a good thing. To put things to rest once and for all."

She gulped down the last of her wine and made her way back into the house. Kirby had already gone to bed. She poked her head in to see him reading.

"All right?" he asked.

Trixie smiled. "Yep, just a busy few days."

"Coming to bed?"

"I'm just going to take a look at some things for the shop, then I'll come."

At the kitchen table, Trixie pulled out the photo album and her notebook. A plan was required. She needed to speak to the suspects. She needed to speak to Anna. But in what order? Should she ask Anna's permission to investigate? But why would she permit Trixie at all? Trixie owned a vintage store. She wasn't an investigator. She wasn't the police. Trixie shook her head. No, she needed to investigate first. As discreetly as possible. If she went to Anna asking but turned up nothing, surely that would only make things worse. Bringing up memories with still no hope of finding out what happened. She didn't want to do that to Sharon's children. To Tanya's siblings.

Although Trixie was still completely unsure whether what she was about to do was right, one thing suddenly became clear. She needed a will.

"Of course, I need a will. And who else but Mitch Lawson to help me with that!"

Trixie couldn't help but laugh, never before noticing she had this diabolical streak. Maybe she was a natural investigator after all.

Jumping online, she was surprised but pleased to see that Mitch had a half-hour appointment available the very next day.

"If that's not a sign, then I don't know what is."

Of course, it would have made sense to have Kirby with her, but she wasn't actually planning on getting the will written. And he was leaving the next morning anyway. This was just an initial meeting. And of course, somehow she would mention Tanya at the same time, despite having no idea exactly how she would do this. She could only hope the universe really was on her side.

Chapter 16

Trixie dropped the kids off at school as early as she could, ensuring she was in Mitch's office at nine o'clock on the dot. She was a little concerned Mitch may not be aware of her last-minute booking and hoped he wasn't running late. She needed to be back in time to open Paraphernalia by ten.

The office was in a stone cottage on the main street of Wattlebury. The door was painted bright red, which seemed unusual for a law office. Stepping inside, she was surprised and a little anxious to see one of the school mums at the reception desk.

"Susannah! I didn't know you worked here." Trixie hoped she had composed herself as the woman with long black hair in a green silk shirt looked up from her computer.

"Trixie! Lovely to see you. I saw you booked an appointment overnight. Is everything ok?"

Trixie wasn't sure if the receptionist at a law firm should be asking private questions, but she just brushed her off.

"Absolutely fine," she said. "I just happened to notice this slot was free, so I thought, why not!"

"Well, take a seat, and Mitch will be out soon."

The waiting area was neat and tidy, if a little old-fashioned. She sat down on a dark wooden chair with a red striped seat and picked up a magazine from the black coffee table. The magazine was over five years old and had a somewhat obscure member of the royal family on the front cover. Flipping through, Trixie stopped at the recipe pages and wondered if anyone would notice if she tore out the recipe for cauliflower pizza crust.

"Trixie Travers, good morning."

Trixie looked up, slightly startled. She hurriedly put the magazine down and, smiling, took Mitch Lawson's outstretched hand.

"Good morning, Mitch," she said. "Thanks for seeing me."

"Not a problem," he said. "This way." He stepped to the side and indicated she should walk to the office with the open door.

It appeared red was Mitch's favourite colour. In front of what appeared to be the original fireplace, flanked by two tall timber bookshelves, was a large wooden desk inlaid across the top with red leather. She sat down on a chair that matched the one in the waiting area, and looked up at the painting above the fireplace, which showed a dot painting in reds of all shades, featuring Uluru, the famous rock from central Australia.

"So, it was a will you were after?" Mitch asked as he sat down and poured them both a glass of water.

"Yes, I think it is probably time. At least I'd like to know the process and what Kirby and I would need to organise to get this done."

"Oh yes, Kirby's your husband. He's the helicopter pilot?"

Trixie nodded. Kirby was famous in Wattlebury for being a helicopter pilot. Just as Mitch was known as the footy club president, having held the position for many years.

"Yep," said Trixie. "And you're still the footy club president?"

"Sure am. Maybe just one more year," he said with a smile and a shrug. Trixie had a feeling he had been saying 'just one more year' for a while now.

"You grew up here too, but I don't think we were ever at school at the same time," said Trixie.

Mitch shook his head. "No, I believe I'm quite a bit older than you are."

Trixie laughed. "Maybe not as much as you think," she said, trying to be kind. "You have kids, right?"

"My two boys are out of the house now," he said. "One's in London, and the other's in Sydney. We have a chef and another lawyer."

"A chef!" Trixie was genuinely impressed. "Is that the one in London?"

"Yes," he said with a smile. "I'm hoping to get over there this year, have a meal or two in the restaurant he works in."

"That would be amazing," Trixie said. "Nice for them to be out of the small town, I suppose, but I have to say, I do like still being in Wattlebury."

"Me too," said Mitch. "I briefly thought about leaving here when I was at uni, but I think I was always destined to take over Dad's practice."

"Yes," said Trixie. "I imagine so. I bet the locals rely on you, too. Someone they've always known, that they can trust."

"It is nice," he said, before leaning to one side and pulling some papers out of his desk. "I'm quite different to Dad though. Took a while for some of them to get used to me."

Trixie smiled. "I'm sure they coped."

"Now, this is all the information I have on wills," he said, placing a pile of papers in front of her. "There's a checklist. But you and your husband, you both run your own businesses, right?"

Trixie nodded.

"Company, sole trader?"

"I'm a sole trader, and I believe Kirby is a company," she said.

Mitch kept asking her questions, making it clear that preparing a will for two people who ran their own businesses and had two children, plus some land, might be a bit more complicated than she anticipated. Even though the whole meeting was a ruse, as they neared the end of the meeting, she was feeling decidedly concerned about not already having a will, and almost forgot why she was there in the first place.

"Well, we have a lot to think about," Trixie said, looking down at the pile of papers in her hand.

"Was there anything else I could help you with?" he asked.

"Actually," Trixie hesitated, wondering if she was going to regret what she was about to ask him. "This is going to sound weird, but well, I had Anna Treloar drop some things into my shop the other day. She didn't tell me anything about them, and when I pulled it out, there was a photo album."

"Ok," he said, frowning, clearly confused at the direction this conversation had taken.

"I just thought, seeing you're a little bit older than me, you might remember."

"Remember? Remember what exactly?"

"It's just, I think the photos are all from the day Tanya Stewart went missing."

Mitch's face seemed to go a little pale, and he began to rub his hands together. "Tanya Stewart. I haven't thought about her in years." His eyes went down to his hands as he said this, before darting quickly up to meet Trixie's.

"Sorry if this is bringing up bad memories," Trixie said, watching him closely.

"Bad memories?" he said. "No. I mean, it's all very sad, but I didn't really know Tanya very well."

"But you knew her?"

"Um, well, I suppose, yes," he said. "We'd been kind of hanging out with the same group of friends around that time."

"So did you go to school with her?"

Mitch shook his head. "No, I think I'd finished school at this stage. I was maybe two or three years older than Tanya. But this is a small town, not a huge number of kids to hang out with. And I mean, Tanya was probably hanging around kids older than maybe she should've been."

"Oh, really?" Trixie thought his comment was interesting. "Why was that?"

"Not sure. Having a single mum, maybe she was by herself a lot, not being watched? Like I said. I didn't know her well."

"What was she like?"

Mitch frowned and then looked at the ceiling. "She was a good enough kid, I suppose. Could be a bit loud sometimes, but I think she was just trying to show off in front of us, being the younger one. But why do you ask? I mean, won't you just give the album back to Anna?"

Trixie knew she didn't have a good answer, but she tried anyway. "Yes, you're right. I'm going to talk to Anna about it. It's just that I hadn't heard of the mystery before. I guess it's on my mind, and when I realised you would have known her, I couldn't help myself. Sorry, I don't mean to pry."

"Sure, sure," he said. "I mean, it is still unsolved. No one knows what happened to her. It's like she vanished into thin air."

"Did you see her that day?" Trixie asked, knowing full well he had.

"Um, I don't know. I mean, I guess I would have. It was the big one-fifty celebrations. You knew that?"

Trixie nodded. "Yes, Mum and Nan told me."

"Right, well, the whole town was there, so I wouldn't be surprised if I ran into her. But I don't remember anything specific."

"And did anyone say anything afterwards? Did anyone notice her acting strange? Or anyone else acting strange? What did everyone think had happened?"

"Gosh, you're starting to sound like a detective now," Mitch said, with a chuckle.

"Sorry! Sorry!" Trixie hurriedly stood. "I'll get out of your hair. I'm just interested. After all these years, wouldn't it be nice to know what happened?"

Mitch nodded. "It sure would," he said. "But, unfortunately, I have another appointment."

"Yes, of course," said Trixie. "And thanks for these," she said, holding up the pile of paperwork. "I'll have a chat with Kirby, and we'll arrange another time."

Mitch showed her out, Trixie waving goodbye to Susannah as the red door was closed behind her.

Had she learnt anything? She wasn't really sure. But she did know one thing. Mitch Lawson knew a lot more than he was letting on.

Chapter 17

Trixie raced back to Paraphernalia, desperately hoping there would be no one waiting for her. Yet, when she pulled up to the barn, braking hard enough to cause dust to fly up behind her, she saw the Professor sitting at the wrought iron table.

"Sorry, Professor! Sorry!" she slammed the van door shut and rushed over to unlock the barn.

"Not a problem, my dear," he said. "I'm rarely in a hurry these days. It was rather pleasant to sit here listening to the birds and the sheep in the distance."

"Well, come in, come in," she said. "Although it is going to take a moment for this place to cool down." She raced around, turning on fans. It was stuffy inside, and Trixie wondered what she would do when the weather got super hot. Perhaps she'd have to keep the shop closed on hot days.

"And how's it all been going?" he asked. "Has the town cottoned on to how amazing Paraphernalia is yet?"

"Ha! Not quite yet. But it has only been four days. To be honest, I'm not all that good at marketing the place. Most of the town probably has no idea I'm here."

"Well, that will change soon enough," he said. "And a big sign out on the road wouldn't hurt!"

"Uggh, of course," she said. "I had meant to do that, but completely forgot. I'll get that sorted. I should have had it done when I got the main sign done weeks ago."

"All in good time, all in good time," he said. "And that being said, how are you going with the transistor? No rush, of course. The cricket doesn't start until Thursday next week."

"If you don't mind waiting, I could probably have it finished in twenty minutes," said Trixie, walking over to her restoration desk.

"I'd be happy to wait all day," he said. "I'll make myself comfortable."

"We can chat while I work," said Trixie, settling into her chair and turning on the lamp.

"Certainly! What would you like to natter about?"

"Well, actually, I do have a topic," Trixie said. "Do you know anything about when Tanya Stewart went missing?"

"Tanya Stewart, now let me think," he said. "That name rings a bell. It was quite a while ago, wasn't it?"

"Yes, in the eighties. Were you here in the eighties?"

"I've been here forever!" he said. "Well, aside from the year I lived in Beijing. Or the six months I was in Stockholm. And there were a few years I spent most of my time in the US or the UK. But aside from that, I am a permanent fixture of Wattlebury."

Trixie smiled to herself as she unscrewed the back of the transistor radio, knowing the Professor must have more stories he could tell than she would ever have time to hear.

"Well, were you here when Tanya went missing, or were you trekking through Europe?"

"I don't trek!" He let out a guffaw. "But yes, I believe I was here at that time. I think I was still working at the University of Adelaide, driving in most days. There weren't any bus services back then."

"Uh-huh," Trixie managed as she concentrated on soldering some wires back into place.

"Now, Tanya Stewart. That was a very sad case. The anniversary day. I don't think her mother actually knew she was missing until the next day. The mother had quite a few jobs, I think. Worked late, so she didn't notice Tanya was gone until the next afternoon, if I recall correctly."

"Gosh, that's a long time for no one to realise you were gone," she said. "But does that mean she could have gone missing on the Sunday, rather than the Saturday?"

"Possibly, although I don't recall that being a big issue. There may have been a sighting? Somewhere on the other side of Adelaide."

"The other side of Adelaide? Really?"

"Look, my memory could be playing tricks on me, but I think that was the case."

"I haven't seen that mentioned in any of the newspaper reports," said Trixie.

"Have you been doing some investigating?" the Professor asked, tilting his head.

"Not really," Trixie said, holding the radio up to the lamp. "It's just, well, I probably shouldn't keep telling everyone this, but Anna Treloar brought in a box of cameras for me to potentially sell, and there was a photo album at the bottom of it."

"A photo album?"

"Yes, and I've worked out that it seems to be all photos of the day of the celebrations. It was Sharon's album, Tanya's mum."

The Professor shook his head. "So sad," he said. "Something a mother never gets over."

The pair were quiet for a while. Trixie was pondering this new information. A sighting? By whom? And where exactly? Was it never reported in the news? And if not, how exactly did the Professor know?"

"Do you remember anything more about the sighting?"

"No," he shook his head. "And I could have my wires completely crossed. But you know who would know?"

"Who?"

"Margaret Doyle," he said.

"I don't think I know who she is."

"Margaret used to work in the police station," he said. "She was there for years and years. Used to manage the switchboard before doing all the administration work."

"And where would I find Margaret now?"

"Well, she's up at the retirement village. Moved there when her husband died. I think your Nan would know her. They were friends."

Trixie paused for a moment, concentrating on closing the radio back up, but also pondering this new information. If only she could walk into the police station and ask about the sighting. A ridiculous idea, of course. However, the Professor seemed to be on to something. Margaret sounded like the next best thing.

"Voila!" Trixie stood and walked over to the professor, the radio in her outstretched hand.

The Professor clapped his hands together. "Wonderful!"

"You'd better check it works first," Trixie said as he took it from her.

The Professor gripped the dial on the side. It clicked, and then immediately they heard the distinct sound of static. Moving to another dial, the Professor twisted whilst watching a red arm move across the station numbers. Within seconds, the sound of Vivaldi filled the room.

"It works!" said the Professor. "You're amazing, Trixie. Well done!"

"Professor, I have a feeling you would have had no problems

fixing this yourself," she smiled.

"Not with my eyesight and arthritic fingers. No, without you, my mother's transistor would have been relegated to catching dust on the top of the fridge."

"Well, I'm glad I could help," said Trixie. "And now, I'm wondering if you could help me? If you could answer just one more question."

"Certainly, my dear," he smiled, Vivaldi still playing.

"Kev Carrington. What do you know about him?"

"Well, I'd never buy a car from him, that's for sure."

"And why's that?"

"As dodgy as they come. I think he's settled down in his later years, but there were always rumours that the cars he sold weren't as pristine as he made them out to be. And I wouldn't be surprised if that business wasn't a front for something more underhanded."

"Really?"

"Look, I don't know him; it's just things I've heard," said the Professor. "But if you're going to pursue this, looking into Tanya's disappearance, then all I can say is, be careful when it comes to Kev. I have a feeling he knows people you wouldn't want to run into in a dark alley."

"Do you think he could be involved? Do you think he knows what happened to Tanya?"

"I wouldn't be surprised," said the Professor. "But then again, he's one of those men who gets looked at when anything nefarious happens in Wattlebury."

Trixie nodded. "And Mitch Lawson. What do you think of him?"

"What, you think he's got something to do with Tanya's

disappearance?" The Professor seemed genuinely surprised by this.

"Not necessarily," said Trixie. "Just something I spotted in the photo album. It's probably nothing." She didn't dare tell him that she had already gone and spoken to Mitch and felt something was off. She didn't want anyone to know she was taking this investigation seriously. It was highly likely she would end up looking foolish at the end.

"As far as I know, Mitch has always had a very upstanding reputation," he said. "Hard worker. By the book. I haven't heard anything otherwise. But then again, he is divorced from his wife, so she may have a different opinion."

"Perhaps," said Trixie. "But it's good to know there's no gossip about Mitch."

"At least not that I've heard," he said. "The Silver Ladies would know more than me, though. I bet between the three of them, they hear all of Wattlebury's gossip."

Trixie laughed. "They probably spread half of it!"

"More than likely," he said with a smile, before holding up the transistor. "Well, thanks for this. I'll leave you to your shop. I hope you have a good day today."

Trixie farewelled the Professor and began pottering around, worrying there would be no customers, then wondering whether Paraphernalia would be one giant flop. This thought had crossed her mind at least ten times a day since she'd opened.

However, it turned out today wasn't the day to be concerned. She had a steady flow of people in and out, even making it difficult for her to stop and grab lunch. A fortune was not made, but a few bits and bobs left the store, and some of the items requested, which she didn't have in stock, provided inspiration for her next clearance sale jaunt.

By the time it hit two o'clock, she realised she hadn't thought about Tanya at all. But that was about to change.

Chapter 18

Trixie felt she might be on a roll, and she didn't want to lose momentum in her investigation. Even though she was constantly questioning why exactly she was doing this, it seemed she may have already gotten herself in too deep. She couldn't let it go, and the time between closing the shop and school pick up seemed like the perfect opportunity to go shopping for a new car.

At least that's what she told Kev Carrington when she rocked up to his car yard that afternoon.

"What, the Morris J getting too old for you?"

Trixie smiled. She didn't know Kev Carrington from a bar of soap, but it seems he knew her, or at least her van. She'd parked down the street; for some reason, it occurred to her that this was what a private investigator would do. So she knew he hadn't seen her drive up.

"I will never give up Morrie!" Trixie said. "But I have been considering getting something a little bit more practical with the kids when Kirby is away."

"Do you think you're an SUV type? All the mothers seem to have them these days," he said.

Trixie inwardly rolled her eyes but smiled and replied. "No, just something small. A Honda Jazz, maybe? Or a Corolla? What do you suggest?"

Kev toured her around the car yard, unable to resist comments like, "When hubby comes down," and "I don't suppose you care about the fuel efficiency," and "This one has enough cup holders for your fancy coffees." But Trixie did her best not to react. A mental note was made to never buy a car from him, but as that wasn't why she was here, she didn't want to get on his bad side.

Eventually, Trixie started talking about how long he'd been in town.

"I've been doing this nearly fifty years! Quit school in year nine and came and worked for me old man."

"Wow! You'd have seen a lot!"

"More than I can tell your delicate ears," he smirked. "But you're right. I've seen a heck of a lot. Know as much about this town as anyone."

"Funny you should say that," said Trixie, even surprising herself at how skilled she was becoming at manoeuvring the conversation to her liking. "I was actually talking with Nan and Mum the other day, and they brought up this missing girl. Um, what was her name again? Um, I think it was Tanya, Tanya Stewart. Do you remember that?"

Kev started coughing, turning away, before punching his chest and taking a deep breath.

"Sorry about that, don't know what came over me."

Trixie thought she knew *exactly* what came over him.

"That's ok," she said. "Do you remember her? How she went missing?"

"Yep, I remember. But I don't know anything about it. Was the talk of the town for a few weeks. But she was never found, and everything died down."

"But you said you know a lot about this town," Trixie pressed. "You must have heard rumours. About what happened to her?"

"Ha! Plenty of rumours! Everyone had a theory. Just none of them were true."

"They weren't?" Trixie found this an odd turn of phrase.

"Well, of course not. If they were, she'd be found, wouldn't she!"

Trixie nodded. She had to agree. Although what if one or more of the rumours were true, but the police just didn't follow them up?

"Well, what do *you* think happened?"

"No idea," he said, turning to walk back towards his prefab office. "Nothing to do with me."

"But you did speak to Tanya, didn't you?"

Kev stopped in his tracks and glared at Trixie. "What exactly are you trying to say?"

"Nothing." If Trixie were in a comic, she realised there would be the words 'gulp' above her head. "Nothing at all. I was just curious."

"Well, maybe you'd better stop with all the questions," he said. "Now, did you want to talk more about that Hyundai, or do you need to chat with hubby first?"

"Yes, I will need to talk to Kirby before I make such a big decision," said Trixie, almost gagging as she said the words. "Thanks for your help, Kev."

He grunted. "Send hubby round when he's back."

Trixie smiled politely and went back to her van. "What an absolute jerk!" Trixie said to herself once she'd pulled the door shut. "Can't believe he's still in business! Doesn't he know it's usually the woman choosing the family car? Unbelievable!'

Turning on the van, she pulled into the street and made her way to the school. "Although I have to say, a fancy iced coffee would go down rather well right now, if only I had a cup holder." She laughed as she made her way through the streets of Wattlebury.

What she'd said to Mitch was true. She loved her town. Trixie had never once wished to live elsewhere. She'd lived in Adelaide for a year while she completed a TAFE course in interior design. She'd even done a few woodworking and electrical courses. But she was back within the year, back with her mum and dad. She worked in the antique shop in town, learning as she went, helping clients choose pieces, before moving into restorations. Trixie had loved visiting clearance sales with the owner, learning how to spot pieces that would be perfect for the shop, or items she knew regulars would adore.

She'd continued until she was pregnant with Meg and had then stayed at home until she had Joe. By the time she was thinking about returning to work, the antique store had been closed down and was replaced by a bike shop. For a few years, she felt a little lost, but worked on renovating their own house, and turning Speckled Hen Farm into a thriving hobby farm with veggies, chickens, sheep and even some ducks. She loved it and loved the small produce stand they had at the end of the road. But she missed the antique business, and it was always in the back of her mind that, somehow, she would return to the industry.

When the idea of using the barn as her own vintage shop came to her, things really started to fall into place. She was more excited than she had been in years. She and Kirby worked hard to clear out the barn and get it up to scratch. It wasn't long before she headed out to clearing sales again, using her small amount of savings for the initial stock. It was obviously still early days, but Trixie was excited about what the future held for Paraphernalia. Although now it seemed her time slipping abilities had thrown a spanner in the works.

As she reflected on her conversation with Kev, there was no doubt that he had been very uncomfortable and didn't want to speak about Tanya. He'd been so proud of his wide-ranging insights into the town, yet as soon as she offered up the opportunity for him to demonstrate them, he shut her down. In her opinion, Kev couldn't have acted more suspiciously if he tried. But did that mean he was a kidnapper? A killer even? Trixie had no idea what the connection could possibly be. Tanya was fifteen. Too young to be looking for a car. Could she have been looking for a job? Did it have something to do with her mother?

She was sure of one thing. Kev knew something. Trixie just needed to find out what.

Chapter 19

"I think you need to ring Anna," said Fern the next morning. She had popped in on her way to volunteering for Meals on Wheels.

"You do?" Trixie asked as she began setting up a new display on one of the tables. She thought it might be fun to play into the time travel theme, so she was setting up a clock, watch and timepiece table. The large hourglass in the centre was one of the items she was most excited about.

"I do," her mum said. "It's great that you've spoken to people, but word may start to get out. This is Wattlebury after all. It won't take long for people to talk. If Anna or Jason gets wind of it, well, who knows how they might react."

"Yes, I know, you're right," said Trixie. "But what do I say? I mean, who am *I* to investigate? I run a vintage shop and have two kids. I'm not a detective!'

"I guess you can just talk about the photo album, say it intrigued you, and you couldn't help but notice the two people Sharon had highlighted."

"She might think I was snooping. I should have rung her as soon as I found it." Trixie groaned.

"Or maybe she *wanted* someone to find it," said Fern. "Did you ever think of that?"

"Nah," said Trixie. "Surely not. I just think she had no idea it was in there. Maybe she never knew about it?"

Fern shrugged. "I still think you should ring her. Before you go any further with this. You wouldn't want to cause drama."

Trixie knew her mother was right. The last thing she wanted was to stir up things in Wattlebury. The town was too small for that. Most importantly, she didn't want to cause Anna and Jason pain. Maybe they would tell her to stay out of it? They'd take back the album and all the cameras, and that would be the end of it.

Picking up a pocket watch, clicking it open and winding it so she could watch the second hand tick round, Trixie wondered, if Anna did ask her to stop investigating, would she be able to make that promise?

"Mum, before I forget, do you know a Margaret Doyle. Is she a friend of Nan's?"

"Yes, they used to play bowls together," Fern said. "Why?"

"The Professor said she worked at the Police station and she may be able to help."

"You really are investigating this, aren't you?" Her mum was grinning.

"Uggh. Leave me alone," Trixie rolled her eyes. "Isn't that what you wanted?"

"Sorry, sorry!" Fern put her hands up. "Back to Margaret. I think the Professor could be right. I'm not sure if Margaret's the type to disclose confidential information, no matter how long she's been retired, but it is certainly worth a shot. Maybe Nan could give her a call?"

Trixie quickly told her mum what Professor Crowe had said about the sighting and then stood in the doorway, waving as Fern drove off for her Meals on Wheels shift.

It was overcast, cooler than it had been in days. Last night, in between pondering the likelihood of Mitch or Kev knowing anything about Tanya's disappearance, Trixie had come up with a vision for a roadside sign that she could make herself. It seemed the weather meant that some physical labour wasn't out of the question.

First, though, she would call Anna.

"I've been going through the boxes," Trixie said when Anna answered. "I wondered if you wouldn't mind popping in at some stage? I've just got a couple of questions."

"Could we do it over the phone? I'm on the afternoon shift today." Anna was a nurse at the Mount Barker Hospital.

"I think it would be better face-to-face," said Trixie. "If you don't mind?"

"Ok, I'll try and get in there on my way to work," said Anna, not sounding particularly enthusiastic.

Trixie thanked her and hung up. She immediately began to feel her chest tighten. What on earth was she going to say? How could she explain it? Why *had* Trixie begun questioning suspects in the forty-year disappearance of Anna's sister?

"Delivery!"

Trixie looked up, surprised to see a young man standing in the door holding a bunch of flowers.

"Are you Trixie Travers?"

"Yes, I am," she said. Who on earth could have sent these?

"Perfect," he said. "These are for you. Do you mind just signing here?" He held out his black gadget, and she squiggled a signature with her finger. "Have a great day!"

Trixie took the bunch of flowers, confused for a moment, before smiling as she guessed the sender. Taking the card off, she opened it.

"Amity!" Amity was her best friend since primary school. She lived in Melbourne, was single, and loved her work in finance. They saw each other as much as they could, but with two kids, Trixie found it hard to travel, and Amity lived a very social life, so she was always very busy. But they knew they were always there for each other.

Dear Trix, I'm sure you've had an amazing first week at Paraphernalia. You're chasing your dreams, and I'm so proud of you! You deserve this. Love Tee.

Trixie was surprised to feel tears in her eyes. It hit her how tense she had been. Even though it had only been a few days it felt much longer. So much had happened, and the pressure she had put herself under, mixed with the sudden time travel experience and the apparent evolution of herself as a detective, was a lot to cope with. To read that Tee was proud of her made her feel very emotional.

"Get it together, Trix," she told herself, moving to a shelf that was lined with vessels of all different kinds. Trixie found a small metal watering can that she thought would be perfect to hold the flowers.

"Those look lovely," said a voice behind her. Trixie spun around to find Janine, her very first customer, standing there, a smile on her face.

"Oh yes," said Trixie. "I'm very lucky. I just need to find the best spot."

"On the windowsill," Janine turned and walked towards the side of the barn. "Just here."

The spot she had chosen was indeed perfect. The worn timber sill had a jar of buttons sitting on it, and the glass of the window rippled as you looked through it. The effect behind the flowers was beautiful.

"Thanks, Janine!" Trixie smiled. "Now, how can I help *you*?"

"Ah, well," Janine said. "I'll potter around, but there's something I thought you should be made aware of."

"Oh?" she raised her eyebrows.

"There's just been a bit of talk, and I'm sure it's nonsense, but I thought it wouldn't hurt to get the details from you, first hand."

Trixie felt her stomach clench, realising the Wattlebury rumour mill was obviously turning.

"What is it?" Trixie walked behind her counter, feeling more comfortable having a slab of timber between herself and Janine.

"Some people have been saying that you've been asking questions."

"Questions?"

Janine nodded. "About Tanya Stewart."

"Ok," said Trixie, trying to sound nonchalant.

"Do you know what I'm talking about?"

"Jainine, I can't really say anything."

"Well, have you been going around town making enquiries?" Janine persisted with her questioning.

"I'm sorry, I'm just not sure why you're asking me this?" Trixie placed her hands on top of the bench, pressing down, an effort to remain calm.

"I could say the same of you." Janine crossed her arms across her chest.

"Look, was there a specific reason you've come here? Is there a particular problem?"

"I just wanted to warn you that you could upset people if you keep this up."

"I have no intention of upsetting anyone, but in this instance, it isn't any of your business," said Trixie, before tilting her head. "Unless you're personally involved? Is there anything you want to tell me?"

Janine huffed. "Of course not. I'm just looking out for you. But if you don't want my help, well, there's nothing I can do."

"I appreciate your concern," said Trixie, moving from behind the counter. "But I'm fine. Now, was there anything else I could help you with?"

"Not today." Janine didn't say anything further; she just glanced back at Trixie, frowning, before leaving.

Trixie watched her leave, and as soon as she was sure Janine was gone, she quickly slumped into the Chesterfield.

It was one thing hoping she was doing the right thing; it was another to know the whole town was aware of what she was doing and was, it appeared, not happy about it. She had always managed to stay fairly under the radar. Knowing so many eyes were currently on her made her decidedly uncomfortable.

Head in her hands, Trixie took a deep breath in an effort to move on from her encounter with Janine.

"Trixie, are you ok?"

Trixie looked up. It was Anna.

Chapter 20

"Anna! Hi!" Trixie stood up, brushing her hands down her top in an attempt to calm herself.

Anna was wearing blue nursing scrubs and had her brown hair pulled into a ponytail.

"You looked a bit overwhelmed," said Anna, taking her handbag off her shoulder and placing it on the floor next to the couch. "Is everything ok?"

"I just had a rather unpleasant visitor," she replied. "But nothing I can't handle."

"Are you sure? Should we call someone?"

Trixie shook her head. "No, nothing like that," she said. "But it did actually have something to do with you."

"Me? Really?"

"Do you have time for a cup of tea?"

"Um, I suppose. Do you have coffee?"

"Sure," she said. "I have a pod machine in the back. Is that ok?"

"That's perfect," said Anna.

Trixie indicated Anna should follow her, and the pair went into the rear storage room, where a miniature kitchen had been fashioned. Trixie had even managed to hook up running water with vintage taps running into an aluminium tub. Next to it was a brass trolley, the tea and coffee station.

"Wow," said Anna. "Even your storage room looks amazing. You do have an eye, Trixie."

Trixie turned to her, smiling. "Oh! Thank you!"

"I don't have a decorative bone in my body."

"I'm sure you do!" said Trixie, pressing the coffee machine. "It's just about finding your own style."

"Well, that I certainly don't know."

Trixie smiled. "We can work on that, whenever you're ready."

"Three kids, nursing, and a farm. I don't have much time for anything except getting through the day."

"Yes, it's hard being an adult," said Trixie, handing her the mug of coffee.

"Oh my gosh!" said Anna. "Some days I wonder how on earth I got here. I'm sure I was in high school just the other day."

Trixie laughed, nodding, as she prepared her cup of tea.

"Well, high school is kind of what I want to talk to you about," said Trixie.

"It is?"

"Let's take our drinks and sit on the couch." Trixie led Anna back into the barn, hoping they would be left alone whilst they spoke.

"High school?" Anna asked as she sat down. "Did we go to high school together?"

Trixie shook her head. "No, I'm pretty sure you'd left before I started."

"Sorry, then I'm confused."

Trixie took a sip of her tea and then held it with two hands in her lap.

"It's about the box you gave me, the box with the cameras."

"Now I'm really confused. My mum's cameras have something to do with high school?"

"Your sister," Trixie said. "Your sister went missing when she was in high school."

"Yes," Anna frowned.

"I'm sorry," said Trixie. "I realise I'm not doing this very well. Hang on a moment. I'll just grab something."

Rising, she went to the counter and pulled out the photo album.

"This was in the box," said Trixie, holding the album out to Anna.

Taking it, Anna looked down before looking up at Trixie. "I'd totally forgotten about this. I didn't realise it was in there."

"I thought that was the case," said Trixie.

"Did you only want to return it to me? You sounded so serious on the phone."

"Well, do you know what the album is?"

"I know it used to drive me crazy. Mum was obsessed with it. I know it was photos of Tanya. I never looked at it, though. I hated how much it absorbed Mum."

"Open it," said Trixie. "It's not just photos of your sister."

"It isn't?" Anna raised her eyebrows before flicking through some of the pages. "I don't understand what I'm looking at."

"It's photos from that day. The day of the Wattlebury 150 years celebrations. The day Tanya went missing."

"But they're all different types of photos, right?" Anna glanced up at Trixie.

"Yes, they're all different. I think your mum collected them. Got them from other people who had taken photos on the same day."

"But why?"

Trixie leant over and turned to the pages with the marks against Mitch and Kev. "She was trying to work out what happened to Tanya. And I believe she thought these two people had something to do with her disappearance."

"Really? This is what Mum was working on all those years? She was investigating?"

"I think so," said Trixie. "And the thing is, what I wanted to tell you, and I'm really hoping you don't mind, but I've been investigating too."

"What?" Anna's eyes widened. "*You've* been investigating?" She then glanced at her watch. "And I'm sorry, but I really need to leave in a moment."

"I know, I'll be quick," Trixie took a sip of tea before continuing. "When I saw the album and learnt about your sister, I couldn't believe no one knew what had happened to her. That she is still missing. And when I saw the people your mum had marked as suspects, Mitch and Kev, well, I'm sorry, but I just couldn't help myself."

"Mitch and Kev?"

"Mitch Lawson and Kev Carrington."

"Really?" Tanya peered at the photos. "Is that who's in the photos?"

"Yes. I asked my Mum and my Nan, and they're certain that's who's in the photos."

"And you said you had investigated? What does that mean exactly?"

"Ah, well, first I went to the library and printed some newspaper articles."

"Ok, that's not too bad, I suppose," she shrugged.

"Ah, yes. Well, the thing is, then I also went and spoke to Mitch and Kev." Trixie winced a little in anticipation of Anna's response.

"You did what?" This time Anna stood up. "I'm sorry, this is just a bit too much. Too much information."

"I'm so sorry, Anna," said Trixie, also standing. "Here, you go to work, take the album, and if you want to talk about this another time, well, I'll be here."

"No," said Anna.

"No, you don't want to talk about it?"

"No, I don't want the album. I hated that album. It took my mum away from us. I don't want it, so if you want it, you can have it."

"Are you sure? Maybe Jason would want it?"

"I can assure you, Jason will not want it."

"Ok," said Trixie, taking the album from Anna. "Well, I can hold onto it. But I won't do anything more. I'm so sorry to meddle."

"What did they say?" Anna stared at Trixie.

"Who? You mean Mitch and Kev?"

"Yes, what did they say?"

"Ah, well, I didn't ask them anything outright, just kind of how they knew Tanya, their memories of that day. They didn't say much."

"So you don't think they know anything?"

"I wouldn't say that."

"You wouldn't?" Anna frowned. "Why?"

"I'm no expert, I don't even know why I spoke to them. I just felt the way they reacted, both differently, but it felt like they knew something, and they seemed uncomfortable."

Anna nodded and then looked to the ground. She didn't say anything for a moment, and Trixie didn't dare speak. She couldn't imagine what Anna was thinking in that moment.

"Why do you care?" Anna looked up. "Why have you started looking into this?"

"Ah, well, that's hard to say." Trixie knew she couldn't tell Anna about the time travel. Or about the fact that she was in one of the photos. "I guess I just felt compelled to do something. It seems Tanya has been forgotten. Your mum put in so much work. I feel sad that it was all for nothing."

"All for nothing," said Anna. "No matter what Jason and I did, there was always Tanya. Nothing we did was enough for Mum. Tanya took our mum away from us. And yes, you're right. It was all for nothing. But do you really think you can find something out?"

"Oh, I have no idea," said Trixie. "And I would hate to bring back painful memories. So I'll stop. I'll put the album away, and if you want it back, it will be here waiting."

"I don't think you should stop," said Anna, quietly.

"You don't?"

Anna shook her head. "I've resented my Mum all my life. Resented her for not feeling like Jason and I were enough for her. But now I know it wasn't just pining, spending hours staring at Tanya's face. Now I know she was searching for clues, and that there may actually have *been* clues in those photos. I feel guilty," Anna's voice quivered. "Guilty for resenting my Mum. And even after I had my own kids, when I would try to imagine what it must have been like for Mum, I never asked her. I never asked her about Tanya, about what happened that day, about the years after. I thought I was in the right. I was stubborn. I thought Mum just didn't love us enough."

Trixie kept her eyes on Anna, watching as tears fell down her cheeks. Trixie couldn't help but pull Anna into a hug, and after a moment, she hugged Trixie back.

"Now I'm really going to be late," said Anna, pushing away. "But I've decided. And I'm sure Jason would want this, too. If you want to investigate, for whatever reason, then I think you should. I know Jason and I couldn't do it. It's too painful. But if you could find out what happened to Tanya, then it wouldn't have been for nothing. Mum's pain. Our pain. It wouldn't have been for nothing."

Anna paused, stared at Trixie, then picked up her handbag. Without another word, she left the barn.

Chapter 21

"So she gave you permission," said Fern. "You have her permission to investigate."

Trixie found herself once again out the back of Silver Gum Cottage with the ladies, chatting over drinks whilst Meg and Joe ran under the sprinkler on the lawn.

"I mean, we already knew that," said Rhada.

"We did?" Trixie frowned as she sipped her riesling.

"You're in the photos! Of course, you investigate."

"That doesn't mean she had permission, Mum," said Fern.

Rhada shrugged. "Well, I doubt Trixie would do much without Anna's permission. She's too much of a goody-two-shoes."

Fern laughed, and Trixie raised her eyebrows with a smile. Rhada wasn't wrong.

"Where's Maggie?" asked Trixie.

"I can't remember," said Fern. "Either doing a shift at the Chocolate Bar or a shift at the pub."

"What do you need Maggie for?" asked Rhada.

"I wanted her opinion on what Mitch and Kev told me."

"Yes, I think she will be very interested in your conversations," said Fern. "Especially with Mitch."

"Come on, Mum, tell me," said Trixie. "What exactly happened with them?"

"I think it was just a little fling," said Fern. "A friends with benefits kind of thing."

"Mum!" Trixie was shocked that her Mum knew of such things.

"I'm not as out of it as you think," said Fern, sipping her drink.

"But isn't Maggie older than Mitch?" Trixie asked.

"Yes, a few years older," she said. "But Maggie has never been one to settle down.

"What about when she had Caleb?"

"Well, you know Maggie's always been a very good Mum," said Fern. "The best. But Maggie was just never meant to be married. To be with just one man."

"Did she live with Caleb's dad?"

Fern shook her head. "Nope, I don't think that was ever on the cards. Oh, the two of them are very good parents. They worked things out with Caleb really well. He always comes first. They just chose not to live together. It was like that from the start. I think that almost made it easier rather than trying to force something that was never going to end well."

"Mum!" A pair of dripping children raced up to the table. "We're hungry!"

"There's a whole fruit platter right here," said Fern, pushing over the plate laden with pineapple, mango, strawberries, peaches and apple. The pair of them shoved mango in their mouths, and each took two strawberries with them as they headed back to the sprinkler.

"So, back to Maggie and Mitch," said Trixie, popping some mango in her own mouth.

"Well, that was a few years before Caleb was born," said Fern. "I think Mitch liked having an older woman to call on, but it wasn't anything serious. They both had fun and then went their separate ways. I think probably around the time Mitch met his wife."

"His ex-wife," said Trixie.

Fern nodded.

"But seeing as Maggie isn't here," said Rhada. "Let's get back on track. Your Mum mentioned something about Margaret Doyle."

"Oh yes," said Trixie. "Sutton seemed to think you knew her, and she might be helpful? Said we should ask her about a possible sighting of Tanya."

Rhada nodded. "He could be right. Margaret could be useful."

"Do you think you could give her a call and see what she knows?"

"Of course I can," Rhada smiled. "Now, when are you planning your first slip?"

"What do you mean?" asked Trixie.

"You're investigating now, right?" said Rhada. "So when are you going to slip back and see what you can find out?"

"To be honest," said Trixie. "I'm hoping I can avoid it."

"Avoid it!" Rhada laughed.

"Why not?" Trixie crossed her arms.

"For one, we know for a fact that you do time travel," said Rhada. "We have the picture to prove it!"

Trixie rolled her eyes. "Maybe I'll change the past."

"Ha!" said Rhada. "But how on earth do you think you're going to solve this without time travel? No one else has managed it?"

"Yes, Trix," said Fern. "If you've got one thing on your side, it's the fact you can time travel. The police could only dream of being able to."

"That doesn't mean I should," said Trixie.

"Why are you so against it?" asked Rhada.

"I don't know," Trixie shrugged. She felt like a teenager again, pouting and refusing to listen to what her mother and grandmother told her.

"You do know," said Fern. "And if you don't talk about it, you'll never get over it."

Trixie couldn't help but roll her eyes before letting out a big sigh. "It's just never been enjoyable to me. It's always happened at awkward times. I feel panicky, worried I'll never get back home, and as I've said, it makes me feel ill. I've not had a single positive experience."

"That's because you've let the time slip control you," said Rhada. "You've got to learn to be in control."

"I have no idea how to do that," said Trixie. "You've never taught me."

"Because you never wanted to learn," said Fern.

"You were a stubborn one," said Rhada. "And don't try and act like you weren't because you know darn well what you were like."

Trixie couldn't help but let a smile creep onto her face. She knew the pair of them were right. Overall, she was a good kid, but when it came to time travel, she wouldn't listen to a word they had to say. She'd just hoped it would go away.

"Well, what am I supposed to do?" said Trixie. "Surely I'm too old to learn now."

Both Fern and Rhada burst out laughing at this.

"Too old!" cried Fern. "You're thirty-six. You're still a spring chicken!"

"Besides," said Rhada, "You're never too old for anything. That's my life motto!"

Rhada wasn't wrong. She was constantly trying out new things. From joining an orienteering club, to plastering a wall in the garden, and even visiting the local Men's Shed, so they could teach her how to rewire a lamp.

"Ok, ok," said Trixie. "Well, give it to me then. What are your top tips?"

"Breathing and visualising," said Rhada.

"So exactly what I already know," said Trixie.

"Yes, Trixie," said Fern. "You do already know this. It's just about being really intentional. It's much easier to visualise a time and place that you've just come from. It's a very different thing to visualise a specific time and location in the past."

"Uggh," said Trixie. "It sounds exhausting. How can I possibly visualise a time and place I've never been to!"

"In this case, you're at a great advantage," said Rhada.

"Oh, am I?" Trixie let the sarcasm drip. "How is that?"

"The album, of course," said Rhada. "You have an album filled with photos of the exact times and places you want to go."

"Gosh," said Fern. "I wish I had that when we were trying to go back to the Proclamation."

"Oh yes!" Rhada laughed. "Gee, that painting was utterly wrong, wasn't it!"

"Proclamation?" asked Trixie. "Are you talking about the Proclamation of South Australia? In 1836?"

"The very one," said Rhada. "It was quite the debacle. We kept ending up in some sort of meeting of a bunch of old men."

"We worked it out eventually," said Fern. "It seems a lot of the people in his painting of the Proclamation were actually portraits of his friends!"

"We discovered it was painted twenty years after the Proclamation. The artist wasn't even in South Australia at the time of the Proclamation."

"Hadn't he only arrived a year before he painted it?" Fern asked.

"I think you're right," said Rhada, laughing.

"So, did you finally get there?" asked Trixie. "And what on earth did you need to go to the Proclamation for?"

"That's a story for another time," said Fern. "But yes, we did get there."

"So what helped?"

"Going to the site of The Old Gum Tree," said Rhada. "Where the Proclamation was held. Instead of focusing on the people, we focused on the Gum Tree."

"So is that what I should do?" asked Trixie. "Should I go to the site of the anniversary celebrations?"

Fern and Rhada looked at each other.

"Perhaps," said Fern. "Although it may not be necessary."

"Yes, I'd try with just the photos at first," said Rhada.

"But what about time? How do I know what time to pick? And should I be travelling at the same time of day in the present?"

"No, you don't need to travel at the same time," said Fern. "It couldn't hurt, but it usually isn't necessary. That being said, time slipping is a tricky business, so anything you can do to avoid errors is a good thing."

Trixie let out a long breath. "This all sounds hard, complicated and exhausting."

"It can be," said Rhada. "But is all about perspective. And how much you want to do this."

"Well, you both know I have no desire to do this whatsoever."

"Really?" Fern raised her eyebrows.

Trixie wanted to challenge her mum, but Meg and Joe lumbered up again, complaining of being cold and requiring towels. It was time to head home.

As she collected her things, Trixie couldn't help ponder how quickly things had changed. A week ago, Trixie would have been adamant that she would be thrilled to never time slip again. But was that still the case?

Chapter 22

"We should have left five minutes ago!" Trixie called down the hallway from the front door.

It was Saturday morning, and they would be late for swimming lessons, again. Joe couldn't find his goggles, and Meg had been so engrossed in a book that even though Trixie had asked her multiple times, she had only just started putting her suncream on.

Trixie sighed. There was nothing she could do. She knew Joe's goggles were under his bed. They were always under his bed. And Meg did not need help, thank you very much. So Trixie stood there, holding the wooden door as she sipped her coffee, wondering if she would have time to make another one before the kids sorted themselves out.

"Found them!" Joe bellowed from his bedroom before pounding down the hallway.

"Go jump in the van," said Trixie. "I'll round up Meg."

Joe rushed through the door before Trixie called "Shoes!" Joe raced back in, grabbed his thongs from the basket next to the front door, and, without putting them on, made his way to the van.

"Meg! I'm sure your suncream is fine!"

"I don't want to get sunburnt on my back like I did last time!"

"You'll be fine!" Trixie was rolling her eyes, glad her daughter couldn't see her. Last week, Meg had returned home with a tiny sliver of red on her lower back, where the rashie top had ridden up and obviously hadn't been slathered in cream.

Eventually, Meg came down the hallway, holding her swimming bag and carrying the large pump pack of suncream. "I'll do some more when I get there."

They finally managed to arrive at the swimming pool, just as the teacher was ushering the class into the water. Trixie found herself a spot under an umbrella at a blue-painted wooden table, saying hello to the parents who were also regretting signing their kids up for eight-thirty swimming lessons. At least it was an outdoor pool and only for the summer, but Trixie questioned whether she would do this again next year.

Today, Trixie brought a book. She didn't plan on reading a word. It was her wall. Her barrier to conversation. Today, she wasn't in the mood for chit-chat. Normally, she was happy to natter away for an hour each Saturday, knowing she was going home to the peace and quiet of Speckled Hen Farm. Today, however, she needed to think. Specifically about time travel.

After tossing and turning all night, Trixie, in the early hours of the morning, had finally accepted that she was going to have to time travel, whether she liked it or not. Firstly, as Rhada had pointed out, it was already a fact. She was in Sharon's photos. It was done. Secondly, she couldn't get Tanya out of her head. If it was Meg that was missing, and it seemed all hope was lost, but someone, somewhere, had the ability, the skills, the special talent that might just solve this mystery, then she would want them to do absolutely everything they could. In this case, Trixie was that person. She needed to be that person for Sharon. For Anna and Jason. She was the person with the ridiculous 'talent', and it seemed she was the only person who had any chance of solving this mystery.

Today, Trixie needed to focus on the fact that she had been approaching time travel the wrong way her entire life. Instead of being in a panic, dreading the situation and resisting it, she needed to embrace it, to go with the flow, connect with the energy that was needed to accomplish a time slip. As she thought about all the other times she had slipped, she recognised there was a particular feeling that came with all of them. Of course, in the past, this had caused her to immediately go into panic mode. Whether it happened in a split second, like it had with the camera, or within a few minutes, as it had done on most other occasions, there was a very specific energy that she felt through her body. Fern and Rhada seemed to think she should have some sort of control over this energy, and once she harnessed this, she would be able to time slip to a time and place of her choice. At the moment, this all sounded implausible to Trixie, but she was willing to give it a try.

At the very least, now that her time slip genetics had kicked back in, she wanted to be more in control in the future for when a slip snuck up on her when she wasn't expecting it.

Glancing up, she spotted Meg in the pool wearing her purple goggles and the blue and white check bathers she had chosen just after Christmas. Trixie smiled at her little face, listening intently to her instructor before she dove, triumphantly surfacing, holding a pool weight.

Meg would almost certainly have the time travel gene, and it was only a matter of time before her daughter experienced her first slip. Trixie's mum had done her very best to prepare her, and still Trixie was shocked when it happened. She'd been almost eleven and had come home from school in tears after her first big fight with her current best friend. Sobbing on her bed, she had suddenly felt grass on her face, rather than her damp pillow. Even now, she could remember the feeling of her heart racing as she sat up, turning her head this way and that, trying to find her bearings. She was on the lawn of her own school. To this day, she has no idea what time frame it was, but she was fortunate that it was either the holidays or after school, because there were only a few kids in casual clothes playing on the playground, a distance away.

"Breathe, 1, 2, 3, breathe, 1, 2, 3." The mantra her mum had drummed into her came into her mind. She started taking the deep breaths she had always been instructed to do. It took her a few goes to slow her breathing, but when she eventually got into a rhythm, she closed her eyes, feeling the now familiar sensation wash over her, and found herself back on her bed.

"MUM!!!" she had screamed. No doubt the sound of her voice had sent chills through Fern. Her mum had raced in and, from the look on Trixie's face, had known exactly what had happened.

Trixie wanted to prepare Meg, just like her own mother had. So far, she had done nothing at all, putting her head in the sand, hoping it would skip Meg. She had even dared to think that possibly the time travel gene had ended with her. Of course, that was fantasy. In reality, the only way to help Meg was to accept her own situation and to learn and practice as much as she could before passing on all she knew.

"Can we get a sour strap?" Joe asked before even reaching for his towel, his lesson having finished.

"Not today," Trixie said.

"But Mum!"

Trixie ignored him, turning, searching for Meg. She finally spotted her, standing in front of the pool safety sign. "Honestly, how many times does she need to read that?" Trixie said under her breath.

Grabbing the bags, Meg's towel and thongs, they scooped her up on their way out the gate.

"What are we doing today?" asked Joe as he was clicked into his car seat.

"After lunch, Nan and Granny are picking you up and taking you to the movies and then you're having a sleepover."

"Yay!" Joe was clearly excited.

"What are we seeing?" asked Meg.

"Oh, I can't remember what it was," said Trixie. "But I know it's something you'll enjoy. Plus, you'll get popcorn and a drink."

"Yes!" Joe cried out again.

Trixie glanced at Meg. She knew her daughter would be wondering if a movie was really the best use of her Saturday afternoon. Trixie had made plans with her Mum to take the kids so she could do some time travel training. She wanted some peace to see if she could get the hang of it, without worrying about what would happen if she travelled when she was alone with the kids.

Unfortunately, that thought had caused her to spiral a little, realising how often it was just her with the kids and what would happen to them if she slipped away. Fern had spent some time on the phone with her the previous evening.

"Trix," said Fern. "First of all, they're smart kids, so they won't panic. However, it is very unlikely to happen, and if it does, you will get the hang of returning quickly."

"How can you be so sure?"

"Because you returned quickly with the camera, and you were very out of practice," said Fern.

Trixie took in a deep breath. "Shouldn't I explain it to them, though? I haven't spoken to either of them about my time travel. I was hoping I'd never have to."

"Well, yes," said Fern. "I do think it's time you explained it to them."

"But what if they tell all the kids at school?" asked Trixie. "You know that's exactly what Joe will do."

Fern laughed. "And who's actually going to believe a five-year-old when they tell everyone their mum can time travel?"

Trixie had to laugh as well. The obviousness made her relax a little.

As they sat down to lunch, Trixie decided it was time to tell them. To tell her two precious children that their mum could time travel, and that it was likely Meg would be able to as well. But not Joe.

"Oh, no fair!" Joe said.

Trixie sighed. Of course, she should have expected this reaction from Joe. She shook her head, but had to realise that to Joe, time travel would sound super cool, and the fact that he couldn't do it would be bitterly disappointing.

"Look, I'm sorry, buddy," said Trixie. "It's just time travelling seems to only be something the girls in our family can do."

"But I *might* be able to. Maybe I'll be the first boy to do it!"

Trixie shrugged. What could she say to that? "I don't know, Joe. Maybe. But I wouldn't hold your breath."

Joe frowned. "Hold my breath? Is that how you time travel?"

Trixie chuckled, shaking her head. "No, no, sorry. That's just a saying. I wouldn't hold your breath means I wouldn't expect something to happen, as it is very unlikely. And unfortunately, it is very unlikely you will be able to time travel."

"Ok," said Joe. "But I bet I can. You just wait and see." Joe returned to his sandwich, and Trixie looked at her daughter. She was staring off into the distance, the cogs clearly moving in her brain.

"What do you think, Meg? Do you have any questions?"

Meg glanced at her mum but didn't say anything. She still had a lot to process.

Trixie let her be, picking up her own ham and avocado baguette and taking a bite. It seemed this conversation had gone a lot better than she'd expected. But surely it wasn't as simple as that?

"Mum," said Meg. "What I don't get is how, scientifically, our bodies can be in one place and then another in an instant?"

Trixie held in a sigh and instead smiled at her daughter. It was typical that her daughter had jumped straight to one of the more complicated aspects of the news. "I don't know Megs, I don't really understand it either. But, I think if you did want to research it, maybe start with Albert Einstein. It's a physics question you're asking. I think he wrote about it. And when I was a bit older than you, I read 'A Wrinkle in Time'. It's a fiction book, of course, but I found that helped a bit."

"Is it good?"

"I remember loving it," said Trixie. "And guess what the main character's name is? Meg!"

Meg's face lit up. "Have you got the book? Can I get it?"

Now Trixie did sigh. "Gosh, I don't know," she said. "I wonder if maybe Granny still has it."

"Can I ring her now? So she can bring it with her?"

Trixie handed Meg her phone.

Chapter 23

As she waved to the kids, Trixie wondered how much of the film Meg would actually watch, now that she had 'A Wrinkle in Time' in her hot little hands.

It made her realise that, despite them being her own flesh and blood, it didn't mean they experienced the world in the same way she did. When Fern had first told Trixie about the fact that she would be able to time travel, Trixie's stomach had sunk. Another way for her to feel different to the kids at school. A big way. Trixie had immediately complained about how unfair it was, why this was happening to her, and how she could stop it from happening. That had never changed, it seemed.

Joe and Meg, on the other hand, saw it as something exciting or intriguing. Not scary. Not annoying. At least, not today. Trixie did wonder how Meg would react after her own first time travel experience. Yet, Trixie had to admit, Meg would probably immediately record data in a notebook and want to discuss the experience in depth to better understand it. Meg probably wouldn't freak out, cry, and hide under her covers for hours, whilst her mother tried to coax her out with food.

"Ok, Trix, enough of this," she told herself. "You've got to get cracking."

Trixie had her day planned. As much as she could. She was going to lock herself in Paraphernalia and time slip. Simple.

She had the camera ready. But she also had a collection of items that she had a significant emotional attachment to, one particular person. Her grandfather. She missed him and would love to see him again. In front of her was a photo of her grandfather as well as a selection of ribbons that had belonged to him. He'd been an amateur chicken breeder and used to show them at the Royal Adelaide Show.

Today Trixie was dressed in a long striped skirt, a white shirt and brown loafers. She was hoping that whatever era she ended up in, her outfit wouldn't make her look too out of place.

Trixie placed a carton of milk and a container of salad in the fridge of Paraphernalia, before returning to pull the sliding door across and locking it securely. She didn't want anyone interrupting, thinking the shop was open when it wasn't.

She had been planning on lighting a candle, just to set a calm mood, but it occurred to her that she might time travel longer than she anticipated and did not want to burn down the barn. So instead, Trixie had brought a selection of essential oils and an electric diffuser that would turn off automatically should she not be around. Trixie had been advised that being as calm as possible would help her to remain more in control of her time slip.

Plugging the diffuser in, she set it up on the windowsill, just behind the Chesterfield. She picked up the photo of her grandfather and took a seat.

"Ok, Trix," she said out loud to herself. "Whatever happens, you can handle it. All you have to do is breathe."

Trixie set a timer for five minutes. She closed her eyes, breathed in the fragrance of the oils, and did her best to switch off her mind. It was hard at first, her mind flicking to her worries about time travel, wondering what the kids were doing right at that moment, and feeling the back of her calves begin to stick to the leather of the couch. Finally, just as the timer went off, she felt she might actually be relaxing.

Trixie stared at the black and white photo of her grandfather, probably from some time in the sixties. He was sitting at a wooden table, wearing a shirt with an open collar, a game of chess in front of him. Trixie closed her eyes and imagined herself sitting opposite her grandfather, playing the game of chess with him.

For a long time, nothing happened. Trixie breathed in and out, constantly having to bring her mind back to the chessboard. She found herself imagining what the table would feel like, what the room might smell like, what the weather was like outside the window. Would her grandfather smile at her, or would he remain stern like the face in the photo? Would Rhada be nearby? Was she the one taking the photo, or was it someone else? Trixie presumed her nan knew how to play chess, although for some reason she just couldn't picture her sitting down to play.

Then her fingers started to tingle. As soon as she noticed, Trixie immediately felt some of the familiar panic begin to surface in her chest. Taking a long, slow breath, she focused on the tingling and the image of her grandfather, willing herself to remain calm and allow the time slip to happen. A buzzing started to form in her ears. Not loud, but a hum just above the surface. Her eyes pulsed slightly, and her head felt heavy. Finally, the feeling of an icy breeze washed over her, and then she was still.

Trixie knew she needed to open her eyes, but she couldn't. She was too scared. Yet, what if her grandfather were there in front of her? And what if he could see her?

It was the noise that forced her to open her eyes, a shocking sound very out of context to Paraphernalia or to the game of chess she had visualised.

"Come on, Bessie," a man's deep voice said as an animal's bellow rang out.

Trixie was sitting on a hay bale, the straw poking into her legs. She was in her barn. She hadn't moved location, only time it appeared. She almost laughed, but sucked it back in when the voice spoke again.

Turning her head to the right, Trixie saw a farmer bent over a cow's hoof, which had been tied into place. He appeared to be trimming it, attempting to solve whatever problem was embedded in the bottom. Glancing around, it was impossible to guess what year it was. Was this the man they'd bought the farm from? Or had she travelled back many more years?

She was frustrated with herself for not travelling to her grandfather. And yet, she had to admit that intentionally travelling to another time, whatever the location, was pretty cool.

"Ok, Trix," she thought. "Time to get back."

Closing her eyes again, she commenced her slow, deep breathing. Trixie was surprised to notice she felt no panic in her body. She was calm, focused, and very quickly felt the familiar wave wash over her.

Opening her eyes, she let out an audible gasp. She had done it! She had returned to the barn. Glancing behind her, the diffuser was still on, and the mist was flowing. Her watch told her she had maybe been gone for three minutes.

"Holy crap," Trixie said, standing and putting her hands to her mouth. She had done it.

"But, hang on."

Jumping up, she ran to the fridge. Swinging the door open, she laughed when she saw the salad and the milk. She had, in fact, returned to the right time and place. All with intention. Reflecting on that day in years to come, she realised it was at that moment she had become her future self.

Trixie Travers, Time Traveller.

Chapter 24

Trixie had the rest of the day to herself. It had been a long time since that had happened, and she was going to relish it. Today, she didn't need to prepare for the opening of Paraphernalia. She didn't need to clean. The house may not be spotless, but it was good enough. There was no dinner to prepare, because her kids were away. That Saturday afternoon and evening, Trixie could do whatever she wanted.

And she had no idea what to do.

As she had been so prepared, Trixie made herself a cup of tea and sat outside the barn with her salad. Cars could be heard travelling past the farm. Trixie realised it had been a while since she'd restocked the Speckled Hen Farm's stall at the gate. Perhaps she could spend some time today tending to the garden and see if there was anything to sell.

Or not.

Trixie also knew she really needed to focus on getting the word out about Paraphernalia. 'If you build it, they will come' was not a great motto for a shop. Especially one located on a farm on the outskirts of town that no one really knew about. This afternoon, she could work on her sign, as well as spreading the word by taking photos of her stock and sharing it with the world.

Perhaps tomorrow.

What Trixie was surprised to notice was her mind kept flicking back to Sharon and Tanya, and more specifically, the photo album. It seemed this mystery wasn't going to let her have even an afternoon's rest. It was tugging at her, and despite her disappointment in not yet being able to set her destination and slip there, Trixie knew the investigation didn't entirely hinge on her ability to time travel. At least, not yet. There was more she could do.

"I'm going to need somewhere to spread out," Trixie said to herself. She had decided that instead of gardening or marketing, she was going to spend the afternoon investigating, and that meant going through all the photos and newspaper articles with a fine-tooth comb.

Packing up and grabbing the box of cameras, Trixie made her way back to the farmhouse. She cleared the kitchen table of all the piles by simply dumping them into a laundry basket and pushing it into Kirby's office. Grabbing a bottle of cleaning spray, she wiped down the table, wanting to ensure there were no remnants of Vegemite or Milo to ruin a photo. Once it was spotless and dry, Trixie began methodically laying out all the items she had.

The cameras were interesting, but Trixie wondered why Sharon had so many? Were they all her own? Had the owners just given them to her when she had come calling about photos of the 150-year event? Or were they completely unrelated to the photo album?

She lay the negative pages side-by-side, repeating rows of brown plastic, with the canisters standing to attention next to them. Trixie wondered if she should get them developed and if it was still even possible?

The photo album was placed front and centre. Although Trixie doubted herself, knowing Sharon would have analysed it over and over, she didn't have Sharon sitting next to her to reveal all she had found. Yes, there were notes and markings, but Trixie felt like something was missing. Was there a notebook out there somewhere, with all of Sharon's notes and ideas? And could Trixie ask Anna about it? Or was that pushing things just a little too far?

"First, champagne," Trixie said, making her way to the kitchen fridge. She found a bottle of sparkling wine rolling around in the bottom drawer and popped it. Grabbing a crystal glass, because it seemed like that kind of day, she poured the wine before inserting a stopper and placing it back in the fridge. Now it was time to start.

Trixie decided she was going to attempt to lay out a timeline based on Sharon's work, but including not only Tanya, but Mitch and Kev. It wouldn't be easy, but there was at least one set of photos that had the orange numerals displaying the date and time at the bottom, as well as Sharon's notes.

The wine went down rather quickly, but Trixie didn't notice as she sipped and peered. Not until the glass was empty, of course. By that time, one page of her notebook was filled, and the next page was beginning. She poured another glass and resumed her review of the photographs. There were several people who, although potentially not connected, were seen talking to Tanya, Mitch, and Kev. Of particular note were those people who had spoken to two or even all three of them. A coincidence? If Trixie had learnt anything from watching Murder She Wrote and Midsomer Murders, there was no such thing as a coincidence. Her problem was, she had no idea who these people were.

As she scanned through the photos a third time, searching for anything odd or interesting, she noticed something that got her rather excited. At the back of one of the photos, a man was standing with a rather large contraption on his shoulder. A video camera. She took a photo of the photo and sent it to her mum immediately.

"Do you know who this is holding the video camera?"

As Trixie impatiently waited for Fern to respond, she had this sense that she had had a breakthrough. Would the video from that day still exist? And if so, who had it? Could Sharon have spotted the same thing? There was no mark against this photo, though. Not that this meant anything necessarily. Yet, Trixie imagined someone with a video camera back in the eighties would have been very unusual. No doubt people would have spoken of it, and she found it hard to believe Sharon wouldn't have searched for it, just as she had done with these photos. It was surprising it wasn't in the box with the albums, but could that mean there was another box somewhere?

Fern didn't respond. Trixie couldn't blame her. She was looking after her grandchildren. Instead, Trixie decided to text Anna. She had given her permission to investigate. Surely she wouldn't mind a question about the existence of a videotape.

Before she poured a third glass of wine, Trixie decided food was in order. She pulled together a rather impressive charcuterie board for herself and returned to the table. After her fourth examination of the photos, she realised the Silver Ladies were going to have to help her. Two other people needed to be identified, the people who were seen talking with Tanya, Mitch and Kev.

Trixie's phone beeped.

I think there were some videotapes in a box. I'll try and have a look when I can.

She quickly responded to Anna. *Great! Thank you.*

Now what was she to do? With a few glasses of wine under her belt and a moderately successful time slip today, Trixie felt inclined to just skip waiting for the video and instead travel to the time and place she was looking at.

"Don't get too cocky," Trixie thought to herself, shaking her head. "You couldn't even get to your grandpa. There's no way you'll land next to the owner of the video camera. And what use would that be anyway?"

With her children on a sleepover, Trixie realised now was the perfect time to head to bed.

Chapter 25

"I wouldn't call it a complete and utter fail," Fern said, unable to contain her grin despite the encouraging words.

Trixie had arrived at Silver Gum Cottage early, before Joe and even Meg were awake. Both Fern and Rhada had been up, and Maggie had stumbled out of her bed once she heard chatter in the kitchen. Trixie was now describing her recent time slip, much to the amusement of the Silver Ladies.

"I got home in one piece at least," said Trixie.

"Was a farmer really fixing the hooves of a cow in your barn?" Maggie couldn't help but seek further clarification.

"Yes!" Trixie moaned. "I don't know how I can be any clearer."

Glancing around, Fern, Maggie and Rhada were all smirking.

"Ok, enough," she said. "Can you at least help me work out how to get exactly where I want to be?"

"Look, Trix," said Fern. "Why don't I do a bit of research, go back through some of my old notebooks, and see if I can come up with a plan?"

Nodding, Trixie sipped her cup of tea. "Sounds good. For now, though, I want you to help me identify some more people." She pushed the photo album over, flipping to a page she had bookmarked.

"Do any of you know this man, and," flipping to another page. "This woman?"

Peering closely, each woman looked in turn before frowning and shaking their head.

"No idea," said Maggie.

"Sorry, Trix," said Rhada. "I don't recall either of those faces."

"So not locals?" Trixie asked.

Fern pulled the album towards herself and flipped the pages, looking at each marked photo in turn.

"They're not anyone I recognise," said Fern, shaking her head. "It doesn't mean they aren't locals. Or weren't locals at the time. But I can't place either of them."

"But both of them were seen speaking to Tanya," said Trixie. "And you can see the man is also speaking to Kev. So I can at least ask Kev."

"Maybe Anna or Jason will know who they are?" said Rhada.

"Maybe," said Trixie. "But they were very young at the time. If these people didn't hang around in town, they might not have any memory of them."

"It's still worth speaking to them," said Rhada. "If you're going to investigate, you have to follow up every lead."

"Well, don't you sound like a detective," Trixie giggled. "Is that all the episodes of Vera you've watched, Nan?"

"I'd be quite happy to be compared to Vera, thank you very much," said Rhada, taking a bite from her marmalade-covered crumpet. "Actually, I did a bit of my own detective work yesterday."

"You did?" Maggie sounded surprised.

"Oh, Margaret Doyle. Did you call her?" Trixie had forgotten about Professor Crowe's lead.

"I did," said Rhada. "Unfortunately, she didn't tell me much."

"That's disappointing," said Trixie. "Did she mention anything about the possible sighting?"

"Actually, yes. Someone had said they had seen Tanya in Port Wakefield with a woman. But they never got any confirmation of that, so she thinks it was a mistake," said Rhada. "But the good news is she still has all her marbles, and had absolutely no hesitation in telling me what she knew. I have a feeling she is going to be very useful for future cases."

"Future cases? What are you on about, Nan?"

Rhada shrugged, smiling.

Trixie shook her head. "Meanwhile, I actually have a useful update. Anna said she was going to look for the videotapes," said Trixie.

"What videotapes?" asked Maggie, frowning.

Trixie slapped her forehead. "Oh, I forgot," she said, pulling the photo album back towards herself before flipping the pages. "Here, look." Trixie pointed at the man with the video camera.

"That's Geoff Blackman," said Rhada. "He used to take that video camera everywhere. He was so proud of being the first person in Lilly Pilly Creek to own one. Drove his wife Pam mad, if I recall."

"Geoff Blackman." Trixie was noting this name down. "I doubt he'd still be alive."

Rhada shook her head. "No, but it was only four or five years ago that he passed. In his nineties."

"So is it worth trying to chase up the video tapes?"

"No idea," said Rhada. "I think both his daughters live in Adelaide now. And his son has moved off the farm. The grandson runs it now. No idea if it would be there, or with the girls, or chucked in the bin. Knowing Pam, she would have chucked it all."

"Here's hoping Sharon was on the ball all those years ago and Anna has a copy," said Trixie.

"So, when are you going to time travel next?" Fern asked, handing Trixie another cup of tea.

Trixie couldn't help but roll her eyes. "Ah, how about never."

"Come on, love," said Rhada. "You'll get the hang of it. It was the first time you intentionally time travelled. That's a pretty big deal, you know."

Sipping her tea, Trixie couldn't bring herself to answer. Not wanting to time travel in the first place, and now having barely accepted it was her destiny, she had little patience for the expectation that she would get there if she worked hard. Why should she work hard at something she didn't really want to do? If the universe was trying to tell her something, that she was indeed a time traveller, then why make it so hard?

"I just wish I could press a button and be exactly where I needed to be!"

"What, like a time machine?" laughed Fern. "Don't be ridiculous. You know they don't exist."

"Oh, don't they?" Trixie arched one eyebrow. "Because I actually saw one the other day."

"You did not!" Maggie burst, eyes wide.

"I did," said Trixie, before taking a long sip of her tea, the Silver Ladies staring at her.

"Whose was it?"

"Professor Sutton's," said Trixie. "He brought it to show me."

"Are you saying you've told him you can time slip?" asked Fern.

"Oh, god no!" said Trixie. "I'm not telling anyone that. No, it was just all pure coincidence."

"Coincidence," said Rhada. "You know there's no such thing as coincidence."

"Maybe not," said Trixie. "But it wasn't because he had any sort of inkling about us. He's completely oblivious, I'm sure. But maybe the universe is helping me. Making time travel at the push of a button a possibility."

"So, it's not possible now?" said Maggie. "You're telling us all about this time travel machine, but does it actually work?"

"Well, no, it doesn't actually work. Yet."

Fern and Maggie couldn't help but laugh. Rhada finished her last crumpet, a smug look on her face.

"Professor Sutton is one of the smartest people I know," said Trixie. "Probably one of the smartest people in the world. If anyone is going to work out time travel, it's him."

"But it serves no purpose when you can, you know, actually time travel," said Maggie.

"Can I?" Trixie looked at Maggie. "Can I really time travel? I'm not so sure. All I can do is accidentally time slip with no rhyme or reason. What good is that?"

"Well, it's a hell of a lot more than Professor Sutton can do, that's for sure." Maggie raised her eyebrows and tilted her head.

"Alright, alright," said Trixie. "I've had enough of this conversation." She pushed her chair out and stood up. "I'm going to wake the kids."

"There's no need for that," said Fern. "When they wake up, I can message you. Why don't you go and enjoy yourself? I think the Farmer's Market is on. You should pop down."

Trixie pictured the rows of trestle tables under striped marquees, filled with fresh produce, homemade candles, secondhand books, and plants. Her mum was right. A visit to the Farmers Market all by herself sounded like an amazing idea.

"Are you sure?" asked Trixie. "I mean, you've had them all

afternoon and all night."

"Of course I'm sure," said Fern. "I'll message you as soon as they wake. I know Meg will be ready for home."

Chapter 26

A while ago, Trixie had considered signing up for a spot at the Wattlebury Farmer's Market. They had enough produce from the farm, alongside some of the vintage items she had started to collect before the opening of Paraphernalia. Yet, upon enquiring, she soon discovered these spaces were hot ticket items, and as she couldn't commit to weekly attendance for an entire year, she quickly gave up that plan.

Wandering down the aisles, she had to appreciate that such tight regulations meant the quality of products on offer where superb. A few loaves of sourdough were first to go in her basket, and then cheeses from the new Butternut Cheesery over in Lilly Pilly Creek.

The market was always busy, which was pleasant but also a little frustrating when there was a line-up to taste the local olive oil or to discover the fresh pesto had already sold out. It also meant, as a local, you knew many people striding down the aisles, slowing you down as you said hello or stopped to chat with those you couldn't simply acknowledge with a smile and a wave. One of those people was Mitch Lawson.

"Nice to see you again, Trixie," said Mitch. He was wearing tan pants, a navy shirt, and a flat cap on his head, very much the country gentleman. "Any progress on the will?"

Trixie was initially confused by this question until she recalled her subterfuge. "Oh, ah, Kirby is still away, so I haven't had a chance to talk to him."

Mitch nodded. "Sure, sure. And, ah," he hesitated. "Any progress on your enquiries, you know, about Tanya?"

She was a little surprised at this question, but then of course, she hadn't exactly been subtle. He obviously knew her questions were more than innocent chatter.

"Um, well, not much," said Trixie. "It's still quite a mystery. But the photos I have of Sharon's are interesting." *Why not try and bait one of the prime suspects*, she thought to herself.

"Oh, are they?" Mitch furrowed his brow. "In what way?"

"Well, some of them are blurry, but I could have sworn you were with Tanya in more than one."

Mitch sighed. Trixie clenched her hand around the basket of produce she was carrying.

"You did know her quite well, didn't you?" Trixie said, attempting to be gentle and kind, in an effort to get him to open up. What she did not expect was to see tears in his eyes.

Mitch nodded.

"I'm sorry, Mitch, I didn't mean to bring up bad memories."

"Well, you have," Mitch replied, and Trixie felt as though she had been punched in the chest. She focused on the dirt at her feet. "But it's ok," he said. Trixie looked up.

"It is?"

"Yes," he nodded. "It's about time someone found out what really happened to her. And I'm sick of pretending."

"Pretending?"

"Pretending I didn't know her," he explained. "It was my Dad who made me keep quiet."

"Keep quiet about what?"

"About our relationship?"

Trixie was embarrassed when she gasped out loud.

"You were in a relationship with Tanya? But weren't you a lot older than her?"

"Yes, four years older," said Mitch. "And of course that's nothing now. But she was in high school, and I was at Uni. It didn't look great. At least, my dad told me so. But she was a lovely girl. Smart, funny, and really excited about the future, considering the tough life she had."

"Tough life?"

"Well, I would have thought being the only child of a single mum would be hard for anyone."

"Of course," Trixie nodded. "So you were hiding from everyone? Hiding that she was your girlfriend?"

"We both were," said Mitch. "We knew this town wouldn't be impressed. So we decided we were going to keep everything a secret until she had finished school and was at Uni too. We planned to move to Adelaide, or maybe even Melbourne. She wanted to become a vet, so it all depended on where she got in."

"That makes sense," said Trixie. "But then she disappeared?"

Mitch nodded, the tears welling again. "Tanya had told me something a few days before," he said. "Something that would change both our lives. We had another fight on the day of the celebrations, and that was the last I saw of her."

"You fought at the 150-year celebration? Or later that night?"

"At the main event. In the afternoon."

"And what had she told you?"

Mitch sucked in a large breath. He glanced at Trixie before looking down at his feet.

"She was pregnant."

"What!" Trixie clamped her hand over her mouth, shocked at her own outburst. "Oh, sorry, Mitch. Sorry. I just didn't expect you to say that.

"It's ok," he said. "It is shocking. And actually, you're the first person I've ever told."

"Really? You never told anyone? Not your mum or your dad? Not Tanya's mum?

He shook his head.

"What were you fighting about?"

"I was trying to do the right thing, to help her. But she refused. Said she was going to sort everything out herself. I asked her what that meant, but she wouldn't tell me. She just walked away."

"And you never saw her again?"

"Never saw her. Never heard from her."

"But did you tell the police all of this?"

Mitch shook his head. "No, my Dad forbade me from even telling them about our relationship. I didn't have the chance to tell them anything else. He actually made me stay in the city for a while. We pretended I was on placement for Uni."

"And now, all these years later? Why are you telling me?"

"Because I haven't been able to stop thinking about it since you came to my office."

"So it wasn't a coincidence that we met today?"

"Oh, it was a total coincidence," he said with a slight smile. "But I told myself, if I did run into you, anywhere, it was a sign I had to tell you."

"Thank you," said Trixie. "But you know I really should tell Anna about this."

"I know," said Mitch. "I have nothing to hide. I should have said something years ago, but no one seemed to believe they could find the truth. It's like everyone gave up."

"Not everyone," said Trixie. "Sharon never gave up."

Mitch nodded, now letting the tears roll down his cheeks, staring at the ground. "Neither should I," he said. "I did nothing to help. I was the opposite of helpful." He lifted his face and looked into Trixie's eyes. "But I'll help now. What can I do? How can I help?"

Trixie reached out and gripped his forearm, attempting to comfort him. His emotions appeared genuine. Trixie was strongly doubting that he had anything to do with Tanya's disappearance.

"I don't know," said Trixie. "Not yet, at least. But I'll let you know. I don't want to give up."

Mitch nodded, forced a smile, and then, putting his hands in his pockets, nodded, turned, and walked away.

Chapter 27

"Did you have any idea Mitch and Tanya were in a relationship?"

Trixie was sitting in Anna's lounge room, perched uncomfortably on a lumpy upholstered wooden chair as she asked this question.

As soon as she had finished talking with Mitch, Trixie had, quite brazenly, she realised later, rung Anna to ask if she could come over. Fortunately, Anna wasn't working that day and was happy for Trixie to pop in. Jason mustn't live far away, because he had already arrived at Anna's by the time Trixie called her mum and then found the farm.

"Course we didn't," Jason said, impatient with Trixie already. "I mean, I was probably six. Anna was maybe ten. We had no idea what was going on."

"Do you think your mum knew? About her being pregnant?"

"If she did, she never mentioned it to us," said Anna. "Not once in all those years."

"It's just, she had Mitch listed as a suspect," Trixie told them. "I'm not sure if it's because she saw them together in these photos," Trixie pointed to the album. "Or if she knew something more."

"Who knows?" said Jason. "I'm sorry, Trixie, but I just don't see how we can help you?"

"Do you remember anything else? Was anything else happening around that time?"

Jason sighed and leaned back in his chair, placing his hands on the back of his head, feet on the coffee table. He shook his head but didn't say anything. He clearly thought Trixie was wasting their time. And perhaps she was.

"Honestly, we were too little to remember," said Anna. "But I have been thinking about our conversation. I haven't found the videotapes.

But I've found something else you might find useful."

Jason pulled his feet to the floor and sat up. His facial expression made it clear Anna hadn't spoken to him about this previously.

Anna stood and walked over to a sideboard. The entire top of the sideboard was covered with photographs. Anna slid open a drawer and pulled out a small red book of some sort.

"This is Mum's diary from that year," said Anna, holding the book out to Trixie.

"Have you read it?" Jason asked his sister.

Shaking her head, Anna sat down. "No, I couldn't bring myself to read it. I think it would be too sad."

"Did you want to read it, Jason?" Trixie asked, apprehensively holding the book out to him.

"Nup," said Jason. "Have at it. I've got no interest in reading it. Just as long as you don't share anything private, go for it."

"Of course," said Trixie. "I would never share anything without your permission."

"I just hope it helps," said Anna. "It's not very big. I can't imagine there's much in there, but there might be some clues."

"Thank you," said Trixie. "I really appreciate it."

"Is there anything else we can do?" Anna asked.

Trixie shook her head. "No, I don't think so." She stood, gathering her bag and her phone. "I'll get out of your hair."

Anna walked her to the door. Jason remained in the living room. He obviously found her annoying and nosy.

"Thanks for this," Trixie said, holding up the diary. "I promise I'll look after it."

"I know you will," said Anna, giving a small smile before closing the door.

Trixie hopped in the van and couldn't resist giving the diary a quick flick through. She was surprised at what she saw. The diary may be small, but it was filled with lines of tiny writing. It appeared Sharon had crammed a lot of information into the tiny book. Trixie only hoped it might help her crack the case.

She found herself laughing. "Crack the case! Honestly, who do I think I am?"

Realising it wouldn't look great if she sat outside of Anna's house whilst she read their mother's diary, Trixie drove away. She also knew the kids would be waiting for her. Despite desperately wanting some more quiet time, to sit and read the diary, she knew she was pushing her luck, with not only the kids, but the Silver Ladies.

"Mum, Granny let me have a piece of chocolate cake for breakfast!" Joe was grinning, a crumb of chocolate cake still lingering in the corner of his mouth.

"Oh, did she now?" Trixie raised her eyebrows, a smile on her face.

"Granny said I could!" said Joe, sounding rather defensive. "And Meg had some too!"

"It's ok, buddy," said Trixie. "We'll just make sure we have healthy food for the rest of the day. Now, can you go and grab your things so we can get home?"

Walking into the lounge room, she found Meg sitting on the couch, her bags at her feet, reading A Wrinkle in Time. She didn't even glance up when Trixie sat down next to her.

"How's the book?"

Meg gave a slight nod and continued reading.

"I'll leave you alone," Trixie said. "But as soon as Joe's ready, we'll be getting in the car, ok?"

Her daughter didn't respond, but Trixie knew she had heard her. Rising, Trixie smiled, remembering the joy of being so consumed with a book. Although the experience of the main character's time travelling would be nothing like what Meg would go through one day, it was at least a way for her to put context to her own abilities.

"Mum!" Trixie called out. "I'm here for the kids."

Eventually, she found Fern, Rhada and Maggie outside. Rhada was watering plants whilst Fern and Maggie played a game of cards.

"I'm back, finally," said Trixie. "Sorry for taking so long."

"I cannot believe Tanya was pregnant," Maggie said. "And you were the first person to find out about it, Trix!"

Trixie had quickly filled her mum in on the news on her way to Anna's. Clearly, the Silver Ladies had been discussing the revelation.

Trixie shrugged. She was as surprised as the rest of them.

"Did Anna and Jason know about Mitch? Or the baby?" asked Fern.

Trixie shook her head. "But they were both so young, they don't really remember anything about that time. I did get one thing, though."

"Oooh," said Maggie. "Do tell!'

"A diary," said Trixie. "Anna gave me Sharon's diary from the year Tanya went missing."

"That sounds like it might be a treasure trove," said Rhada.

"I hope so," said Trixie. "It's full of impossibly small writing, so let's hope I can actually read it!"

"It's certainly one way of travelling back in time," said Fern, an unusual tone to her voice.

"A much more convenient way," said Trixie. "At least for me."

"I'm reaaaady!" Joe called through the screen door.

"Well, thanks as always for looking after the kids," said Trixie. "We'll leave you in peace."

"Never a problem, sweetheart," said Fern.

"You know we love having them," said Maggie.

"Make sure you report in about the diary!" Rhada called, waving the hose in Trixie's direction.

"I'll send in a write-up, shall I?" Trixie laughed.

"That would suffice," said Rhada, winking before turning back to her roses.

Chapter 28

Trixie didn't get the quiet afternoon she was hoping for.

Meg promptly finished her book and wanted to discuss it at length. The problem was, Trixie had read it so many years ago, she didn't have the clarity required to adequately answer Meg's questions. But she did her best, especially when Meg moved into the factual situation of their own time slip condition.

"So, do we tesser?

"Tesser?" Trixie's mind started scrambling, trying to dig out the meaning of the word and its importance in the book.

"That's how they travel," said Meg. "They tesser. They use their minds and energy to travel."

"I forgot they used that term in the book. Well, yes, I guess that's what we do. We tesser too," said Trixie. The memories of A Wrinkle in Time were coming back to her.

"In the book, they mostly travel to distant planets and other locations, but that's not what you do, is it, Mum?"

Trixie wanted to sigh and tell Meg her mum didn't do much of anything. But she knew what Meg was asking. "No, we can't travel to other planets. At least, I don't think we can. We travel to other times and places in our own world. From my experience, it's usually to times and places we are familiar with or have some sort of connection to."

"So, *how* do you time travel? How do you get to where you need to go? How do you tesser?"

Trixie hesitated before replying. "I don't."

"What? Of course you do?"

Shaking her head, Trixie, for the first time, felt truly embarrassed about her lack of knowledge and experience. She had never had as much as a sliver of the curiosity Meg was already displaying. If she had, perhaps she would have been able to get to where she needed to go. She would have solved Tanya's disappearance, or at least have a chance of doing so. Now, her only hope was the diary.

"What I mean is, I don't really know *how* I do it."

"So Mum, can't you time travel to a particular place in time? Like if you said right now you wanted to go to see them building the pyramids in Egypt, you wouldn't be able to?"

"*I* certainly wouldn't be able to," she said. "Maybe Nan or Granny could. I don't know. I've never asked them."

Meg's eyebrows shot up. "You've never asked them!"

"Sorry, Meg," Trixie said, feeling sad. "The thing is, I'm very different to you. Time travel never excited me. I never wanted to learn about it. I just wanted it to go away. I hated everything about it. It made me feel sick. I had no control over it. I'd never know when I was going to slip next. You were the best thing that happened to me in more ways than one. As soon as I fell pregnant with you, I stopped slipping. Up until the other day."

"The other day? You mean you time travelled?"

"Well, not deliberately," Trixie said. "I picked up a Polaroid camera and wham! I was in another place and time."

"Where?" Meg asked, leaning over the table, eyes wide.

"Oh, here," she said. "In the Wattlebury main street. Some time in the eighties."

Meg rolled her eyes. "And you mean the nineteen eighties, right?"
Trixie nodded.

"Ugh, so boring. It would be so much better if it were the eighteen-eighties. Or the sixteen eighties. Imagine how different Australia was then!"

"Yes, well, I did travel somewhere else. Yesterday, actually."

"You did?"

"It's probably not that interesting either. I don't know the exact time, but I'm sure it was earlier than the eighties."

"And where did you go?"

"The barn. A farmer was caring for a cow."

"What, our barn? That's not interesting!"

"It may not be interesting to you," Trixie said. "But it was to me. It was the first time I had sat down and tried to intentionally travel. The first time I chose to time slip."

Meg stared at her mum's face, appearing to analyse her expression. "Wow, Mum. That sounds cool."

Trixie smiled. "Actually, it was. Cool and frustrating."

"Why was it frustrating?"

"Because I was *trying* to go somewhere else."

"Oh. Where?"

"To my grandparents' dining room," she explained. "I had a photo I was looking at. It didn't work. But I suppose I have to take small steps." Trixie shrugged.

"Absolutely, Mum. It was your first try. That is amazing!"

Trixie smiled, recognising the echo of her own voice in her daughter's, the way she encouraged her kids. Sometimes she had realisations that maybe she wasn't as much of a shambles as a mother as she felt most days.

"What age did you first slip?" Meg asked.

Trixie knew this was coming. Knew Meg wanted to know when *she* was going to start time slipping. It was one of the things Trixie most dreaded. But now that Meg appeared to have a genuine interest, maybe all the training Fern and Rhada had tried to do with her would actually work for her daughter.

"I was a few years older than you. Nearly eleven," said Trixie. "That's one of the reasons why I wanted to tell you. Because there's a lot we can do to help prepare you."

"Who can?"

"Me, and Nan and Granny," said Trixie. "I wasn't the best student, but Nan and Granny are very good teachers, if they have someone who listens to them. I thought maybe you and I could both become their students."

"What, learn how to time travel together?" Meg was smiling.

Trixie smiled too. "If that sounds ok to you?"

"That sounds amazing! When can we start?"

Trixie laughed. "We're going to have to talk to them about that. But not today. Meg, do you have any more homework you need to do? You know, for actual school?"

Meg groaned. An unusual response for her. "I suppose I can go and do my spelling words again. I usually do them fifty times, but I've only done them twenty."

"Well, off you go then," said Trixie.

Watching her daughter leave the room, Trixie shook her head and smiled. The two of them were so different. Trixie realised it was because of her daughter that she was going to force herself to take this time travel business seriously. Without Meg's enthusiasm and the fact that, as her parent, she needed to prepare her daughter as much as possible, Trixie knew she would continue to bury her head in the sand for as long as possible. Even when that behaviour could be disastrous.

Chapter 29

Trixie reached for her cup of coffee, picked up the diary, and curled her legs up on the couch. The air conditioning was on so that, despite the pulsing heat outside, she was comfortable.

She spent the next few hours reading Sharon's diary. The kids flitted in and out, asking questions which mostly revolved around which snack they could eat next. Fortunately, there wasn't much fighting, as the two of them managed to find ways to entertain themselves for most of the afternoon.

Sharon was clearly an experienced diary writer. It started on January the first, and had an entry for almost every single day, even if some of them were as simple as *Normal day today but I cooked apricot chicken for the first time and the kids loved it.*

Trixie didn't read the whole thing, though. She decided to skip to March eleventh, the day Tanya went missing. Perhaps unsurprisingly, there was no entry. Nor any for the entire week. Until March nineteenth, when Sharon wrote, *The police think she's a runaway. I'm going to have to find her myself.*

Flicking backwards, Trixie decided to read from September onwards, attempting to get some insight into what was happening in Sharon and Tanya's world in the weeks leading up to that fateful day.

Her coffee was empty, the air conditioning was starting to feel a little too cool, and her foot felt like it was falling asleep. Trixie was just about to put the diary down and get up when she saw it.

Tanya's Dad is back from Broome, and he wants to see her.

"What!" Trixie said aloud. It was the last thing she was expecting. No one had mentioned Tanya's Dad. Not a single person. Not Anna. Not Jason. Not even the Silver Ladies, whom she thought might have remembered this fairly significant piece of information. That was, if they had ever known who he was.

Trixie quickly read further, trying to find out how long he hung around. Sharon mentioned Terry a few times. They'd met up. The first meeting seemed to go well, but the next one, not so great. Terry wanted to see Tanya, but Sharon didn't want to put her daughter through the anguish of having her father leave again. Eventually, she'd taken Tanya to meet him at a Pizza Hut in the city near where Terry was staying at his mum's. She'd left the young kids with a babysitter, so it was only Tanya, Terry and Sharon. Sharon had noted that the meeting went much better than she expected. But she was still nervous. He'd never stuck around anywhere long, and she couldn't work out why he'd made an appearance now. When Sharon had asked him, all he'd said was he didn't want to wait until it was too late.

Putting the diary down, Trixie lay back on the couch and stared at the ceiling. She was confused. It seemed quite obvious that Terry may have something to do with Tanya's disappearance. But why wasn't he on Sharon's suspect list? From what she could tell in the diary, Terry was still around, or at least still in Adelaide, in the days before Tanya went missing. But once Tanya disappeared, there was no more mention of Terry. Did Sharon know something but just hadn't written it in her diary? Should Trixie find this weird, since Sharon apparently captured almost everything in her diaries?

But most importantly of all, Trixie needed to find out who this Terry person was. And if he was still alive.

"Terry? Tanya's dad?" Fern was asking.

"Yes, Mum, Terry. Do you know him?" Trixie said into her phone as she walked up and down the back verandah.

"I've never heard of him before," said Fern. "I never knew who Tanya's dad was. I don't think anyone did."

"So, how do I find out?"

"Trixie, you're the detective," said Fern.

Trixie cleared her throat. "Only because you insisted. Why won't you help me?"

"Of course, we'll help you, but I'm not sure how we can. What do you suggest?"

Sighing, Trixie swapped the phone to her other ear. "I have no idea, Mum."

"How about we all meet at The Chocolate Bar and see what we can work out."

"The Chocolate Bar? I don't know. The kids have school tomorrow."

"Make it an early tea," Fern said. "I'm pretty sure The Chocolate Bar will be the best location for this."

Trixie was confused by her Mum, but she wasn't in the mood for cooking (she rarely was), so it didn't take much for her to hustle the kids into the car and meet the Silver Ladies at their usual table.

"Milkshakes?" Odette asked as Meg and Joe sat down.

The pair looked at Trixie, hands pressed together, pleading.

Despite shaking her head, she agreed and then ordered a lemon, lime bitters for herself. The Silver Ladies ordered the cherry ripe mocktail drink of the day. They all ordered their food before Trixie turned to question her mum.

"Why were you so insistent on us coming to The Chocolate Bar?" Trixie asked Fern as they waited for their drinks.

"Who knows the most about Wattlebury?" Fern asked.

Trixie glanced at Rhada and Maggie.

"Not these two," Fern laughed. "No, there are two other people here who can be relied upon to have heard all the comings and goings of this town for years and years."

"Who?"

Fren cocked her head as Odette came back to the table carrying a tray of drinks.

"Oh! Odette!" Trixie exclaimed.

"Yes, my dear?"

"Um, well, ah-" Trixie's cheeks turned pink. She hadn't meant for Odette to hear that. "I just wanted to ask you a question."

"Can you take a quick break?" Rhada asked her.

Odette finished placing all the drinks and put her tray on the main bar before pulling up a chair.

"How can I help?"

"I suppose you've heard," Rhada began. "That Trixie is doing some investigating. About Tanya?"

"Why would she have heard?" Trixie asked. Had the Silver Ladies been talking to Odette and Rupert without her knowledge?

"Oh dear Trixie, still so innocent," Maggie laughed. "O and Rupert hear everything!"

"Which is precisely why we think Odette can help you with your current puzzle," said Rhada.

Trixie sipped her drink, wincing a little at the sourness.

"So, what is it?" Odette asked.

"Trixie," Fern said, nodding at her daughter.

"Ok," Trixie rubbed the back of her neck. "Well, I've recently come to discover that Tanya's father had come to visit her in the days before her disappearance. But I don't know anything about him except that his name is Terry. I'd like to try and find him. No one else has mentioned him, and no one seems to know who he even is."

Odette closed her eyes, resting her chin on her hands, not saying a word. Trixie glanced at the Silver Ladies, who sat quietly, sipping their drinks. In the silence, Meg and Joe were doing an excellent job of letting the entire cafe know they had extremely large milkshakes by perfecting their slurping. Trixie glared at them, which only encouraged them to slurp slightly less noisily. Before she could say anything, Odette spoke.

"I do recall Sharon meeting with a man a few times here, over the years. He was never anyone I recognised in any other context except with Sharon. And his ute."

"Ute?" Trixie asked.

"He drove a very memorable ute. I remember it clearly."

"You do? Why?"

"Because the name on the side was so funny," Odette smiled. "Fuzzy's Fencing."

"Fuzzy's Fencing?"

"Yes, and it had a picture of the bear, you know, that cartoon. Fuzzy Bear. Was he from The Muppets? I don't remember. But I do remember that it was on the side of his truck.

"And do we think Terry was Fuzzy?"

"I have no idea," Odette said. "Either he was Fuzzy, or he worked for Fuzzy."

"That's a pretty good lead," said Fern. "I can't imagine there were many businesses called Fuzzy's Fencing."

"I wonder if they still exist?" said Rhada.

"Is there anything else you need from me?"

The Silver Ladies looked from Odette to Trixie, who shook her head. She was excited to look into Fuzzy's Fencing, but beyond that? She had no idea.

"Thanks, Odette," Trixie said. "Thanks for your help."

Odette smiled, pushed herself up out of her seat and made her way back behind the bar.

"So, what are we thinking?" asked Maggie, leaning in close to Trixie. "Do you think Tanya skipped town with her Dad?

"I can't work it out," said Trixie. "If she did, wouldn't it have been pretty easy for Sharon to find that out? Why was she still investigating? She must have spoken to him?"

"It's certainly suspicious," Fern said. "I just can't work out why. Did he have something to do with Tanya going missing, or is the story of Terry something else entirely?"

"All I know is," said Maggie. "Fuzzy's Fencing is one of the most Australian-sounding businesses I've ever heard."

Meg and Joe paused in surprise as Trixie and the Silver Ladies burst into laughter.

Chapter 30

"I still can't believe Mitch told you Tanya was pregnant," said Maggie, recalling that morning's conversation.

"I know!" Trixie said. "By the end of it, he was crying."

"Poor bloke." Maggie shook her head.

Trixie was nodding, taking bites of her squid ink and cocoa pasta as she spoke. "The main thing I took from it was, firstly, he knew Tanya was pregnant. But also, his Dad sent him away and refused to let him talk to the police. Mitch said it was because his Dad didn't want anyone to know they had been in a relationship. Mitch said his Dad didn't know about the baby. He didn't dare tell him. He didn't tell anyone. But now he wishes he'd done more at the time to help."

"So, does that rule out Mitch, or put him smack bang at the top of the list?" Fern asked.

Letting out a groan, Trixie put her hands on her head. It hit her again that she had no idea what she was doing and questioned whether she should be doing anything at all. So what if she time travelled when she picked up Sharon's camera? What did that have to do with anything? It was a coincidence. Pure and simple. And whoever said there was no such thing as coincidences, quite frankly, didn't know what they were talking about.

"Were they real tears, Trix? Or crocodile tears?" Rhada asked.

"They seemed real to me," she said. "Whether he was really regretful, or because he killed her and threw her in a ditch, I don't know."

"Whoa," said Maggie. "That's getting rather dramatic, isn't it?"

"Honestly, I have no idea what I'm doing. No idea what to think. And no idea whether I should be pursuing this or not."

"Of course you should," said Rhada with a frown. "Let's not rehash this. It's already been decided. What I want to know is how Kev at the car yard comes into this?"

The Silver Ladies were quiet.

"Mum, this is the best chicken nugget I've had in my life," Joe proclaimed, his mouth full.

"They do a mean chicken nugget at The Chocolate Bar," Trixie smiled, ruffling her son's hair.

Meg was reading her book, eating her spaghetti bolognese with a dark chocolate and tomato sauce, without even looking at her fork. "I'm not all that sure Kev has anything to do with it at all," said Rhada.

"What, you don't think Kev should be a suspect?" asked Maggie.

"What is it all detectives consider?" asked Rhada. "Motive and opportunity?"

"So professional, Nan," Trixie laughed.

"And yet it's true. With the question being, what motive did Kev have?" Rhada sat with her chin resting on linked fingers.

Trixie had to admit, Rhada was right. What motive did Kev have other than having the vibe of a sleaze bag? "None as far as I can see."

"So at the moment," said Fern. "That only leaves Mitch, who has a fairly substantial motive, and Terry. What sort of motive would Terry have?"

"The problem is, we know absolutely nothing about Terry, except he was Tanya's dad, and he drove a ute with a bear on the side of it. At least according to Odette," said Trixie.

"And that, my dear, is your next job," said Rhada with a smile.

Trixie took her last mouthful of spaghetti, raised her eyebrows, and sighed. The fact that in less than a week she had gone from a mum with two kids to a business owner and time travelling detective was something she could barely get her head around.

"I can guess how you want me to do that," said Trixie.

"Well, of course," said Rhada. "Why wouldn't you use the one thing you have that no one else has?"

"Except for you two sitting right there," she responded. "Why can't either of you do it?"

"We can't," said Rhada. "We're too old. We've lost all our energy. It's up to the young ones."

"Plural?" asked Trixie. "Who else do you know? Can't we rope them in?"

"Only, Meg," said Fern. "And she clearly isn't ready yet."

"I'm ready!" The Silver Ladies and Trixie were all a bit shocked to hear Meg pipe up. "Just seems like my body or my mind isn't."

"Don't be in a rush, Meg," said Trixie. "Enjoy this time when you don't have to worry about slipping at any moment."

"Meg here will be fine," said Fern. "She'll be well prepared."

"I will?" asked Meg. "When does this training start? Mum said you were going to teach both of us?"

Fern looked up Trixie. "Oh, did she now?"

"Yep! She did," said Meg, giving Trixie no room for denial.

"Yes," said Trixie. "I thought I'd better get as much help as I can. It seems I don't have a choice."

"No, you don't," Rhada said.

"And hopefully we can get Meg more prepared than I am." Trixie smiled at her daughter, who beamed back. Meg clearly had no apprehensions about time travel. Yet.

"Well, how about after school, tomorrow?" Fern suggested. "I'll prepare the curriculum."

"Curriculum! Come on, Mum. No need to go full on," said Trixie.

"You just leave it to me. You two need the best training you can get. I'm taking this very seriously."

"Well, on that note," said Trixie, looking at Joe, who was resting his head on the table. "I need to get these two kids to bed."

As they drove home, Trixie pondered her next few days. Her mum's training plan. Identifying Terry. And would she need to time travel again to achieve both of these? A shiver went through her as soon as she realised that was the most plausible scenario. What did surprise her, however, was that she wasn't feeling the usual dread of time travel.

Perhaps she had finally accepted it. This was her destiny.

Chapter 31

"Seriously! You're taking me to the play cafe?" Joe was bouncing around Maggie as she tried to pack her handbag.

"Yes, buddy," said Maggie. "I'm totally serious. I might even get you some nuggets if you're good."

"Yes!"

Joe's trip to Mount Barker with Maggie was all part of the time travel training session Fern had planned. The part where they needed Joe out of the way so Meg and Trixie could concentrate.

When Trixie and Meg were finally ushered into the lounge room, they were both struck by what they saw.

"Whoa, Granny, you've created your own school!" Meg said, stopping in the middle of the room. She was in awe of Fern's flip chart stand and presentation on the television.

Trixie couldn't help but smile. Her mum was certainly taking this seriously. She supposed she shouldn't expect anything less from a former teacher.

"Please take a seat," Fern said, indicating the couch. In front was a coffee table lined with notebooks and pens. Rhada was perched on a kitchen chair to the side of the flip chart, clearly ready to assist Fern.

"Today we are going to cover some preliminary time travel information," said Fern.

"Oooh, are you going to explain about worm holes and time dilation and quantum mechanics and cosmic strings?" Meg asked, sitting on the edge of her seat, eyes wide.

Fern smiled, looking bewildered. "No, and honestly, I barely have any idea what you're talking about."

Meg sat back in her seat, her smile disappearing.

"But what I *am* going to talk about is what it *feels* like to travel," said Fern.

"Awful," said Trixie, somewhat louder than she intended.

"Now Trixie," said Fern. "I know you haven't had a great experience, so far, but let's try and put that all aside. Let's start from scratch, and give both Meg and you the best chance from here on in."

Trixie nodded. She knew her mum was right, and she didn't want to be the sullen student, pushing back on everything the teacher was saying. She was here to learn and to be a role model for her daughter.

"As I was saying," Fern resumed. "We will cover what time travel feels like, what to do if you feel a slip coming on, how to control whether you want to time travel or not-"

"You can do that?" Trixie said, this time intentionally loudly. It was entirely new information. She was sure no one had ever told her about this.

"Yes, you can," Fern replied, pursing her lips a little before continuing her previous sentence. "And the beginnings of how to intentionally slip."

"Oooh, this is going to be good," said Meg, leaning forward to pick up a pen and a notebook.

Trixie couldn't help but smile, although inwardly she was groaning. She wasn't the best at taking instructions from her mother at the best of times. To be going through a formal education process with her may be a little more than she could bear. Glancing at Meg, Trixie resolved to focus more on her daughter and less on herself.

"So, let's start at the very beginning, shall we?" Fern grinned and winked at Rhada, who beamed at her granddaughter and great-granddaughter.

Trixie took a deep breath and held her tongue.

Fern flicked over the first page of her flip chart. Trixie had to admit she hadn't seen one of them in years and wondered where Fern had found it. But the thought flew out of her head as she was struck by the brightly coloured image Fern had drawn on the first sheet.

It almost looked like Da Vinci's The Vitruvian Man, although the person portrayed in Fern's image was a fully clothed woman, and instead of being enclosed in a circle and square, the person was standing, arms and legs wide, inside what appeared to be a sundial.

Meg skooched closer to Trixie, grabbing her hand. When Trixie looked down at her daughter, she saw she was grinning. A thrill rippled through Trixie, and she couldn't help but smile along with Meg. She realised this could actually be fun.

As her mum flipped page after page on her chart, Trixie found herself listening intently and actually writing things down in her notebook. Why did all this information feel so new? Some of it she felt was embedded somewhere in her brain, but when she tried to pull it out, it felt as though she was chasing a dream that was always a few seconds ahead. Occasionally, she found herself shaking her head, bewildered, and a little annoyed at herself. Why had she never listened before? Why had she resisted so much? Perhaps her innate terror of time travel would have abated if she'd only been willing to learn.

Fern went through all the different symptoms of time travel. Trixie found it surprising that her mum was speaking of time travel as though it were an illness. But then again, perhaps it was. A genetic condition that meant their bodies weren't quite normal, whatever that meant. And although it didn't affect them chronically, when it was triggered, it certainly manifested in very specific ways.

"A sinking feeling, racing heart, fuzzy head, blurred vision…."

"That's a lot!" said Meg.

"Well, it's different for everyone. And it doesn't all happen at once," said Fern. "Does it, Trixie?"

Trixie wasn't quite ready for the question. "Ah, well, I suppose not. I would mostly feel sick, like I was car sick. Maybe my body was anticipating the slip?"

Rhada nodded. "Yes, that makes sense. I didn't feel very sick, but I would often feel extraordinarily dizzy. It could be a real pain in the butt."

"There's more," said Fern.

"There is?" Trixie asked.

"You can get tingling sensations in different parts of your body," said Fern. "I often found my hair felt like it had electricity running through it."

"That's weird," said Meg.

Fern laughed as she picked up her cup of tea. "It sure is!"

"Ok, so how do we fix it?" asked Trixie.

"Fix it?" asked Fern. "Do you mean, fix time slipping?"

"No," said Trixie. "I mean, fix the symptoms. What can we do about them?"

Fern shook her head and looked at Rhada, who shrugged her shoulders.

"You can't do anything about them," said Rhada. "You just get used to it."

"I have to get used to feeling sick every time I time travel?" Trixie moaned.

"Well, yes," said Rhada. "But you have to remember something."

"And what is that?" asked Trixie, taking a deep breath.

"The symptoms are the key to managing your travel," said Rhada.

"They're the first signs you have that something is going to happen," said Fern.

Trixie frowned and slowly nodded her head. "And the first sign you have so you can stop it happening?" She was almost nervous asking this question, expecting someone to laugh at her again.

"Now you're getting it!" said Fern, lapping her hands.

Trixie laughed. It was fun to see how excited her mum was, and how thrilled she was to be teaching her daughter and granddaughter about time travel, finally.

"Well, how do we stop it? That is the number one thing I want to learn," said Trixie.

"Trixie! Such negativity!" Rhada chided.

"I just kind of feel I should have been told about this years ago!" said Trixie. "Why didn't you tell me I could stop my time travel?"

"Because you need to know how to travel, and return, before you can stop it," said Fern.

"Why?" Trixie was getting rather frustrated and was beginning to remember why she'd never succeeded with her time travel education previously. "Why do I have to time travel at all? Why does the travel have to happen first? Wouldn't it be better for everyone if we all just stayed put?"

"Would it be better, Trixie?" Rhada raised her eyebrows. "Would it be better for Tanya?"

"Tanya! I have no idea if it's better for Tanya. I know absolutely nothing and have no idea if my time travelling is going to do anything at all for her. The diaries I have, and normal detective work, seem at this moment to have a much higher likelihood of success."

"Then why did you travel? Why did the Polaroid camera want to take you somewhere else?" Rhada asked.

"I have no idea!" Trixie ran her hands over her face before glancing down at her daughter. Meg's face was one of shock, and Trixie gulped. "Oh, sorry, Meg. I'm sorry. I know I seem focused on stopping time travel. I would just like to know how. So I feel more in control."

"It's ok, Mum," said Meg. "I guess it's like riding a bike. It's good to learn how to ride, but pretty important to know how to brake."

Sitting down on the couch again, Trixie scooped her daughter into a hug, tears in her eyes. "Yes, Meg, you're so clever. That's exactly right."

Meg allowed Trixie's hug for a few moments before pushing away and looking up at her Mum. "So, are you ok to learn about time travel now, Mum?"

Trixie smiled. "I sure am."

Chapter 32

Trixie spent the next week practising time travel. She intentionally worked on trying to slip, not just trying to stop it. She looked out for the symptoms, getting more and more familiar with her own personal array. The motion sickness wasn't the only one she noticed. She also noticed the pulse in her left wrist seemed to vibrate, as well as a tingling sensation.

The bonus was that, after all her work, she did manage to travel a few times.

The first one was an utter failure. She was trying to get to her first day of school. Instead, she went back to the week before when she was taking Joe to *his* first day of school. Trixie immediately panicked after appearing right near the front gates. No one seemed to notice her sudden appearance as they were all in a rush to get their own kids off for the first day of school. She quickly walked away from the school, heading towards where her van had been parked. She knew she hadn't seen herself that day, so, breathing deeply, she calmed herself before stepping back behind a tree. Her pulse was racing, and when she didn't manage to time slip right away, she began to get worried.

"Trixie, pull yourself together!" she said. "One, two, three, four. One two, three, four."

She breathed in deeply before hearing a noise. "Oh crap," she muttered. What Trixie saw did nothing for her heart rate.

In front of her was her.

Trixie sucked in her breath and held still. Why she was worried, she didn't know. She already knew she didn't spot herself. But she could only imagine what might happen if she did. Making a mental note to ask her Mum this question, she watched as the Speckled Hen

Farm van drove away.

She let out a huge sigh of relief, and in that moment - zap! - she found herself back in her living room.

"Bloody hell!" she cried out. "Am I ever going to get the hang of this?"

The next day, determined not to give up, she attempted to travel to her teenage bedroom. Instead, she appeared in the kitchen of Silver Gum Cottage.

"Seriously!" she said out loud to Fern, Rhada and Maggie, who were all sitting at their table eating tea.

"You time travelled!" Fern cried out, jumping to her feet and clapping her hands. "Well done!"

"And I had absolutely no intention of coming here," Trixie groaned. "What day is this?"

"It's the Thursday of the first week of school," Rhada told her.

"What, so last week. Humph," Trixie was not impressed. "Why didn't you tell me I arrived in the middle of tea?"

"I presume we don't want to influence you," said Fern.

"Influence me?"

"Worry you. Panic you. Jinx you," Maggie piped in.

"You're all utterly maddening," Trixie said.

"Yes, but you're clearly doing something right," said Rhada.

"You've slipped, Trixie!" said Fern. "And I can only presume from this conversation that it was intentional?"

"Intentional, yes," said Trixie. "But I was trying to get to my teenage bedroom."

"Well, it's progress, dear," said Rhada. "Keep trying!"

Trixie rolled her eyes. "I'd better be getting back to the future. I'll see you there."

"Bye!" the three ladies called out as Trixie left the kitchen and walked out to the backyard.

She was calmer this time, and it only took her a few moments to return to her own house. It was an improvement, but she was still utterly frustrated. Why couldn't she travel to the exact time and place she meant to? What was the trick? She hated to admit it, but it seemed like she needed her next time slip lesson.

That Friday, Trixie picked up the kids and headed straight to Silver Gum Cottage after school. Once again, Maggie was happy to take Joe under her wing. Meg and Trixie resumed their positions on the couch.

"So, Trixie, you've been having some success?" Fern asked, once again standing next to her flip chart.

Shaking her head, Trixie responded. "I wouldn't call it success," she said. "I've travelled. Sure. But technically, I could already do that. What I want to be able to do is travel to exactly where I want to be. When I want to be. And at the moment I can do neither. I need to know the trick."

"Trick?" Fern asked.

"The hack. What is the secret to travelling properly? Travelling wherever and whenever I need to. Especially if I'm going to solve this case, which people seem to expect me to do."

"I don't know if there is any trick, Trix," Fern said, unable to stop herself smiling at the word play.

Trixie sighed. "So, how exactly do I do it? Teach me. I'm ready. I want to know."

"I need you to remember one key thing," said Fern. "It's all about energy. And energy is all about clarity of thought."

"Clarity of thought?"

"The energy you are putting out directly connects to what you want to achieve. If you doubt yourself, if you let your mind wander, if you're distracted, then you can't channel that energy in the right way."

"It sounds almost impossible," said Trixie.

"It sounds like mindfulness," said Meg.

The three women all turned and stared at the young girl.

Meg smiled. "You know, relaxing, clearing your mind, focusing on one thing. We learn it at school."

"Yes, Meg," said Fern, smiling. "Mindfulness. I think you're on the right track. I was going to say meditation, but I think mindfulness is a great description. What have you been taught about it?"

"Well, one thing we learnt this week was Bubble Breathing," she explained.

"Tell us more," said Rhada, sitting up straight, focused on her great-granddaughter.

"Ok, so we sit with our hands in our laps. Then we close our eyes and imagine we are blowing bubbles. We have to do really deep breaths and then very slowly breathe out so we can make a huge bubble that doesn't pop."

The women nodded, smiling, listening intently.

"Then we imagine the bubble floating away. Our teacher said if anything is worrying us, we can put it in the bubble and then watch it float away from us."

"Oh, I like that," said Rhada.

"Or you can imagine it changing colours," said Meg. "But I was thinking Mum could use it to picture herself travelling to exactly where she means to be. Maybe put yourself inside the bubble and imagine travelling back in time."

"Ooooh," said Fern. "That's good. That's really good. A great idea, Meg!"

Meg smiled, glancing at her Mum. Trixie smiled back, once again amazed at the smarts this kid had. Her ability to listen to what Fern was telling them and immediately relate it to something she had been learning was astounding. It seemed Meg was much more likely to become the time traveller everyone needed, more so than Trixie. Perhaps they should all be focusing their efforts on the youngest time traveller in their midst. Except, she hadn't ever travelled, and who knew how long that would take.

"I have a feeling with you, Trixie," Fern said, tilting her head slightly. "That patience may be the key."

"Are you telling me I'm impatient?" Trixie tried to sound offended, but they all knew patience was not her strength.

"Ha ha," said Fern. "You're going to have to spend some time working on this Bubble Breathing. Don't rush to travel. Just work on bringing all your focus to your breathing and the bubbles. Just blow bubble after bubble, before you even start picturing where you want to travel. I have a feeling that you'll sense when the time is right."

"Uggh," said Trixie. "I know you're right, but it drives me crazy. Why can't I just do this? Surely you didn't go through all this palaver every time you wanted to travel?"

"If we wanted to do it properly, we did," said Fern.

"Yes," said Rhada. "Your mum is right. But, I will say, just like everything, once you get the hang of it, you can get in the zone much quicker."

"The best way I can explain it, inspired by Miss Meg," Fern gave her granddaughter a wink. "Is that it's like learning to drive a car. When you're first learning, you have so much to think about all at once, and it *can* feel overwhelming. But you need to practice and practice before you get to the point that it's second nature."

"And how long is that going to take?" asked Trixie.

"Patience, Trixie," Fern said with a smile.

"Ok, ok, so we've covered focus and mindfulness," said Trixie, glancing at her daughter, smiling. "Is there anything else? I need all the tips, because this investigation has been going on for a long time, and I'd rather like to move on."

"What, do you have another investigation in mind?" Rhada asked.

"Absolutely not," said Trixie. "I want to get this done and dusted. I mean, how many mysteries can one town have?"

"You would be surprised," said Rhada, glancing at Fern.

"Enough of that," said Trixie. "I just need to get to the right location. So hit me up with your tips."

"Where exactly do you think you need to go? To find out what happened to Tanya?"

"The 150-year celebrations," said Trixie. "I think the only thing is to go back and try and find Tanya on the last day anyone saw her."

"You mean, literally see her? Talk to her?"

"No," said Trixie, frowning. "I mean, I shouldn't talk to her, right?"

"No way," said Fern. "You need to have virtually no interactions with anyone. Especially such a key person. If you do, you don't know what could happen."

"How easy is that?" asked Meg.

"Good question, Meg," said Rhada. "Fern, I'm not sure what you found, but when I travelled, I felt I didn't exist as strongly in a different place and time. Almost as though I could slip by unnoticed much more easily than in our present time."

"Almost like you're a ghost?" asked Trixie.

"I guess so," said Fern. "That's probably a good description. I think you can slip by, but you can also make yourself known to people. You can talk to them."

"What if you, I don't know, bumped someone?"

"The number of times I had people turn to me, wide-eyed, and say 'Oh, I didn't see you there!'" Fern laughed.

"So I should be able to slip by unnoticed?" Trixie had asked.

"Well, that's certainly been my experience," Fern had told her. "And it makes solving mysteries a lot easier."

"You mean, it makes spying on people a lot easier," Trixie said.

"Spying, investigating, whatever you want to call it."

"And they aren't weirded out?" Trixie said. "You don't look strange to them?"

Fern shook her head. "I don't think so. I mean, I tried to avoid it as much as possible, but whenever I was noticed, or if I did actually speak to someone, I was treated normally, even if they were surprised at first."

"Right," said Trixie. "Let's get back to the point of today. How. How exactly am I going to do this?"

"Look, my top tip," said Fern. "Is that you have to get super clear on the location you are going. So you need to pick a location at the celebrations and visualise yourself there."

"And the best photo," said Rhada. "Is the one you're actually in. Just focus on that. You can literally see yourself there. Because you've been there."

"You've been there?" asked Meg.

"There's a photo, Meg," said Trixie. "There's a photo in the album I was given, and I'm in the photo."

"Really! So you're already a proper time traveller!"

"It seems so." Trixie smiled at Meg and then turned to Fern and Rhada. "Maybe I am already a proper time traveller after all."

Chapter 33

Once the kids were in bed and Trixie had a quick phone call with Kirby, who had promised he would be home by the end of the following week, she pulled out Sharon's photo album once again.

Her mum was right, of course. Trixie had time travelled before. There she was. She had proof. It was possible. And she also knew exactly where she needed to go. What surprised her most, which she hadn't previously noticed in her shock, was that she also knew exactly when. There, on the bottom of the photo, in digital orange print, was the time the photo was taken. 1:23 pm.

Trixie stared at the photo, thinking of Meg's Bubble Breathing. She didn't want to time travel right now, but perhaps she could practice the breathing she would need. Putting the photo aside and only picturing herself in her own lounge room at that moment, Trixie began the bubble breathing. Meg had explained when they were driving home that the best way to start was to breathe in a square. Four breaths up one side, hold four breaths across the top, four breaths down the other side, and hold four breaths along the bottom. As she did this, Trixie marvelled at all the things the children were taught at school these days. Would it have made a difference to her? To her time travel approach? Perhaps. Perhaps not. But she was glad her children were getting these opportunities.

As her mind went over the outline of the square in her mind again and again, her breathing became focused and calm. Trixie began to see what Fern and Rhada were trying to tell her, about clearing her mind and focusing on one thing. For the first time in her life, Trixie was beginning to feel in control of her time travelling. She could finally see there was a chance she could manage the process and not only stop it, which had been the top priority her entire life, but also travel to the right place. The place and time she intended.

Yet, it was all well and good knowing when and where. The next questions were what and who? What exactly was she trying to find out? And who was going to give her that information? The complexities of time travel and the rules surrounding it meant she couldn't walk up to Tanya and ask her exactly what was going on. She also couldn't accuse a potential murderer before it had even happened. If it had happened at all.

What was she trying to achieve by time travelling to the celebrations? Ideally, she would follow Tanya and simply see what happened to her. But did she really want to? What if it was something awful? And how realistic was it that she would be able to remain in a time slip long enough? One alternative was to see who exactly Tanya interacted with and find out if there were other people Trixie could speak to in the present day. A few more leads couldn't hurt, right?

Opening her eyes, Trixie sighed. What was she doing? She had absolutely no idea. Once again, she doubted she should be doing anything at all. Was she meddling where it wasn't needed? And who would the truth help anyway? Yet as always, the idea that she had been given the gift of time travel, and the fact that the Polaroid camera seemed to be wanting her to do something, felt as though she was being pointed to something bigger than herself. A task she needed to complete.

In that moment, Trixie decided to stop second-guessing herself. She was constantly going round and round in circles, and it wasn't helping anyone. Most importantly, it wasn't helping find Tanya. What if she could bring some closure to a family? What if her time travel ability could actually solve this case?

Standing, Trixie brought the album to the kitchen table, along with her notebook. It was time to make a plan. At the moment, they had three suspects. Mitch Lawson. Kev Carrington. And now Terry of Fuzzy's Fencing. Trixie slowly lifted the photo of herself, marked 1.23 pm, and placed it on the table. She then flipped through the album looking for any other time-stamped images. Within minutes, she had a row of photos laid out on either side of the original.

Rifling through the kitchen drawers, she found a mish-mashed selection of sticky notes, some in the shape of strawberries, others orange stars, along with a block of small fluorescent squares. Items from the table were removed to the kitchen benches, and Trixie began working, placing notes above and below the timeline. Referencing the timeline she had written down in her notebook, Trixie tried to identify the 'who' and 'what'. If she landed back in time at 1:23 pm, who should she be looking for, and in what direction should she go?

It quickly became apparent that Mitch was the closest person to her location in the photo. Tanya next. Kev was too far along the timeline. Trixie doubted she would catch up to him before she was brought back to the present. The most interesting thing was that Terry was nowhere to be seen. Trixie went back to the album and scanned all the photos in the album that remained. He wasn't in any of them either. If Terry had anything to do with Tanya's disappearance, it didn't appear to have happened at the celebrations.

Trixie knew with certainty that she time travelled. What she didn't know, couldn't know, was whether she would solve this mystery. Yet, it seemed she had no choice. She had to slip and see if there was anything she could do. And being as prepared as possible was key.

In her notebook, she began writing out a time travel schedule centring on 1:23 pm. She could assume she arrived within a few minutes of this photograph, but there was no way of really knowing. Just because she couldn't be seen in any other photos didn't mean she hadn't arrived a lot earlier than this. Therefore, she extended her schedule two hours either side of this point in time. It was too long. She had never time slipped for anything more than forty minutes. But she wanted to ensure she had everything at her fingertips.

The plan was set.

"Now, I just have to travel to a specific time and location, for the first time in my life."

Trixie shook her head. At this moment, with absolutely no confidence in her own abilities, it felt utterly impossible.

Chapter 34

"Maggie's working at the pub today." Fern had rung first thing. "We thought we might have lunch there."

Trixie really wanted to time travel. She had planned to somehow wangle to drop the kids off with the Silver Ladies after swimming and slip back to 1989. Now she had been thwarted because she was yet to inform her mother of the plan and was too nervous to do so. She had no realistic excuse, and Trixie had to admit that the idea of a chicken schnitzel with diane sauce sounded like a pretty good backup option.

What she didn't expect when she went up to the bar to order drinks for herself and the kids was to discover Kev Carrington pondering life over a pint of Coopers Pale Ale.

"Afternoon," he grunted with a nod when he realised who was next to him.

"Hi Kev," Trixie replied.

"Still sticking your nose in where it's not wanted?"

Trixie frowned, surprised at how comfortable he was with such a blunt remark. Glancing at the beer in front of him, she wondered how many of them he'd had.

"Pull your head in, Kev," said Maggie, who had clearly overheard him.

"Well, she is," he said, locking eyes with Maggie for a moment before looking back down at his hands. "Bringing up the past and getting people all worked up again."

"Maybe people should get worked up," said Maggie.

"Maybe they should," he said, turning to look at Trixie. "But maybe people shouldn't go around pointing fingers when they don't know all the facts."

"The facts?" asked Trixie, feeling emboldened by Maggie's self-assuredness. "What facts am I missing?"

"Plenty," said Kev, taking a gulp from his glass.

"Like what exactly?" asked Maggie, folding her arms across her chest. "If you don't want fingers pointed, then maybe you should help the people who are just trying to do the right thing."

"Bringing this all up again ain't doing the right thing."

"Of course it is!" said Maggie.

"I'm just trying to do the right thing by Anna and Jason," said Trixie. "By Sharon. And of course, for Tanya."

"So why don't you just tell her what you know?" said Maggie. "Or do you think you'll implicate yourself?"

"I had nothing to do with it!" said Kev, glaring at Maggie.

"I never said you did," she replied. "But all your guff sure makes it sound like you have something to hide."

"Ain't got nothing to hide," he said.

"So, tell us these so-called facts." Trixie raised her eyebrows and then sipped the pinot noir Maggie had just handed her.

Kev started glancing around the pub, making it pretty obvious to everyone there that he didn't want the wrong people to overhear. Luckily for him, it didn't appear anyone could care less what he had to say. Except for Trixie, although she did her best to look nonchalant.

"She was goin' to Melbourne," he whispered.

"Melbourne?" Trixie had lowered her voice and leaned in. "How do you know that?"

"Because she was hitchin' a ride with one of me freight guys."

"Hitching a ride with who exactly? And why?"

Kev took another gulp of his beer before turning to face Trixie.

"She told me she was going to live with her Dad," he said. "He was moving to Melbourne, and she was going to live with him. Problem was, he didn't know. She was gonna surprise him. Don't know why she asked me. Clever kid, I guess. Knew I got cars shipped all over. So I gave her the name of me Melbourne guy. That's it. I know nothing else. Nothing at all."

"Well, who is this Melbourne guy? Is he still around?"

"Got no idea," said Kev. "Might have retired. Might have moved. I haven't used him for years."

"Do you think you still have his number?"

Kev shrugged. "A landline, maybe. Dunno if I have a mobile. Maybe I do somewhere in the office."

"Do you mind having a look?" Trixie asked, her heart racing. This was a real, actual lead. Kev was right. This was a fact. Something she could actually look into.

Kev shrugged. "I suppose. When I have time."

Trixie wanted to roll her eyes. His complete disregard for a missing person was staggering.

"Do you remember his name?"

"Mickey Blue," he said. "At least that's what everyone called him. No idea if that was his actual name. All I remember was he had a Smurf toy and a Mickey Mouse toy tied to the front of his truck."

"Weird," said Trixie.

"Oh, it's a thing, Trix," said Maggie. "They often tie toys to the front of their rigs. Some trucker thing."

Kev let out a laugh that quickly turned into a cough before he downed the last of his pint.

"I'll see if I can get you his number," Kev said as he slid off the barstool. "But I don't want no one knowing I spoke to ya. Keep me out of it."

Trixie nodded and watched him limp out of the bar.

"That's the earliest he's left in years," said Maggie, smiling at Trixie. "You sure got under his collar."

"At least I finally have some concrete information," said Trixie.

"I wonder if he ever told anyone else about his Melbourne contact?" Maggie asked.

Trixie nodded. "And if it took that much effort to drag that tid-bit of information out of him, I wonder what else he knows?"

"Mum! I'm dying of thirst!" Joe was now trying to climb onto the stool Kev had just evacuated.

"Sorry, Joe-bo," she said. "Maggie, the kids both want a raspberry lemonade, please."

"Coming right up!" Maggie winked at Joe before grabbing two butcher glasses and the post mix soft drink gun to squirt lemonade into them. She then grabbed a bottle of raspberry cordial and slugged it into both, before plopping a straw in each.

Somehow, Trixie managed to get two glasses of raspberry lemonade and her own glass of wine back to the table by the front window, where Rhada and Fern were sitting with Meg.

"You will not believe what Kev just told me," Trixie said, interrupting whatever Fern was telling Meg, as she slid into her seat. She passed Meg her soft drink and then helped settle Joe in his seat, pulling the drink up close enough so he didn't spill it before he'd even taken a sip.

"Mum," Meg groaned. "Granny was just getting to the best part."

"The best part of what?"

"When she time slipped onto a concert stage," Meg said.

"What?" Trixie had never heard this story. "Ok, Granny can finish that story in a moment. I promise. But this is important."

"What is it?" Rhada asked.

"I have a lead! A real lead!" said Trixie. "Tanya was going to Melbourne. And Kev knows who she was getting a ride from."

"Who?"

"Some bloke called Mickey Blue," said Trixie. "Ever heard of him?"

Both Fern and Rhada shook their heads. Trixie wasn't surprised. Why would they know some Melbourne truck driver?

"Doesn't sound like a real name, though," said Fern.

"I know," said Trixie. "But Kev promised to try and find me his number." She took a sip of her wine. "I mean, knowing my luck, it will be a dead end. But it's something, right?"

"It's more than something," said Fern. "Even if we don't find this guy, you now know that Tanya was going to Melbourne. But why?"

"Her Dad," said Trixie. "She was going to live with her Dad."

"I didn't know he was from Melbourne?" said Fern, looking at Rhada, who shrugged.

"No, Kev said he was moving there," said Trixie. "I guess at the very least we can try and find him and see if Tanya made it to Melbourne."

"I don't think she did," said Fern. "Everyone always said the last place she was seen was at the town celebrations. You'd think they would have questioned her Dad."

"Maybe they did?" said Trixie. "Maybe he lied?"

Neither Fern nor Rhada had a response to that.

"Now, Granny," said Meg. "Back to the stage story!"

Chapter 35

By the time the kids were wolfing down their chocolate sundaes, Fern, Rhada, and Trixie had made next to no progress in their plans to identify Mickey Blue. Trixie had started googling on her phone, but nothing of relevance seemed to appear.

"Mum, I need to go to the toilet," said Meg.

Looking down at her daughter, she smiled at the ice cream and chocolate sauce she had around her face.

"And a face wipe too!" Trixie stood and walked with Meg towards the ladies, but before they reached the door, a tall figure stood in front of her.

"I saw you talking to Kev. Don't think I don't know what you're up to."

Trixie was shocked to see Mitch's father, Bruce, pointing his finger at her.

"Hello, Mr Lawson. Are you ok?" said Trixie, putting her arms around Meg's shoulder and pulling her close. She was hoping Fern or Maggie might spot what was going on and intervene.

"No, I'm not ok!" he said rather loudly. "You're bringing up things that should be left alone. You're causing more problems than you realise, and it's all for nothing."

"Nothing? A missing girl is all for nothing?"

"Tanya was always going to be a lost cause," he said. "I'm sure she got herself mixed up in something she shouldn't have. She was always bad news, just like I told Mitch."

"Mitch doesn't seem to agree with you."

"Mitch could never think straight when it came to that girl," he said. "Luckily, I was around to put a stop to things."

Trixie opened her mouth, unable to speak for a moment.

"How exactly did you do that?" she finally managed to ask.

"Never you mind," he said. "If I were you'd I'd leave things alone."

"You haven't really given me a good reason why?"

"I don't need to give you a reason," he said. "Just don't say I didn't warn you."

Without another word, he turned and walked over to a table full of older men, all of them staring at her. It sent a chill down her spine. Meg tugged at Trixie's arm, and remembering the toilet, quickly guided Meg in that direction.

"That man was mean," Meg called from the cubicle. Trixie was leaning against the tiled wall, eyes closed.

"He wasn't very polite, that's for sure," said Trixie.

"Why was he so angry?"

"To be honest, I'm not really sure," said Trixie. It was true. She was very confused, but her alarm bells were certainly ringing. It hadn't ever occurred to her that Mitch's dad might be involved, even when Mitch spoke about him. But at that moment, he was rising in the ranks to become her top suspect. She couldn't deny that Bruce Lawson seemed to have a lot of reasons to get rid of Tanya, especially if he did know about her pregnancy. The scandal for the family might have been more than enough for him to sort the problem out himself. Or get someone else to do it.

"Did you notice Bruce in the album?" Fern asked when Trixie and Meg returned to the table and told the Silver Ladies about their encounter.

Trixie shook her head. "No, but then of course I wasn't looking for him. And I might need your help to spot him. I imagine he'll look a tad different."

"It seems so obvious," said Rhada, frowning. "I mean, he is the type. Always so concerned with the family's reputation. I wouldn't put it past Bruce to drive a body out to the Flinders and bury it."

"Nan! You can't say something like that!"

"Why not? You're all thinking it."

Trixie and Fern looked at each other and shrugged. She was right. Trixie's first thought had been to picture Mr Lawson tossing Tanya's body into his boot or the back of a ute before driving out of Wattlebury.

"Can I have another one?" It was Joe, face covered in chocolate sauce, holding up his bowl to show he had licked it clean.

"Joe! What a mess!" Trixie said. "Nope, no more ice cream. It's time we head home."

"Aw, do we have to?"

"I thought maybe we could fill the blow-up pool," Trixie said.

"Oh, yeah, let's do that!" said Joe.

Trixie stood, collecting her bag and phone, making sure the kids had everything.

"You go home and check out the album," said Fern, as they all waved goodbye to Maggie, leaving the pub. "Message me if you think you've spotted Bruce."

"But let's not put all our focus on him," said Trixie as they walked out to the car park. "Don't forget we've just found out about the Melbourne trip, too. We need to find out about this Mickey Blue fella. Not to mention Tanya's Dad."

Trixie pulled the van door open, ushering the kids in, ensuring Joe was properly clipped into his car seat.

"Your suspect list is overflowing," said Rhada.

"*My* suspect list?"

"You're a detective now, Trix, whether you like it or not," said Fern. "All these threads will start to come together, and that will be the time."

"The time for what?" Trixie asked, getting into the van and winding her window down.

"The time to travel, my dear," said Rhada, winking. "The time to slip into the photos and discover the truth."

Fern tapped the side of the van in farewell, and together the two women walked away across the car park.

Trixie sighed, turning over the ignition switch, allowing the van to shudder into life. She didn't argue any more. She realised there was no fight to be had. She *was* going to have to time travel. It seemed she was the one destined to find out what happened to Tanya, whether she liked it or not.

As Joe prattled on about what toppings he would put on an ice cream sundae if he could make anything he liked, and Meg piped in with her thoughts, Trixie mulled over all the new information she had been given today. What was more likely? That Tanya had been kidnapped by this Mickey Blue bloke? Or had Bruce Lawson done away with her? Trixie had to admit the second option seemed much more likely at this stage.

Pulling into the Farm, her thoughts turned back to Tanya's father. She presumed Tanya hadn't made it to Melbourne. If she had, she wouldn't have been declared missing. But it would be nice to know if that was in fact her plan, to move to Melbourne to be with her father. What she didn't know was whether he was still alive. Would Anna know, and would she be able to put her in touch with him?

Before she even got out of the van, she shot a text message to Anna asking her just that. By the time she had Joe and Meg slathered in suncream and splashing around in the pool, Anna had responded.

As far as I know, he is still alive. Last I heard, he was back in Adelaide. Terry Weber. This is the number I have for him.

Trixie's heart was pounding.

Chapter 36

Trixie waited until the kids were in bed that evening before calling Tanya's father. It took her a while to work up the courage. Could she call him? She could, couldn't she? Should she? Would she?

"Just bloody do it," Trixie said before quickly pushing the number on her phone.

"Hello," a man's voice answered.

"Ah, is this Terry Weber?"

"Who's asking?"

"Oh, um, well, my name is Trixie Travers," she said. She felt her throat catch and her confidence waver. "From Wattlebury."

"Wattlebury? What's up?"

"I'm sorry to bring this up, it's just, I'm kind of helping Anna and Jason, you know, they're-"

"I know who Anna and Jason are? What do you want?" his voice had gone from gruff to stern, verging on angry.

"Look, I just had a quick question. When Tanya went missing, was she planning on coming to Melbourne to live with you?'

"What are you saying? And who are you to ask this? Helping Anna and Jason. What does that mean?"

"I know, it's not really anything to do with me, and it's a long story. But I'm kind of investigating what happened. And someone told me Tanya was planning to move to Melbourne to live with you."

"Did they now," he said. "I'd be careful who you listen to in that town. Full of gossip mongers."

"Yes, sorry, I'll leave you alone."

"What, you're gonna give up that easy?" Trixie thought she almost heard a chuckle on the other end of the phone.

"Well, ah, I'm not sure what else I can say. You can either answer my questions, or I'll say goodnight."

"Investigating, you say? Tryin' to find out what really happened to Tanya?"

"Uh, huh," said Trixie.

"Well, I'd kinda like to know that too," he said. "Before it's too late."

"Too late?" She realised she'd heard that phrase before.

"I'm dyin' love," said Terry. "To be honest, I can't believe I'm still here after all these years. It'd be nice to know what happened to Tanya before I go to sleep and never wake up."

"Oh, I'm very sorry to hear that."

"Not your fault, love," he said. "Too many ciggies. That's the problem."

"Ah," said Trixie. "Well, I would like to find out what happened. And it seems a few people are talking now. I've been told some things that the police never heard, as far as I'm aware."

"But why are they telling you? Are you a cop or something?"

Trixie laughed. "God no. I own a vintage store."

"You've got me baffled, love. What's a vintage store owner got to do with finding my daughter?"

"Look, Terry, it's a rather long story and a weird one. But Anna brought in some of Sharon's stuff, and one thing has led to another, and it seems I've suddenly become a detective, whether I like it or not. And the thing is, I think Tanya deserves to have this looked into. Don't you?"

"I sure do," he said. "And I'll tell you all I know. Which is nothing. But the nothing I do know could help you."

Trixie frowned. This old Aussie bloke seemed to have turned into a whimsical poet. "And what nothing do you know?"

"Tanya hadn't made any plans with me. The last time I saw her, only a few days before, I mentioned she might like to come for a visit to my new house. She just shrugged at me. Made me feel sad. She was getting older. I thought maybe she didn't want to bother with her Dad any more. So no, I don't think she was planning to come to Melbourne to live with me. At least, if she was, she didn't ask me."

"Thank you, Terry," said Trixie. "Is there anything else you think I should know?"

"Nope, but I am curious. What do you think happened?"

"I have no idea," said Trixie. "But everyone else seems to think something bad has happened. So I'm trying to find out what and by whom."

"So who's on your list?"

"My list?"

"Come on, detective," he said. "Who's on your hit list? Who do you think ended my daughter's life?'

"Gosh, well, I don't think I can really say. Nothing concrete."

"Am I on the list?"

Trixie's eyes bulged. What was she meant to say to that?"

"Of course I bloody am," he said, answering his own question. "And so I should be. I'm the deadbeat Dad. But I just want to say, Tanya was hanging around some people I wouldn't trust as far as I could throw them. And ever since that woman came to live with them, I think she grew up way too quick."

"Women? What woman?" Trixie had no idea who he was talking about.

"Oh, that foreigner," said Terry. "Didn't anyone mention her? Some woman came to board in the house. Sharon did that sometimes to make money. I can't remember her name, but I think Tanya became friends with her and got mixed up in an older crowd."

"I'll have to ask Anna and Jason if they know," said Trixie. "But I have heard Tanya was hanging out with some older kids, so that does make sense."

"Yep, well, I'd look into them," said Terry. "I'd been worried Tanya was going off the rails a bit, and when she went missing, well, I'll just say I wasn't totally surprised."

Trixie paused and then asked, "Do you mind one more question?"

"Sure," he said.

"Are you Fuzzy? Of Fuzzy's Fencing?"

"How the hell did you know that?"

Trixie couldn't help but laugh. "The owner of the cafe in Wattlebury remembered you. Or your ute at least. So you are Fuzzy. But why Fuzzy?"

"Love, if you could see me, you'd know why. I have a huge beard, and back in the day, I had a decent head of hair too. Not so much today. But everyone calls me Fuzzy."

"Sounds perfect," said Trixie. "Thanks for your time, Terry. I'll let you know if I find anything."

"Thanks, detective," he said. "I still ain't got a clue why you're doing this, but thanks a lot. I hope you work it out."

Putting her phone down, Trixie let out a long, slow breath. A woman? What was going on? In one day, so much new information had been thrown at her. Now she had to find not only Mikey Blue, but also a mysterious woman. Yet something was tugging at her brain.

Had she actually heard about this woman before? The more she thought about it, the more familiar the idea of someone living in that house seemed. But where would she have heard it?

Trixie yawned. Glancing at her watch, it was only just after nine, but she felt exhausted. It was bedtime. There was nothing else she could do tonight. Perhaps the Silver Ladies might remember something about this woman.

Was Terry right? Was she really a detective after all? The simple act of asking questions, questions the police had potentially never asked, seemed to be pulling in a lot of leads. Was it really only a matter of time before she discovered the truth?

Chapter 37

"Just so I'm clear," said Fern. "Terry says there was a woman boarding in Sharon's house, and he thinks she was leading Tanya astray?"

Trixie had the Silver Ladies on a video call, set up in the kitchen whilst she drank her coffee and flipped through the photo albums.

"That's what he said," Trixie replied. "Although I'm not sure how much use it is."

"Well, if you could find her, you could at least talk to her," said Maggie. "If she and Tanya were close, she might have some idea about what was going on in Tanya's life."

"But on that topic," said Trixie. "Maybe we should be chasing down the people who were in this group. This gang of older kids that Tanya was hanging out with. They might be easier to find than a foreign boarder from forty years ago."

"Yes," said Rhada. "You're probably right. But how do we find out who they were?"

"Mitch, of course," said Fern. "He's the centre of this wheel. In fact, it keeps spinning back to him every time we head off in another direction."

"Or back to the Lawson family," said Trixie. "After yesterday, my money is firm on Bruce."

"What about this Mickey Blue Eyes chap?" asked Rhada.

"I can't work him out," said Trixie. "Is he a red herring? Or is Kev intentionally trying to lead us astray?"

"Look at you talking all detective-like," Maggie said with a grin.

"Ha ha," said Trixie. "You're all the ones pushing me to investigate this. How about you support me!" Trixie took a sip of coffee, but then smiled, acknowledging that she was getting into the swing of this sleuthing business.

"You definitely have to find him," said Fern. "That's what they do, isn't it, chase down every lead."

"I just feel I have so many more leads since last night," said Trixie. "Mickey Blue, this mysterious woman, and then the group of older kids. Not to mention Bruce. I mean, I probably need to ask around about him, right?'

Fern, Rhada and Maggie didn't answer. They just glanced at each other.

"What?" asked Trixie.

"Well, I wouldn't poke that bear too much," said Maggie. "To be honest, I think he might very well have had something to do with this. And if that's the case, I wouldn't risk it. I'd just send the police his way."

"So you think I should tell the police about our conversation?"

"Not yet," said Maggie. "I'd find out everything else you can. But I wouldn't be asking too many questions about him. If you hit a dead end with everything else, then maybe you go to the police. You just don't want to keep Bruce on your radar. You never know what he might do."

Trixie frowned and took a long sip of her coffee. Maggie was basically telling her to keep her head down, or she might end up like Tanya. Again, she wondered what on earth she had gotten herself into.

"Right, back to the photos," said Fern. "Did you find Bruce?"

"Is this him?" Trixie asked, angling the album towards the phone camera. She leaned her head around and attempted to point at a man in a group on the edge of the photo.

Fern shook her head. "No, that's Wally Pfitzner. Keep looking."

Trixie flicked the page and peered at the photos. "Oh!"

"What! What is it?" Maggie asked, moving her face closer to the camera as though she would be able to peer down at what Trixie was looking at.

Trixie brought the album back up to the camera.

"This," said Trixie. "Remember, I showed you this before. We didn't know who this woman was that Tanya was speaking to. Could this be the boarder?"

The three women moved their heads in closer before laughing as they almost bumped heads.

"One at a time, I think," said Rhada. "Me first."

One by one, the women peered at the photo.

"Well, I have no idea who she is," said Fern. "So yes, perhaps that is her. Maybe ask Anna?"

Trixie nodded. "Yes, that's what Terry said. They were still young, but I guess she might remember someone who lived with them for a while?"

The Silver Ladies all nodded.

"Or, you know, you could go and ask her yourself?" said Fern.

"Ask the mysterious woman?" Trixie was confused. "But we don't know who she is."

"Just walk up to her and say hi."

"Mum, what are you going on about?"

Fern smiled. "Take that photo, time slip, and find out who she is?"

Trixie laughed. "Oh, I do love your faith that I could actually do that!"

"You can, dear," said Rhada. "You just need to believe it yourself.

And a good kick up the butt."

"I'm not sure how a kick up the butt will help me," said Trixie.

"You need to get over yourself, Trix," said Maggie.

"Stop all the palaver," said Rhada. "Stop making it so hard on yourself. You know how to slip. You know what you need to do. It's the doubts that are messing you up. Not your skill level. It's all the questions you keep asking yourself. Forget it! Just do it!"

"That's very easy for you all to say," said Trixie.

"There you go! Doubting yourself!" said Fern. "When none of us here doubt you in the least, do we ladies?"

"Absolutely not!" said Rhada.

"You will totally nail it," said Maggie.

"Well, there's nothing I can do about it today," said Trixie. "Kirby isn't back until the end of the week. I can't exactly slip off with the kids here."

"We could take them for you, of course," said Fern. "But why not try tonight. I found nighttime travel much easier. Quieter and less distracting."

"But I won't see anything," said Trixie. "No one will be there."

"You're forgetting, Trix, you can travel to any place and *time*. Any time of day. You don't have to travel to same the time of day."

"Oh, right," Trixie slapped her forehead. "I knew that. Sorry. I still just don't believe I can do what you're asking me to."

"That's what today is for," said Rhada, looking directly into Trixie's eyes. "I want you to work on yourself doubt. Every single time you notice yourself thinking you can't do it, you need to change that thought, tell yourself you can time slip whenever, wherever, and however you choose. This is your destiny. You are a time traveller."

Trixie held eye contact with her Nan for a moment before nodding. She was right. And deep down, Trixie knew she could do it. She just had to believe in herself.

Chapter 38

Trixie found that cleaning the entire house was the best meditation for her. She followed her Nan's advice, and as she tidied and vacuumed and folded the clothes, she listened to her thoughts. Whenever she noticed she was doubting herself, she flipped it. She imagined she was talking to Meg and Joe, knowing that she would never speak to them the way she spoke to herself. Even if it didn't help her time travel, she had to admit that by lunchtime, she was feeling very positive.

"Can I have two-minute noodles?" Joe had asked when she'd called them in for lunch. Joe had been in the scrub at the back of the house building a hut, and had returned covered in dirt, twigs in his hair. Trixie smiled, grateful for the life they had on the farm.

"Sure can," she said. "What would you like, Meg?"

"Can I have a triple-decker egg?"

"Absolutely!" Meg had found the recipe online, although it was Trixie who had named it the triple-decker egg. Using three buttered slices of bread, she cut a hole in the middle one, cracked an egg into it, and toasted the stack in the sandwich maker until it came out golden and crisp. Meg had one almost every day.

Once the kids were eating at the outside table, Trixie made herself a plate of scrambled eggs with mushrooms, tomatoes and feta cheese before joining them. As the children ate and chattered, Trixie realised she felt the most calm she had in a long time, savouring every mouthful of the eggs. She stared out at the garden, appreciating the patch of green lawn surrounded by her native cottage garden. It was a warm day, but not sweltering as it had been. There was even a cool breeze which tickled the wind chimes down the far end of the verandah.

A willy wagtail drank from the bird bath, and one of the farm cats emerged from underneath a lavender bush, stretching both back legs before wandering off towards the chook shed, no doubt hoping to spot a mouse. A cow could be heard in the distance, and the occasional crow cawed from their perch in the pine trees on the edge of the far paddock.

Trixie picked up a piece of feta with her fingers and placed it on her tongue, enjoying the salty tang of the cheese. Meg had a spot of yolk on her chin, and Joe's lips were circled in yellow as he picked up the bowl and slurped the last of the noodles' broth.

"Mum, can I go back to the hut?" he asked, jumping up so quickly he knocked the wooden deck chair onto the verandah behind him.

"Sure, but can you at least put your plate inside?" Trixie said. "And make sure you take a water bottle. It's hot out there."

Without another word, Joe dashed inside with his plate, letting the screen door slam behind him.

"What are you going to do for the rest of the afternoon?" Trixie asked her daughter.

"I've been doing some research on quantum physics," Meg replied.

Trixie almost choked on her final spoonful of eggs, coughing and pounding her chest. "Oh, ok. That sounds, um, interesting."

"Well, if I'm going to learn everything there is to know about time travel, I need to start somewhere."

"That's the goal, is it? To learn everything there is to know about time travel?"

"Of course! Why else would I have been given this ability?"

Smiling at her daughter, she stood up. Trixie knew she shouldn't be so surprised by her daughter's completely different approach to life and to time travel. No doubt Meg would eventually surpass her by leaps and bounds. For now, though, it was up to Trixie to try and understand as much as possible herself, so that she could at least guide Meg's first few trips. Trixie only hoped that wouldn't be any time soon.

Trixie returned to her house cleaning meditation, and Meg reclaimed her possie on the couch in the study where she had a laptop perched on a side table and a notebook in her lap. As Trixie tidied the desk, emptied the rubbish bin, and dusted the windowsill, she observed Meg, pausing and rewinding the video she was watching, making notes in her book, and then flipping through a large dictionary at her side. Trixie shook her head and smiled as she left the study, pulling the wooden door behind her. Most days, she couldn't believe she and Kirby were responsible for creating these two amazing humans.

As Trixie made her way to her own bedroom to remake her bed, before tackling the pile of washing that needed to be put away, she started to plan her own time slip. She would try again this evening when the kids were in bed. It wouldn't be a long slip, but Trixie needed to know she could do it. That she could travel to a certain time and place. And this time it was going to be to the Wattlebury 150 years celebrations.

This was not part of the 'official' investigation. She would need more than a quick jaunt for that. No, tonight would be a practice run. Something to test, to evaluate. Maybe Trixie was more like Meg than she realised.

Sitting on her bed, folding the clothes, she stared out the window. Trixie focused on her thoughts, on her abilities, working to build her confidence, knowing deep down she was more than capable of time slipping properly, if only she didn't let her fears get in the way.

As she folded, she glanced towards her wardrobe and spotted a pair of tweed pants she hadn't noticed for a long time. Something about them made her heart leap. Why, she had no idea. But in an instant, she had a vision of herself wearing those brown tweed pants, with a crisp white shirt and jacket. She jumped up and pulled out the pants, laying them on the bed. Then, on her hands and knees, she rifled through the bottom of her wardrobe until she found the brown lace-up leather shoes she hadn't worn in years. Trixie didn't think she had a white shirt, but she did have a white t-shirt, which she pulled from a drawer.

"What about a jacket?" she mused, before walking to Kirby's wardrobe and opening it. Sliding back hanger after hanger, she finally put her hands on a dark brown corduroy blazer. "Perfect!"

She pulled on the outfit before turning towards the full-length mirror in the corner of the room.

There was the person Trixie had been looking for all these years.

Trixie Travers, Time Traveller.

"It just needs one more thing," Trixie told herself as she made her way to the barn.

Once inside, she flicked on a lamp and walked over to the desk where she had repaired Professor Crowe's transistor. She pulled open a drawer and found a small silver key. Unlike the many random keys she had in bowls around the shop, this key actually had a lock it fit into.

On the other side of the room was a tall glass-fronted cabinet. She unlocked the door and reached inside, pulling out a worn, navy velvet box. Without even locking up the cabinet, she opened it up.

A gold pocket watch.

It was a beautiful specimen, one she'd had in her collection for many years. Trixie always thought she would sell it one day, yet she hadn't put it on display when Paraphernalia opened. For some reason, she had kept the box closed and pushed it to the back.

The cover of the watch was delicately engraved with a ring of cogs in a variety of shapes and sizes, intertwined with a flowering vine. Then, slightly off centre, and as though viewed from a distance, was a small cottage surrounded by a picket fence, a large gum tree towering over it. To the left of the cottage was an elaborate monogram, which Trixie read as S.C.J., although it was worn and difficult to read.

The long chain of the watch had a bar and clip at one end. Trixie slid the watch into her trouser pocket and then clipped the other end of the chain to one of her belt hooks. Placing her hand into her pocket, she gripped the cool metal. Holding the watch, she was literally holding time in the palm of her hand. It connected her to the concept of time in a visceral way.

Her outfit was complete.

Grinning, Trixie had an overwhelming feeling.

"Now, I'm a time traveller."

And of course she already was, because as she caught a glimpse of her reflection in an old dressing table mirror, Trixie realised she was looking at a version of herself she had already seen. The version from Sharon's photo album.

Chapter 39

Somehow, Trixie had managed to get the kids into bed half an hour early. Joe had fallen asleep as soon as his head hit the pillow. Hut construction was an exhausting endeavour. Trixie had allowed Meg time to read, but she was not surprised when she checked ten minutes later to find Meg had fallen asleep with her book on her chest. Lifting it off gently and popping it on the side table, she had tucked Meg in before quietly closing the door behind her.

It was time.

And then she waited another hour just to be sure.

Then it was really time.

So, she grabbed a glass of water, brushed her teeth because it felt like the right thing to do, and popped on some mascara to make herself feel put together.

Then it was finally, most certainly, time.

Taking a deep breath, Trixie picked up her glass of water, patting her pocket to ensure the watch was still safe and sound, before walking outside.

She had decided to sit on the back verandah. It would be quiet there. She could see the stars, and for some reason, like the pocket watch, the stars felt as though they connected her to the concept of time. The fact that the light she was seeing was thousands or millions of years old, having time travelled through space to get to her.

She took a sip of her water before placing it on the table next to her. The deck chair creaked as she shifted her weight to get more comfortable. The breeze that brushed her cheek still had a touch of warmth to it. Trixie began Meg's bubble breathing. First, she concentrated on her breathing. In……hold……out……hold……in……

hold……out……hold. She focused on the stars for as long as she could before her eyelids grew heavy. Then it was time to visualise exactly where and when she wanted to be. To support this, she had also changed the date on the pocket watch as well as setting it to midday. She now reached into her pocket to hold the watch.

First, she pictured herself blowing a bubble. She imagined blowing it so large that eventually she could walk into it. Next, she imagined floating in that bubble over the Wattlebury main street towards the area she knew had been blocked off for the celebrations. She tried to remember the types of cars that would have been common on the streets, visualising Ford Falcons and Holden Commodores, in particular the large green station wagon her parents had had for many years. As she floated, she pictured people from the eighties in their fluorescent clothes, big hair, riding skateboards, and wearing Walkmans. Intermingled with this, she added people dressed in costume to celebrate the town's anniversary. Once she felt she had a strong picture in her mind, Trixie began to repeat the date and time in her head, over and over. No doubt it was her imagination, but the watch in her hand seemed to get warmer, almost hot.

Then she felt it. She could only describe it as a ripple of nausea that started from her head and flowed down her body to her feet. Her skin tingled all over before she felt a shudder. Opening her eyes, she recognised where she was. It was the same Lions bench she had sat on when the Polaroid camera had shot her back in time. Yet, looking around, it was much busier, and there was a buzz air.

"I think I might actually have done it," Trixie said under her breath. She pulled out her pocket watch and looked at the date and time. Of course, it hadn't changed. But was it now, in fact, correct?

Lifting her head, she dared take in the scene around her. She saw women wearing long dresses with high necks, carrying parasols. She saw young boys wearing shorts and shirts, and girls wearing dresses with pinafores over them. The men she saw wore suits with waistcoats, and some even wore top hats. For a moment, she panicked before looking again. She also saw men in stonewashed jeans, t-shirts and thongs, and women wearing denim skirts with brightly coloured blouses.

"Yes, I think I've done it," she thought to herself. "I think I've arrived in 1989 on the day of the anniversary celebrations." Standing, she looked to her left and right before heading off confidently to the west, to the main location where most of the photos were taken, right out the front of the Wattlebury Soldiers Memorial Hall.

It felt odd walking down the street of her hometown almost forty years earlier. Not just for the obvious fact that she had literally travelled back in time, but also because no one seemed to notice her. At all. Trixie felt just like the ghost she had imagined, although at one point she had intentionally bumped someone, just to test if they did in fact see her and they did apologise. She remembered Fern and Rhada's explanation that when you time slip, your presence or your energy is different. She supposed there must be some scientific, quantum physics-level explanation for this that Meg could no doubt soon explain. But it did feel like it was going to be easier than she had anticipated to find the people she was looking for, without being noticed.

Yet, that wasn't today's job. Today's job was simply to get to the right place and time, and she needed to confirm that. Weaving her way through the crowd, she glanced around until her eyes fell upon a large, fluttering banner above her. It said it all.

Wattlebury 150 Years Celebrations

"Excuse me," Trixie said, tapping an old man on the shoulder. "Do you have the time?"

The man lifted his wrist and looked at his black digital watch. "It's just after midday," he said.

"Thank you," said Trixie, resisting the urge to hug him. She had done it. She wanted to squeal or skip down the street. But instead, she turned and walked back the exact way she had come, planning to return to the Lions bench for her departure. It seemed fate, however, had other plans, because suddenly she spotted someone in the crowd.

There was the woman from the photo. The unidentified woman she was yet to ask Anna about. She was standing by herself, eating a hot dog and watching a man on a penny farthing bicycle.

What did this mean? Was Trixie supposed to speak to her? Was she supposed to ask her something?

No. No, she wasn't supposed to speak to anyone of significance. She was sure Rhada had been joking when she told her to go up and ask her. But she also didn't want to miss her chance to find out who she was. Slowly, she moved closer, stopping next to a young woman with a stroller. Trixie glanced sideways, trying to make sure it wasn't anyone she knew. There was something familiar about her, but she ignored it.

"Excuse me," Trixie said quietly. The young woman jumped.

"Oh, I didn't see you there."

Trixie smiled. "It's fine. Um, sorry, strange question, but do you know the name of that woman over there, holding the hot dog?"

"Oh, um, I think her name is Geraldine. Something like that."

"Thanks," said Trixie. "She's the one who boards with Sharon, right?"

"Yeah, that's right," said the woman, before the child in the stroller let out a squawk.

Trixie smiled and moved away. She couldn't believe how easy that was. And how unlikely it was that the first person she asked could answer her question. What a fluke. Or was it?

Turning, she quickly walked towards the bench. That was enough for today. More than enough. She had slipped, and now she had a name. Taking a seat on the bench, Trixie realised she was still holding the pocket watch. Taking it out, Trixie quickly changed the date and time to the present. She knew the pocket watch did nothing to help her travel. It wasn't magic. But it did help Trixie focus. Breathing deeply again, picturing the bubble in her mind, she floated back to her present-day lounge room. She felt the familiar feeling of nausea and was pleased. Never had she thought she would be happy to acknowledge the sickly feeling of time travel. But today she was. Within moments, she felt the shudder and knew she was back in her living room.

Opening her eyes, she quickly grabbed her phone, which had been left on the coffee table, and texted the Silver Ladies group chat.

I DID IT!!!!

Chapter 40

The confidence Trixie woke up with that Monday morning was glorious. It had taken her a while to fall asleep with all the excitement, but once she did, she slept deeply. Her phone had begun pinging that night and continued once she woke up. The Silver Ladies chat was abuzz.

By the time the kids were at school, and Trixie was at Paraphernalia, Fern and Rhada, with Maggie's input, were planning her next slip.

"But first," Fern said when Trixie set up a group phone call as she started her coffee machine. "You must ring Anna and find out about this Geraldine woman. What a discovery!"

As she frothed the milk, Trixie explained again what she'd done.

"So you understand what I mean about people not noticing you?" Rhada said.

"Totally," said Trixie. "It was weird, actually."

Rhada laughed. "It is weird. Sometimes I felt like a ninja."

Trixie burst out laughing, imagining Rhada head to toe in black, trying to sneak past people.

"And it seems like you've all worked out what I need to do next?" Trixie said as she carried the phone outside to her little table.

"Do you think you can identify the spot you were in the photo?" Maggie asked.

Sipping her coffee, Trixie nodded before realising they weren't on a video call. "Yes, yes, that should be pretty easy. I could see the stage, and I'm pretty sure I'm standing opposite it."

"The problem is going to be finding Tanya," said Fern. "Have you found a photo that you can try and travel to? One just before the one you're in?"

"I haven't brought the album over with me," said Trixie. "I was a little distracted this morning. But I don't think many have the time stamp just before mine. What do you think I should do?"

"Pick one photo and just go for it," said Rhada. "There's no way of knowing what you're going to find anyway."

"But am I just going to try and follow Tanya? Is that the plan?"

"I think it has to be," said Fern. "And perhaps a backup is to try and find the Mickey Blue truck. She likely went with him"

"You think?" asked Maggie. "What about Bruce? Shouldn't you be trying to find him?"

"I have no idea," said Trixie. "But I was wondering, how likely is it that Bruce actually did something himself? Isn't it more likely he roped in someone else?'

"Oh, Trix, you could be right," said Fern. "And if that's the case, it would almost be impossible to find out who."

"*Almost* impossible," said Rhada. "But don't forget we have time travel on our side."

"But what you're saying is that even if I travel again, I might not find out what happened to Tanya?" With her morning of overwhelming confidence, this thought made Trixie's heart sink.

"Of course, dear," said Rhada. "There's no way of knowing anything."

"Uggh," said Trixie. "I was so sure that once I solved my time travel problem, I'd solve Tanya's mystery."

"And I believe you will," said Rhada. "I truly believe you have been brought in to this for a reason. But we just don't know if your next slip is going to be the thing that cracks the case. I really hope it does. It may do. But there's no way of knowing."

"Maybe I'll just travel and visit myself in the future and ask," Trixie joked, but with a question in her voice.

"No Trix," said Fern. "You know it doesn't work like that. It can't work like that. You can't talk to yourself. And to talk to your future self? I have no idea what that could do."

"Alright, enough of this," said Trixie. "I need to open the shop and focus on my day job."

Trixie hung up the call and took her coffee cup back inside. After making another cup, she ensured the open sign was in position before picking up a feather duster. The barn gathered a lot more dust than she had expected, so it kept her busy and in her own thoughts.

It wasn't long before a car rolled up. It was Jason.

"Hi," said Trixie, a bemused look on her face. "How are you?"

Jason forced a smile, but he didn't seem particularly happy to be there. Trixie braced herself for what he was about to say.

"I've remembered something," Jason said.

"Oh," said Trixie. "Come in. Did you want to take a seat? I've just made a coffee. Can I get you one?" She realised she was babbling. Something about Jason made her nervous.

"Actually, that would be nice," he said, surprising Trixie. Perhaps this wasn't going to be a confrontation after all.

She left him to wander around the shop, inspecting her collection. Trixie had no idea if he had any interest in vintage items.

"Here you are," she said, passing the hot cappuccino to him.

"Thank you," he said. "And also thank you for what you're doing."

"Oh! Well, you're very welcome," she replied. "But if you don't mind me saying, I thought you'd come here to tell me to butt out."

Jason managed a smile before sipping the coffee. "I suppose that's fair enough. And if I'm honest, I wasn't happy the last time I saw you. But I've done some thinking since then."

Trixie nodded, but didn't say anything. Let them talk. That was a detective tactic, right?

"I know I said I didn't remember anything," said Jason, looking down at his coffee. "And I don't. Not really. At least. I don't know if it's a real memory or something I made up."

"Either way, would it be helpful to tell someone?" Trixie spoke gently.

Jason looked up at her. "I think so. I hope so."

Trixie nodded, sipped her coffee, and waited.

"I saw them together. Tanya and Mitch. I saw them a few times. One time I saw them kissing. It wasn't the first time I'd seen Tanya kiss a boy. Normally, I would have run and told Mum to try and get Tanya in trouble. But for some reason this time I knew, somehow, I shouldn't tell mum."

Trixie nodded.

"But the last time I remember seeing them together, I can't work out when it was. They were fighting. It seemed like a big fight, but then it ended with both of them crying. Mitch cried. I remember as a little boy being shocked by this. I couldn't remember seeing another boy cry. Not a big boy. I guess Mitch was an adult. It was the crying I remember."

"How did you see all of this?"

"Well, Tanya used to have to look after us all the time, me and Anna," he said. "She'd take us to the playground and tell us to nick off.

She'd go and meet up with friends or boys in the gazebo. Most of the time, Anna and I would just play in the playground. But sometimes I'd follow. Anna never did. She was always a goody two-shoes. Well, that's what I thought. Now I realise she was the most responsible of the three of us. But I'd sneak up and watch what Tanya and her friends were doing. This time it was just Mitch and Tanya.

"Do you think they were maybe breaking up?"

Jason shook his head. "I had no idea at the time, and I'm still not sure. But it was pretty serious." He looked up at Trixie. "Do you think he had something to do with it?" Trixie hesitated. She wasn't quite sure what to tell him. A lot of it was speculation on her part. She quickly decided to only tell him things she knew first-hand.

"He told me they fought at the celebrations, the day she went missing. About the baby. I don't know anything else. He said she walked away, and he never saw her again."

"Do you think that's true?"

"I don't want to speculate," said Trixie. "I don't know."

Jason nodded. "Ok, well, if you hear anything, would you let me know?"

"Of course," said Trixie. "But are you ok with what I'm doing? Only, the other day I didn't think you were happy that I was investigating."

"I wasn't," said Jason. "To be honest, I'm still not. But it's not got anything to do with you or what you find out. I think we'd all like to know what really happened. It's just hard. I'm not good with emotions and bringing all this stuff up. I'm still not a man who cries. I wish I were."

Jason stood and held his hand out to Trixie. She shook it. It may have appeared awkward, but she realised this was the best Jason could do to acknowledge his appreciation. Trixie smiled and patted him on the shoulder as he walked out.

"Oh, Jason, just one thing," Trixie said. "Do you remember a lady named Geraldine living with you?"

"Geraldine?"

"I think she was a boarder? Lived with you around the time Tanya went missing."

"Oh, you mean Gerry?"

"Maybe? I guess that would make sense."

"Sure, I remember her. She lived in the back room. The sleepout. I think she was one of those seasonal workers. Not sure what she did. I didn't have much to do with her."

"Were she and Tanya friends?"

"No idea," he said. "But I doubt it. Gerry was a lot older than us, even Tanya. Maybe they spoke. Why do you ask?"

"No real reason," she said. "Someone just mentioned her the other day. I thought if they were close, maybe she would know something about how Tanya was feeling at the time."

"Nah," said Jason. "I doubt it. And probably a waste of time anyway. I'd have no idea how you'd find her now."

"No worries," said Trixie. "I'll cross that off my list. You're right. Probably barking up the wrong tree with that."

Jason nodded. "I do really hope you find out what happened to our Tanya."

Chapter 41

Customers came in and out during the day, and Trixie was surprised to have one of her busiest and most profitable days so far. She sold a dining table and eight chairs, a cuckoo clock, a bundle of picture frames, and a tiny antique brass navigation set containing a compass, a miniature telescope and a magnifying glass.

At lunch time, she placed the 'Back in 15 Minutes' sign on the door and raced back to the house to grab not only lunch, but the photo album and brought them back to the barn. Sitting at her work desk, lamp on, she once again went through each photo with a fine-tooth comb. She was searching for photos that contained Tanya, Mitch, Bruce, Kev, and, perhaps stretching it a bit, she searched for Mickey Blue's truck. She even made note of the woman she now knew as Gerry. But Jason was right. If she were a seasonal worker, it would be doubtful Tanya would have had much to do with her. And she would be virtually impossible to find now anyway.

Placing her magnifying lamp over the album, she peered at every inch. Several photos could have contained her persons of interest, but they just weren't clear. There were a few that contained Tanya, but she was unable to reference any particular time or location. By the time she came to the end of her examination, she had pulled out only three photos that could be the most useful.

The first photo was the one that contained Trixie herself. It was very clear where she was, and the time stamp confirmed when.

The second photo contained Tanya talking to Mitch. The interesting part was, when she had peered at this photo again, she believed she had found Mitch's Dad in the background, watching them. This photo also had a time stamp, about ten minutes prior to the photo of Trixie.

The third and final photo was of Tanya talking to Gerry. The main reason this one was useful was that it was taken fifteen minutes after her conversation with Mitch, and five minutes after Trixie's photo. The best part, it appeared Tanya was very close to the same location Trixie was in her picture. It also indicated that she may have been walking in a somewhat westerly direction because it was further on from where she had been with Mitch. She hoped this would make it quick and easy for her to locate Tanya. Of course, in five minutes, Tanya could have gone in any direction. For now, though, it was all Trixie had.

"Well, the cricket was amazing!" a voice boomed from behind her. Trixie jumped and knocked her head on the lamp.

"Professor Crowe! You scared the life out of me!"

"Sorry, my dear! You did look rather engrossed in something. Am I interrupting?"

"Oh, it's nothing. Come in!" she called, even though he was already standing in the middle of Paraphernalia.

"You did a great job with the transistor," he told her. "It's like it's brand new. So I've brought you something else." From behind his back, he flamboyantly revealed a large carpet bag.

"Oooh, what is it?" Trixie walked over to him. "Where do you want to put it?"

"This table will do," he said, walking over to an oval oak dining table.

Out of the bag, he pulled a piece of striped canvas, which he laid on the table. He then proceeded to dip his hand in like Mary Poppins. Trixie almost expected him to pull out a standard lamp. What he did pull out was much more shocking.

"Is that a baby's coffin?" Trixie gasped.

"It is," said Professor. "But don't worry. That's not what's inside."

The professor reached into his bag again. This time, he pulled out a wooden stand of some sort.

"You have me completely flummoxed, Professor Crowe."

She could see a smirk on his face as he put a key into the side of the tiny coffin and turned.

"Would you like to do the honours?" he asked Trixie.

Trixie quickly shook her head. She was not ready to find out what on earth the Professor carried around in a tiny baby's coffin.

The lid was lifted, and from inside he pulled out two white gloves which he promptly slid onto his hands. He then, with a glance at Trixie, slowly lowered his hands into the coffin. The item was raised with as much care as you would expect of a newborn baby.

She held her breath.

It was a bird! A stuffed bird!

"Oh, thank goodness," she exclaimed.

"Did you really think it would be a baby?" the Professor laughed as he carefully went about setting it up on the stand. He rested the feet on what Trixie now realised was a perch, and flipped over a tiny clamp which rested gently but securely on the feet.

"Voila."

"It's beautiful," said Trixie. "I'm no orthinologist. I have no idea what that bird is."

"Well done you for knowing the word orthinologist," he said.

Trixie smiled. She was rather proud of herself.

"It's a Paradise Parrot. Native to Australia but has been extinct since the nineteen twenties."

"Really? How sad," said Trixie, walking up to take a closer look.

The bird was mostly emerald green, with dark grey wings and tail, a red stripe above its eyes, splashes of red on its belly and wings, sky-blue tips, and yellow rings around its eyes. It was rather beautiful.

"This is a specimen I acquired many years ago," he said. "I can't tell you anything more than that, or else I'd have to kill you." This caused the Professor to let out a raucous laugh, which rather startled Trixie.

"It is lovely," said Trixie. "But I'm not quite sure why you've brought it to me. Or did you just want to show it off?"

"Of course I want to show it off, but no, I'm hoping you can help me." He gently spun the bird around. "Can you see here, just under its wing, there's a bit of a dent."

Trixie nodded.

"I believe the internal frame has either bent or come undone." He turned the bird again. "And here, the claws appear to be separating. As well as here," he pointed up near the beak. "There is something of a hole."

"Don't you think you should get a professional to do this?" Trixie asked. "It looks very precious. I'm worried I might ruin it."

"Oh no, dear," said the Professor. "No, I can't take it to anyone who knows what they're doing. To anyone who has even an inkling of what it is. That's why I brought it to you!"

Trixie felt as though a wet flannel had been tossed in her face. "So you're saying you brought it to me specifically because I have no idea what I'm doing?"

"Precisely!"

Trixie shook her head but didn't dare ask any more. From

everything he'd said so far, it seemed this bird may have come into his possession in a less-than-scrupulous manner, and Trixie did not want to know any more.

"Well then," she sighed. "Could you at least give me some hints as to what you'd like me to do?"

For the next twenty minutes, Trixie and the Professor spoke of all the ways she might mend the bird. She took many notes and realised that before she touched a thing, she would need to do some research on taxidermy, especially for an item that was at least a hundred years old.

Once they finished, Trixie checked one more time. "So you're entirely sure you want me to do this? What if I mess it all up? It would be worthless!"

"Trixie, it's worthless anyway. I could never sell it. But that doesn't mean it isn't worth looking after. And I trust you entirely."

"As long as you're sure," said Trixie, helping him to get the coffin back into the carpet bag.

"Absolutely," he said. "And there is no rush. I just thought it would be a fun project for you. I'll pay for however long it takes you. Have fun!"

Trixie smiled. He was one of the most unusual people she had ever met. But she had to admit, she adored him.

"Can I perhaps pick your brain on something?" Trixie asked.

"I would love you to," he said.

"You brought in your time machine the other day," she said.

"Yes," he nodded.

"Well, if we could, in fact, time travel. If it was real-"

"Oh dear, it is real. Trust me."

Trixie smiled. Little did he know. "Ok, well, if you were to time travel, what would you consider to be the most important thing to remember? So as not to alter time, or change the world as we know it."

"That is a big question," he said. "But a very, very important one. It is something I ponder at night as I fall asleep. Because no doubt, one day very soon, I will have the joyful experience of travelling through time."

Trixie wanted to laugh, but kept her composure.

"And although I can't be sure, I feel that the most important thing is to only ever travel with good intentions, and have your number one goal to be to observe only. Take in all you can, use it as a source of knowledge, of experiencing history, and bring it back to the present day to make a positive impact on the world in your own life. Do not feel you have any right or need to make any sort of impact on the past, big or small. You must leave no footprints. You were never there."

With that, he picked up his bag, tapped an imaginary hat, and left the building.

Chapter 42

You must leave no footprints.

That afternoon, Trixie pulled out her notebook and began writing. She focused on the Professor's concept of leaving no footprints. She knew the photo of her had already left a footprint. Was that a bad thing? Or without that footprint, would she have never discovered the truth about Tanya?

Except she hadn't. Not yet. Now she found herself wondering if the photographic footprint was actually a mistake. Was it leading her in the wrong direction? Did she assume she was meant to be there because she already had been? Just because she had, didn't automatically make it right. Was she wrong to pursue this?

The questions went around and around in circles. She wrote and wrote until a customer popped in with an old typewriter and asked if she could fix it.

"It was my Great Grandmother's," the woman explained, as Trixie lifted off the cover and blew away some dust. It was a blue Imperial Good Companion and looked well-loved. Trixie wondered about all the words that had been written on the machine. She could see letters imprinted on the ink tape still inside.

"Do you mind leaving it with me?" asked Trixie. "I'll take a look and give you a call once I know if there's anything I can do."

"Perfect," the woman smiled. "I'd love to be able to use it again. I just want to be able to peck out a few lines on it. Not write the next great Australian novel."

"It's a beautiful piece, so I do hope I can help," Trixie said, writing down the customer's details on a lined card.

"I appreciate your time. You have a lovely shop here," she said, walking towards the door.

"Thanks, Melissa, I'll give you a call in a few days," said Trixie, before placing the typewriter on a shelf near her workbench.

As she pushed the typewriter back, it bumped the miniature coffin containing the extinct Paradise Parrot. A thought crossed her mind. If she could go back in time and save the last mating pair of the breed, would she? How could it be a bad thing to stop a bird from extinction? And yet, she pondered further, that one act didn't guarantee its longevity. It might only delay the inevitable. And was it inevitable that the bird became extinct? Was everything inevitable? If so, what was the purpose of time travel? Why had her family been given this gift? Gift. Mutation. Curse. Which was it?

Whenever she had spoken to Jason and Anna, the discussion of her investigation only seemed to bring pain. And yet, at the end of each conversation, there was also a degree of hope. Hope that Trixie could actually find something no one else could. What if she couldn't? What if it was inevitable that Tanya was never found? Was it worth all this pain?

Yet, Sharon had left footprints by creating her album. Footprints that Trixie seemed destined to follow. And each and every photographer had left footprints, as had the people in each photo. Were these all without purpose? Or was it inevitable, not that Tanya would never be found, but that Trixie would discover the right path to follow, the right footprints? The paradox was, Trixie could only follow the footprints left for her as long as she did her best not to leave any footprints of her own.

Trixie went to her counter and pulled out an extra-long sheet of butcher's paper, slicing it cleanly. Taking a pencil from a jar, she started sketching a mud map of Wattlebury. She placed the three photographs at the top and marked each location as best she could. She then attempted to map out the best route for her to take, to observe what she needed to.

She wanted to arrive near the location of Mitch and Tanya. It was a specific time and location she could visualise, because she had the photograph. The timing of this photo meant she would arrive before her own image was taken, but not so early that she would risk running out of time to get to the location of Tanya and Gerry's meeting. This was her ultimate goal. It was the last photograph of Tanya. At least, it was the last photograph Sharon had been able to find. Trixie needed to follow Tanya from that moment for as long as possible. She needed to see who it was that changed the course of her life.

Was it Mitch's father, bundling her up into his car and ferrying her away? Or was it Mickey Blue, in his truck, on his way to Melbourne? Then again, it could have been someone else entirely, someone they hadn't considered, didn't even have on their radar. And Trixie needed to remember that she was merely an observer. She wasn't meant to do anything. She could only observe in an attempt to find the truth and bring it back to the present.

Standing, Trixie glanced at the clock. Almost time to go and pick up the kids. She texted the Silver Ladies group chat.

Can I come over after school? I want to run through my plan. I'm going tonight.

It was decided. By writing that simple text, she had set the wheels in motion. She was going to time slip tonight and discover what really happened to Tanya. At least, she hoped she would.

Trixie rolled up her butcher's paper map and put the three photos into an envelope before sliding them into the album. All the lights and lamps were flicked off before she pulled the door of Paraphernalia closed, the album under her arm. Pausing for a moment, she wondered if much would have changed the next time she walked in here.

"The football went straight through the art room window," Joe was telling her as they drove to Silver Gum Cottage. "Do you think Samuel is going to get in heaps of trouble?"

"Did he mean to kick it into the window? Were they playing where they shouldn't be?" Trixie asked as she manoeuvred the van through the streets of Wattlebury.

"No," he said. "We were all on the oval playing marks up, like we do every lunch time. Just Samuel did a huge kick!"

"Well then, it sounds like an accident, so I don't think Samuel should get in trouble."

"Phew," said Joe, dramatically resting his head back on his booster seat.

"Do the big kids really let you reception kids kick the footy with them?" Trixie asked.

"Yep! We sometimes take turns. Like the big kids have turns, and then they'll stand down the other end and kick the balls to us. They give us really good marks. It's cool."

"Well, that's lovely," said Trixie, turning into the driveway. Joe jumped out of the van before the ignition was turned off. Meg was slower, ensuring she had her schoolbag with her.

"I hope Joe doesn't eat all the biscuits before I get there," she said, referring to Fern's biscuit barrel. Trixie smiled. Never in living memory had that biscuit barrel been emptied.

She wasn't surprised to find all three Silver Ladies in the kitchen waiting for her.

"Is it time for a cuppa or do we need to crack out the gin?" Maggie asked.

"We most certainly do not need gin," said Trixie. "At least I don't. No idea about the rest of you."

"Tea it is," said Rhada, grabbing the kettle and filling it from the tap, whilst Fern was dishing out an equal number of biscuits to Meg and Joe, before putting the barrel on the table.

"So, tonight's the night, is it?" asked Fern. "Should the kids stay here, do you think? I can take them to school."

"I was hoping you'd say that," Trixie said with a smile, before sitting down and grabbing a monte carlo for herself. "I'd hate for anything to go wrong, and the kids wake up to no one there."

"Nothing will go wrong, dear," said Rhada, patting Trixie's shoulder. "But all the same. You never know."

"What do you mean? What could go wrong?" Trixie asked, sending biscuit crumbs flying from her mouth.

"Nothing dear, nothing. But when you get to my age, you learn to always be prepared for anything."

Trixie bent down and pulled the brown paper scroll from her bag.

"This is my plan for tonight," she said, rolling it out on the table. Fern and Maggie stood over the table, trying to make sense of what Trixie had sketched out.

"Well, now, where am I going to put the milk and sugar?" Rhada said, standing there holding the items.

"Just plonk them right on top," said Trixie, who moved around to bring the mugs of tea over as well.

Once the four women had made a cuppa to their own preference,

Trixie went back to her bag and placed the three photos on top of the map. "See, this is what I'm trying to represent. Start at location one. Move to location two. And then from location three, hopefully I can follow Tanya and discover what happened to her."

It was silent in the room for a good few minutes, aside from the occasional slurp and crunch. Trixie looked at each woman in turn, trying to read their expressions, but they gave nothing away.

"So, what do you think? Am I crazy to think I can do this?" Trixie couldn't bear the silence any longer.

They all looked at her and smiled.

"Trixie," said Fern. "You can absolutely do this."

Chapter 43

Sitting on her verandah, knowing the kids were safe with the Silver Ladies, Trixie began to contemplate what the night might bring. What was she going to see? Could she handle it? The idea that something awful had happened to Tanya and she would be the one to witness it scared her. But then she remembered what Rhada had told her when she walked her to the car after dinner.

"Trix, the likelihood of you actually seeing what happened to Tanya is very low," she said. "You will be lucky if you can stay in your time slip long enough. I think half an hour would be pushing it."

"So what's the point?" asked Trixie. "If there's no chance of me finding out what happened, what am I doing this for?"

"I didn't say you won't find out what happened," Rhada said. "You are the observer. Observe everything. Take note of everything. Anything could be the clue to what really happened. As soon as you return, write down every single thing you can think of. You never know where it might lead you."

"What if I miss something? Can I go back?"

Rhada shook her head. "That is never a good idea. You run the risk of being seen by yourself. I've heard stories of that happening, and the outcome is never good."

"You're telling me this is my only chance?"

"That's correct," she said. "Make the most of it." And with that, Rhada had shut the van door for Trixie and waved her goodbye.

As she stared out at the stars, Trixie felt her heart begin to race. If this didn't work, then everything would have been a waste. And the hope she had given Jason and Anna would be for nothing.

On her wrist was a watch from her vintage collection that was known for keeping proper time. As the schedule was so important to her trip, she thought it was the best choice.

Along with the envelope containing the three photos, she had another item she hoped might help her quest. The Polaroid camera.

She'd pulled out the film from the box, sure it wouldn't work. But taking one snap of the barn, she was thrilled to see the photo slowly reveal itself.

The Silver Ladies didn't know about this part of the plan. In some ways, it felt wrong to take photographs in the past and bring them back to the present. But then again, wasn't that the journey of every image ever taken? Recording the past to bring it to the future? As a time traveller, if all she could do was observe, then why not take a tool to make her observations easier?

Wearing the same outfit as last time, of course, Trixie decided to stand as she prepared to time slip. She had stuck the photo of Mitch and Tanya to the verandah post. Holding the Polaroid camera in one hand, her other hand was gripping the pocket watch. For a few minutes, Trixie stared at the photo before finally closing her eyes to begin the bubble breathing. She visualised herself floating towards the Wattlebury Celebrations, to a tree just opposite Mitch and Tanya. Breathing in and out, she felt the wave of nausea come over her before the familiar shudder hit her.

Opening her eyes quickly, she almost squealed. She was standing next to a gum tree and, as the crowd parted, there were Mitch and Tanya. Pulling her hand out of her pocket, she quickly noted the time on her watch before lifting the camera to take a photo. The click and then the whirr as the photograph appeared from the bottom of the camera was a little louder than she expected. She glanced around, but, of course, no one was taking any notice of her. Shaking the square plastic, she could see an image slowly revealing itself. It had worked.

"Oh crap," Trixie said, looking up. She had lost sight of Mitch and Tanya. So much for eavesdropping on their conversation. Shoving the photograph into her coat pocket, she quickly began walking to the second location. She had identified it as being opposite the main stage, but in particular, there had been a lady wearing a rather large pink hat. That was what she was searching for as she scanned the crowd.

Although the year was 1989, being in the crowd was rather disorientating, as so many people were dressed in outfits from all the eras that had existed in the timeline of Wattlebury. The good thing was that she did not feel in the least bit out of place in her own brown tweed outfit. However, for the life of her, she could not spot the lady in the pink hat.

Trixie looked at her watch. She had just over a minute to get to the location.

"It's ok, Trix," she told herself as her heart began to race. "This is the one part of the timeline you know happens. Believe in it. Believe in yourself."

Then, just like magic, the lady with the pink hat appeared. Trixie had no idea what to do, so she just slowly walked in that direction, casually glancing this way and that, pretending to smile and take in her surroundings. Then, once she was next to the woman in the pink hat, she paused and turned in the direction of the supposed photographer.

Trixie gasped. There, holding the very camera she herself was holding, was Sharon. And she appeared to be looking directly at Trixie. Sharon lifted the camera, pressed the shutter, before lowering it and walking away.

"That was weird," she couldn't help but say out loud.

"What was that, dear?" the woman in the pink hat asked her. It was Odette from The Chocolate Bar, but a much younger version. Trixie knew her mouth must be gaping, but she quickly composed herself.

"Oh, nothing, just talking to myself," Trixie explained before moving away. Another glance at her watch told her she had two minutes to get to Tanya and Gerry's location, and she was determined not to mess this up. Walking briskly, with the occasional running skip, Trixie made her way through the crowd towards her destination, the Strawberry Van. The Strawberry Van had been a part of every major town event in Wattlebury that Trixie could remember. At the Wattlebury Show only last year, she had taken Joe and Meg to get a serve of strawberries and ice cream. So when she had spotted the familiar logo in the corner of the third photo, she knew she would be able to find Tanya.

Just as she was about to arrive at the van, she realised something must have gone wrong. She wasn't at the Strawberry Van. Instead, it was the van containing the woman who was making announcements on the loudspeaker. She was in the wrong place. Spinning, Trixie quickly tried to work out where the Strawberry Van was.

"Come on, come on," she said, her palms beginning to sweat. There was nothing else to do. She was going to have to ask someone. Tapping a man on the shoulder with an "excuse me", she was shocked to see Kev turn around.

"Are you ok?" he asked her. Clearly, the shock was written all over her face.

"Ah, yes, sorry," she said. "You just reminded me of someone. I ah, I just can't seem to find the Strawberry van. I'm supposed to be meeting someone there."

"Oh, that's over the other side, near the tennis courts," and he pointed across the crowd in the opposite direction.

"Thank you," she said, stifling a groan. She was never going to make it. But she had to try.

This time, Trixie didn't even bother avoiding running into people. Fortunately, most barely noticed her when she pushed past. And if they did, she didn't stop long enough to make eye contact. She didn't want anyone to notice her.

Trixie was puffing by the time she got to the tennis courts, and for a second, she thought she had been sent on a wild goose chase. Panic rose in her as she weaved her way past the Laughing Clowns, but there it was, the Strawberry Van. Gerry and Tanya were in line.

Gerry seemed to be the one talking, with Tanya just shaking her head, not looking at the woman next to her. Trixie wanted to try and get closer, to hear what they were saying, but she couldn't see how without being noticed. Picking up the Polaroid camera, her back to Tanya and Gerry, she pretended to frame a shot before turning slightly and taking a snap of the two of them. She then went and stood between the Strawberry Van and the Lions Club sausage sizzle, attempting to look as though she was waiting for someone.

The Strawberry line didn't move for a long time. Trixie worried people would start to wonder what she was doing, and had to continually remind herself that most people wouldn't even be aware of her.

"Remember, your energy is different when you time travel," she heard Fern's voice in her head. "We don't seem to have as much substance as everyone else. If you keep out of the way, you'll be fine."

Of bigger concern was the fact that the minutes were ticking over, and if Rhada was right and she only had about thirty minutes in total, she might run out of time before she discovered anything of importance.

Glancing back at the van, Trixie was relieved to see they were on the move. Or at least Tanya was. She had her plastic bowl of strawberries and ice cream and was walking away from Gerry, who stared after her. Trixie didn't waste time watching Gerry, though. It was Tanya she needed to keep an eye on. Fortunately, she didn't move fast while she ate her food, but once that was done and tossed into a bin, Tanya seemed to know exactly where she was headed. Making her way further and further from the 150 Year Celebrations, it took a while for Trixie to work out where they were going. Then it dawned on her.

"Kev's Used Cars!"

The crowd was thinning out, and at one point, Tanya glanced around. Trixie quickly turned to look into the window of the local craft shop and was pleased to see Tanya continue. Trixie decided to walk a little slower, keeping some distance between them. She took a snap at one point, and stood to shake it for a moment, before sliding it into the pocket with the others and moving on.

As expected, Tanya turned down the street that Kev's car yard was on, giving Trixie the chance to regain some ground. She then got to the stobie pole on the corner and used it to hide. What she saw was less of a surprise than she might have expected. A semi-trailer truck was parked right out front of the car yard. It wasn't clear if it was Mickey Blue's; it was facing the other way, and even if she could see the cab, it was still too far away to read anything. But Trixie had a strong feeling that's who it belonged to.

Trixie decided to confidently stroll down the street. There was no reason for Tanya to think Trixie was following her. She just needed to appear like she knew exactly where she was going.

As Trixie got closer to the car yard, she saw Tanya duck under the wire chain that surrounded the cars for sale. The yard was clearly closed, but Tanya seemed to know where she was going. Out the front of Kev's transportable office were a couple of orange plastic chairs. Tanya bent down and pulled something out from underneath one. A backpack.

Trixie paused, deciding she was close enough. Looking around, she spotted the community noticeboard. Walking up, she pretended to read the flyers, and even went so far as to pull a tab from a piece of paper advertising a plumbing service.

Tanya ducked back under the chain, struggling a little with her backpack. Trixie manoeuvred herself so she was in a position to take some photos. She had to capture this moment before Tanya drove away. There was no way of knowing if the photos would be useful, but Trixie didn't have any idea what else to do.

Tanya walked to the driver's side, which meant Trixie could no longer see her. What was she doing? Then she heard a loud bang and voices. Tanya walked back around and was followed by a short, blonde man. He stepped up and opened the passenger door of the truck and was just reaching out towards Tanya when the screech of a car was heard behind Trixie. Tanya, the truck driver, and Trixie all looked in the direction of a brown Mitsubishi Colt that was racing down the street. What Trixie was not expecting was for it to jump the curb and come to a halt just next to the truck.

"Tanya! Tanya!" It was Gerry leaping out of the car. "Don't go with him! Come with me!"

Trixie's eyes went wide. What was happening?

"I'll look after you," Gerry said, running up to Tanya and grabbing her backpack. "I'll look after both of you. It will be better with me."

"No, Gerry," said Tanya, trying to pull her bag from the woman. "I should be with my Dad."

"But what if he throws you out? Once he finds out. You know he won't be happy."

Was Gerry talking about Tanya's baby? Did she know?

"I know, but what else can I do?"

"I've been trying to tell you," Gerry said, putting her arm around Tanya's shoulder. "Come with me back to Perth. I'm in a house with heaps of room. And I can find work for both of us. I know lots of people."

"But what about when the baby comes?"

"The Government pays you," said Gerry. "When you're a single mum. You know that. You'll be fine."

Tanya looked up at the truck driver, supposedly Mickey Blue, as though this bloke was going to know what to do. Of course he wasn't! Trixie wanted to run over there, tell Tanya she was making a huge mistake. She should stay in Wattlebury. Or go to her Dad in Melbourne. But she should not go with this stranger all the way to Perth!

"I just don't know," said Tanya.

"Look, if it doesn't work out, I'll get you back to Victoria. Or to South Australia. Wherever you want. You know I'm used to travelling.

And I really want to help you. I'd love to help you. I have lots of friends. We all look out for each other. I promise you'll love it."

Tanya was hesitating, glancing up at the man who was now looking rather put out.

"You need to make a decision, love, coz I've stuck around here longer than I should've already," he said, jumping down from the step.

"Um, oh my gosh, I don't know what to do," Tanya said.

"Yes, you do," said Gerry, guiding her over to her car. "It'll be fine. Your dad doesn't even know you're coming. He won't miss you. It'll be fine."

"If you're sure?" Tanya said again, sounding younger than her fifteen years.

Getting a grip of herself, Trixie pulled up the camera and quickly snapped a photo.

"Of course I am." And with that, Gerry opened the car door and guided Tanya into the seat, before chucking the backpack in the boot.

Trixie kept snapping.

"See ya, mate!" Gerry called out to the truck driver. She jumped in her car and, without even putting her seatbelt on, put the car in reverse.

Taking one final photo of the car, Trixie hoped the number plate would be clear. By the time the final Polaroid had slid out of the camera, the little brown car was gone.

Chapter 44

"Where did you say you got this photo from?" the police constable asked the next morning, as she took the photo Trixie was handing her.

Rhada and Fern had come with her to the police station after dropping the kids off at school. She'd called the Silver Ladies the night before, as soon as she'd slipped back, only a matter of minutes after Tanya had disappeared. They had spoken for almost an hour, going over everything Trixie had seen.

As they were speaking, Trixie had pulled out each Polaroid from her pocket. Some of them were fuzzy, one was black, but there were a couple, including the one of Gerry's car, that were clear. And the number plate could be seen.

This was the photo she was now showing the constable.

"I found it in an album I was given," said Trixie.

"But how do you know it's Tanya?" she asked, taking the photo and holding it up for a better look.

"I just do," Trixie said. "And look, you can see her backpack," she said, handing him another photo of Gerry. "I bet if you checked, someone would mention what type of backpack she had. I don't know what else to say. But you need to find out who owned this car in 1989."

"And how exactly do you expect me to do that?" the constable raised her eyebrows.

"Can't you look it up on your computer?"

"Not from that far back," she said.

"Look, do you want to find out what happened to Tanya or not?" Trixie was now frowning, her hands pressing on top of the counter.

"Of course, the whereabouts of a missing person is important," the police constable said. "But it was almost forty years ago. It's a cold case."

"Ok, well, I know the owner of the car was someone called Geraldine. Known as Gerry. Does that help?"

"Not from where I'm sitting." The woman's expression did not change.

Trixie groaned and was no doubt about to say something she would regret, but fortunately Fern pulled her to one side before stepping up to the counter.

"Is there some other way to go about this? Should we be speaking to someone else? Another department?"

"No," the woman sighed, perhaps registering that this group of women were not going to give up easily. "But I can reach out to the people who run Missing Persons at Head Office. I doubt they'll be able to do anything."

"That would be greatly appreciated," said Fern. "Now, do you want to keep this original photo, or will you take a copy?"

"A copy will be fine," said the police woman. "I'll take it and scan it."

Trixie, Fern and Rhada stepped away from the counter.

"Thanks, Mum," said Trixie. "I was about to lose my mind."

"Of course," said Fern. "It's not an easy thing to explain."

Trixie took a seat and stared out the window. It seemed in an instant all the effort, all the agonising, and then the moment of possible success, would be all for nothing. A license plate from forty years ago. What did it mean? Plus, the gnawing feeling inside that she was lying to an officer of the law. The photograph was from forty years ago, right? Just because it was taken less than twenty-four hours ago didn't mean anything. Surely?

"Here's your photo." The constable had returned and was holding out the photo.

Jumping up, Trixie took the Polaroid and, somewhat calmer now, thanked the constable.

"I look forward to hearing what they find," she said, attempting a kind smile. The constable just nodded in reply and watched them as they left the station.

"Chocolate Bar?" Fern asked.

"Absolutely!" Trixie replied. "A coffee and chocolate is exactly what I need right now."

As they got seated and Rupert took their orders, the ladies didn't say a word. It seemed none of them could think of anything useful to say. It was unprecedented. Trixie felt as though she had been driving down the freeway in a car that had gradually gotten faster and faster until she felt like she'd almost lost control before wham! The brakes kicked in, and with some whiplash, they were now sitting at a set of red traffic lights, wondering if it would ever turn green. There was nothing more to do but wait. And that was not in Trixie's nature.

"Do you think we should tell Anna and Jason?" Trixie asked.

"Tell them what exactly?" Fern said.

Trixie let out a sigh. What could she tell them? "Guess what, I saw your sister from forty years ago and she got in a car with the woman who used to live with you."

"You could show them the photograph?" Rhada raised her eyebrows and shrugged her shoulders.

"What, tell them we just found it?" Trixie asked.

"Perhaps?" Rhada replied. "Maybe it was put underneath another photograph, and you only just found it?"

"As though Sharon hid it?" Fern said. "I'm not so sure about that. Why would she hide it?"

The women were silent again. It would be a hard idea to sell. It Sharon had found it, she would have taken it to the police herself.

"Maybe we shouldn't be getting their hopes up," Trixie said.

"No, probably not," said Fern.

"I'm just concerned the police are going to do absolutely nothing," said Trixie. "I mean, how likely is it that anyone in the Missing Persons Unit actually takes a second glance at this. It's a random photo with no real explanation as to why it was taken or that it really is Tanya."

"Except for the backpack," said Rhada. "That could prove it is Tanya."

"Yes, but it doesn't prove when it was taken."

"If you were a police constable, would you at least consider it a lead?" Rhada asked her granddaughter.

Before she could answer, Odette arrived with their coffees and a plate of their gorgeous chocolates.

"Thanks, Odette," said Trixie. "This is just what we needed."

"Oh? Bad morning?"

"Well, can I ask you something?"

Odette nodded.

"Do you remember a woman who used to live with the Stewarts? I think her name was Gerry or Geraldine."

Odette frowned. "It seems vaguely familiar. I know Sharon used to take in boarders fairly often."

"Even after Tanya went missing?'

"Yes, absolutely," said Odette. "Up until she died, I think she always had someone living in the back room. It was how she made money."

"Gerry lived with them around the time of Tanya's disappearance," said Trixie, as though that might spark a memory. But Odette just shook her head.

"I'm sorry I can't help you," she said. "I don't think she ever came in here."

Odette left, and Trixie sighed again. "It's all been a complete waste of time. All of it."

"Do you really believe that?" asked Rhada.

"Of course it has," said Trixie. "I saw the exact moment Tanya left town, and it doesn't mean a thing. If the police can't do anything with it, there's no way we can. Being able to time travel doesn't make things easier. It makes it harder. Just because we can go back in time doesn't mean the police can, or anyone else, for that matter. It's too hard to find anything today. It's ancient history. Everything has probably been destroyed, or at least put in the deepest, darkest part of their archives."

Rhada looked at Trixie but said nothing, sipping her coffee.

Trixie pulled the plate of chocolates over to herself, considering eating every single last one. Instead, she selected one with a tiny coffee bean and gold leaf on the top and placed the entire chocolate into her mouth. She closed her eyes, appreciating the gooey coffee-infused caramel, coated in dark chocolate.

"Too bad," said Trixie, standing and pushing her chair rather noisily away from the table. "I'm showing Anna the photo. She can do with it what she likes. She can have it. She can have the whole photo album, and I'll wash my hands of the whole thing. I'm not obligated to do or say anything."

Rhada and Fern stared at her, Fern holding a chocolate in front of her mouth, about to take a bite. One of them may have eventually spoken, but Trixie didn't give them the chance, leaving without them.

"Trixie, I can't really speak to you at work," Anna said, standing in front of her in the Hospital waiting room.

Trixie knew she would regret visiting Anna at work, but when she had knocked on her front door and no one answered, Trixie had headed directly to the hospital. Neither the reception desk nor triage would call Anna for her, so Trixie defiantly took a seat in the waiting room, watching out for Anna. Just as she was losing her nerve and about to leave, Anna appeared from behind two double swinging doors. Trixie had raced over.

"I know, I'm sorry," said Trixie. "This will only take a second. I wanted to give you this." Trixie handed Anna the photograph.

"What is it?" Anna peered at the photograph.

"It's a photo of Tanya getting into a car. Gerry's car. Gerry, who lived with you back then. It's Gerry's car, and this is her number plate. I've given it to the Police too, but I don't know if they'll do anything."

A look of understanding crossed Anna's face. "Are you saying Tanya left town with Gerry?"

Trixie nodded.

"But how? Where did you get this? How do you know it's Gerry's car?"

"I just do," said Trixie. "It was in the album." Trixie took the album from under her arm and also handed that to Anna.

"What do you expect me to do with this?"

"I don't know Anna," said Trixie. "It's the best I can do. I've done everything I can. That's the information I have. I need to give it back to you now."

"But Trixie-"

Trixie didn't hear any more. She turned and left, knowing she couldn't answer Anna's questions, no matter how many she asked. It was too much now. She needed to leave. It was time to get back to normal life. And that meant opening Paraphernalia, and perhaps even making a start on Professor Crowe's bird.

That was enough time travelling. It was time to get back to the real world.

Chapter 45

"Oh, Trixie! You've done an amazing job!"

A few weeks later, Trixie was proudly showing The Professor all the work she'd done on the Paradise Parrot.

"I hope so," said Trixie. "All I can say is I've learnt a lot about taxidermy. Especially taxidermy from the late 1800s. That's been quite the journey."

Trixie didn't tell him that she meant a literal journey. One weekend, when Kirby had taken the kids camping, Trixie had time slipped into the offices of one John Gould, a man who had visited Australia in the 1800s, collecting hundreds of bird specimens and shipping them back to England. He was a world-renowned taxidermist and orthonologist, and Trixie had spent a few hours, spread over a couple of slips, observing him. Thankfully, he never noticed her hovering in the background, completely absorbed in his work. Plus, she had found a rather convenient broom closet to hide in.

Combined with a lot of reading and online research, Trixie now felt she had an adequate grasp on this unique skill. Nothing to write home about, but at least the Professor appeared to be pleased.

"I can't wait to get it back home and put it on display," he said. "I have a reunion of sorts this weekend. Colleagues are coming to visit, and I'd quite like to show this off to them."

Trixie smiled. One day, she would quite like to join one of the Professor's gatherings. She imagined they would be rather eye-opening.

As the Professor was carefully placing the bird back into the child's coffin, Trixie's phone rang.

"Trixie? It's Anna."

Trixie was shocked. She had not heard from Anna since their awkward meeting at the hospital.

"Can you come over? Now?"

"What, come to your house?" asked Trixie.

"Yes," said Anna. "I know you have the shop open, but would it be possible to close? It's important."

Trixie frowned. "What is it?"

"I'd rather tell you when you get here, if that's ok?"

Trixie's heart began to race. This could only be something about Tanya. And her first thought? Tanya's body had been found. Of course, Anna wouldn't want to talk about that on the phone. Trixie wasn't sure she wanted to talk about it at all. But it was only right that Anna tell Trixie. She was the one who opened up this can of worms in the first place.

"Of course," said Trixie. "I can close the shop. That's no problem. You want me to come right away?"

"Yes, please," said Anna.

"Ok, I'll see you shortly."

Trixie hung up. "I'm sorry, Professor, but it seems something urgent has come up."

"That's fine, my dear," he said. "I've just got one more tie and then I'm done."

Trixie began racing around the shop, gathering her handbag, ensuring the till was secured, and wondering what else she needed to do before rushing out. The Professor was just closing the coffin and placing it back into the carpet bag as Trixie began flicking off all the lamps and lights.

"Thank you," she said, walking to the door. "I don't mean to rush you."

The Professor strode through, carpet bag in hand. "I'm happy to be rushed. I'm looking forward to getting home myself," he said, before turning and holding out his hand to shake Trixie's. "Thank you again, you've done a wonderful job. You know I'm telling everyone about you. Beware, you might be inundated!"

"Not with taxidermy work, I hope," she said with a smile.

The Professor laughed as he made his way to his green Jaguar.

In her van, Trixie began to feel rather nervous and a touch nauseous. For a moment, she worried she was about to time slip as she was driving, which would be disastrous. But this feeling was different to the now familiar time travel sickness, and she realised that what she was feeling was in fact dread. It could only be bad news, and she wasn't sure she was prepared for what Anna was going to tell her. If it was indeed Anna who was the bearer of the news. Perhaps there would be a police detective or coroner there, having already given the family the awful news that they had found Tanya. Where had she been found? What had happened to her? And most importantly, who had done it?

Trixie realised that getting yourself mixed up in investigating mysteries would invariably lead to bad news. Fortunately, this was a one-time only deal, and Trixie had rather enjoyed the last few weeks, although somewhat uneventful, serving customers, repairing items, and accepting new stock. Everything she had originally planned for herself now that the kids were both at school.

Anna was waiting at the door, and she waved as soon as she spotted Trixie coming up the farm track. She didn't look exactly distressed, almost excited, but Trixie realised the poor woman was probably in shock. Trixie smiled sympathetically as she got out of the car and walked up to Anna, realising she was going to have to maintain her composure, no matter what she learnt once she entered the house.

As Trixie walked into the living room, she saw a woman, maybe in her early fifties, sitting on the couch. She didn't look much like a police detective, or a coroner, or any other person Trixie imagined bringing this terrible news to Anna and Jason. But then again, Trixie had never met, as far as she was aware, a police detective or a coroner, so how would she know. This woman looked sad and was staring at her hands. She was wearing jeans, a long striped shirt, and had a neat brown bob. By her feet was a leather handbag.

"Trixie," said Anna. "I have someone I want you to meet."

Trixie walked over towards the woman, expecting her to stand and shake her hand. Instead, she just glanced up at Trixie and then looked at Anna, waiting for her to speak.

"Trixie, this is Tanya."

Trixie extended her hand. "Very nice to meet you, Tany-." She stopped abruptly before turning to Anna, her mouth wide. "Tanya!"

Anna was beaming, tears in her eyes, nodding. "Yes, my sister."

"Oh my goodness!" Trixie couldn't control herself and quickly turned to find a chair to sit in before she collapsed.

Tanya was looking at Trixie kindly. "I hear I have you to thank."

"You do?"

Anna came and sat down on the couch, close to Tanya, picking up her hand. "Of course she does. Without you, the police would never have tracked her down."

"The police found you? They actually looked?"

Anna and Tanya nodded together, the similarity in their mannerisms and smiles somewhat startling to Trixie.

"Oh, Trixie, good you're here!" Jason had just walked in carrying a tray of tea cups and a teapot. "Isn't it amazing!" Jason was beaming, and now Trixie couldn't help but smile.

"It is truly amazing!" said Trixie. "But tell me, how did this happen? How did they find you? And where have you been all these years?" Trixie then covered her mouth with her hand. "Oh, sorry, sorry, I'm probably being very insensitive."

"It's ok," said Tanya. "Of course, you have lots of questions. It sounds like without all your questions, I would never have been reunited with my brother and sister." She turned to smile at Anna, squeezing her hand.

"It was the photo you found," said Anna. "The license plate."

"They traced it to Gerry, Geraldine Kowalski. In Perth," said Jason. "Tanya was in Perth!"

"Perth! All this time?" Trixie asked, looking at Tanya.

"I've moved a bit since. But yes, I went with Gerry to Perth," said Tanya. "She said she would look after me. Me and the baby."

Trixie couldn't help but gasp. "So there was a baby!"

"Yes," Tanya laughed. "Although she's not much of a baby now. She's in her thirties now and has kids of her own."

"Oh, how lovely," said Trixie, smiling. "But why did you stay? Why didn't you come home?"

The question clearly touched a nerve. Tanya put her head down and began to sob. Anna and Jason looked at each other, sorrow all over their faces.

"She didn't think she could," Anna tried to explain. "Tanya

thought Mum would be so disappointed in her. Getting pregnant as a teenager just like she had. Tanya was meant to go to university, do all the things Mum never got to do."

Tanya nodded and lifted her head. "And it just got harder and harder as the years went by. I didn't want to mess anything up. I knew Mum had Anna and Jason. They'd moved on. They didn't need me stirring everything up. At least," Tanya sobbed. "That's what I told myself."

It was now Jason's turn to get up and sit next to his sister. He put his arm around her shoulder.

"It sounds like Geraldine was a piece of work, though," said Anna, her face turning stern. "From what Tanya's told us, she was rather manipulative. Thought she knew what was best for Tanya and Piper. That's her daughter's name. Our niece."

Trixie nodded with a smile, waiting for Anna to continue.

"Tanya," Anna turned to her sister. "You were only fifteen. An adult who had decided she knew what was best for you, took you away from your family, to the other side of the country, isolated you, and made you believe you wouldn't be able to cope without her. It's amazing you ever managed to get away from her!"

"Get away?" Trixie asked.

Tanya lifted her head. "When Piper turned five, and I was looking at schools for her, Gerry started talking about homeschooling. That she would homeschool Piper, and I could go out to work. I don't know why that was the thing that broke me, but within a fortnight, I somehow managed to get out of there. I moved down to Esperance. We were in a refuge for a bit. But then I found a job, found a house, Piper started school, and we started an entirely new life."

"Gosh, Gerry sounds awful," said Trixie.

"She was," said Tanya. "I'm pretty sure she kept trying to find me for a while. Just a couple of weird phone calls I got. I was scared for a long time, but she never did. I found out years later that she had died. She'd been living in Kalgoorlie. Finally, that chapter of my life was really over."

"But you didn't think of reaching out to your Mum? Or Mitch? Is he the father?"

Tanya nodded her head but couldn't speak.

"Mitch is coming for dinner," Anna explained.

"And your Dad?" asked Trixie. "Does he know?"

"Yes, I spoke with him this morning," Tanya managed to say. "He couldn't stop crying. I'm going to be visiting him tomorrow. He said I was almost too late. I almost missed everything," she stifled a sob, looking at Anna and then Jason.

"You're here now, sis," said Jason. "And that's all that matters."

"It's ok, Tanya," said Anna. Like Jason, she wrapped her arm around Tanya. "We'll make sure you see your Dad. And Jason and I, well, we have all the time in the world."

Trixie smiled, tears forming in her own eyes. She realised she was clutching the pocket watch that had become a permanent fixture in whatever she wore each day. Time travel had given this family a second chance.

SIGN UP TO MY NEWSLETTER

Thank you so much for reading Trixie Travers is Captured in Time. If you enjoyed the book and would like to be notified when new books in the Trixie Travers Time Travel Mysteries series are released, or other titles, I would love it if you would sign up to receive my newsletter. Every now and then you may receive exclusive free bonus material, as well as my latest news or when titles go on sale. If you would like to sign up please visit my website

abbielmartin.com

ABOUT THE AUTHOR

Abbie L. Martin is a South Australian author who lives with her family in a small town very similar to Wattlebury. She has been dreaming of writing and publishing since she was a child, and when she reached her forties, finally decided to take the leap. Whilst also running a business with her husband, and juggling life with three children, Abbie loves nothing better than peace and quiet with a good book and a glass of wine, preferably an Adelaide Hills sparkling.

BY ABBIE L. MARTIN

The Lilly Pilly Creek Ghost Mystery Series

Book 1 - The Ghost of Lilly Pilly Creek

Book 2 - The Bride of Lilly Pilly Creek

Book 3 - The Lights of Lilly Pilly Creek

Book 4 - The Flames of Lilly Pilly Creek

www.ingramcontent.com/pod-product-compliance
Lightning Source LLC
Chambersburg PA
CBHW071141180726

48291CB00007B/2291